ARDATH
acclaimed
People of the Mesa,
Island in the Lake
and
Towers of the Earth,
brings us her most powerful novel yet,
an epic tale of prehistoric survival . . .

HUNTERS OF THE PLAINS

DO-NA-TI
After his first hunt, he was a man. A young,
new hope for a clan whose future was
uncertain . . .

E-LO-NI
His Terrapin wife, the fearless woman who
would carry the bloodline of both clans and
teach the traditions that made them great . . .

Praise for
PEOPLE OF THE MESA . . .

Berkley Books by Ardath Mayhar

PEOPLE OF THE MESA
ISLAND IN THE LAKE
HUNTERS OF THE PLAINS

HUNTERS
OF THE
PLAINS

ARDATH MAYHAR

BERKLEY BOOKS, NEW YORK

HUNTERS OF THE PLAINS

A Berkley Book / published by arrangement with
the author

PRINTING HISTORY
Berkley edition / March 1995

ISBN: 0-425-14645-6

BERKLEY®
Berkley Books are published by The Berkley Publishing Group,
200 Madison Avenue, New York, New York 10016.
BERKLEY and the "B" design
are trademarks belonging to Berkley Publishing Corporation.

PRINTED IN THE UNITED STATES OF AMERICA

10 9 8 7 6 5 4 3 2 1

ONE

THE GRASS, DOTTED WITH PATCHES OF SAGEBRUSH, STRETCHED
away from sky to sky, with sunflower plants rising as high
as Do-na-ti's head. The meandering ravines that broke the
prairie with their runnels were hidden beneath gray-green
and tan-green layers. Above him clouds sailed over, tall and
frightening shapes from which lightning or devil winds
could descend at times to devastate the People who lived on
the land.

Those were gods so remote that even the shaman of the
Badger Clan did not really believe that his rituals and chants
could propitiate them. The boy who was creeping through
the grasses below the giant cloud shapes felt, if he did not
understand, that deep uncertainty.

Today was bright, however, the sun blazing down on the
patches of sunflowers and the endless sea of tall grass.
Constant wind rippled the tops of the grasses and made the
flowers bob erratically, masking any movements of small
animals along the ground.

That made it difficult for the boy to watch his prey at its
digging. The badger he had targeted seemed to be adding
rooms to his burrow among sagebrush roots in the side of a
small hummock. The busy gray-and-white striped shape
appeared and disappeared among swaying sunflower stalks
as it pushed dirt out of its excavations and turned back into
the depths for more.

Do-na-ti slithered forward with the lithe certainty of a snake until he was in the last fringe of brush and flower stalks. So softly had he approached that the badger, now returned to the outer air and busy with something at the mouth of its burrow, was unaware of him.

Yet he knew that as soon as he rose to throw his short spear the animal would be alert instantly. That was why his final sequence of movements was incredibly swift and smooth. With one motion, he was on his feet, his arm cocked, the weapon sent surely on its way to the target.

The badger gave a gruff shriek as the keen chert point buried itself in its muscular back and penetrated lungs and heart. With desperate flops, it reacted reflexively, and at last, thrashing and kicking, the creature died.

Do-na-ti waited until the last reflex movements stopped and a trickle of blood dribbled from the badger's nose and mouth. Approaching a badger that was not quite dead was a perilous matter, which had been known to cause terrible injury to hunters who lifted prey that was still living and were clawed and bitten by their quarry.

The boy stepped forward at last. He looked up at the sky, down at the dead animal, and sang the ritual of thanks for this kill. He marked his forehead with the creature's blood, and then he gutted the dead badger. Having tied the carcass foot-to-foot, he slung its looped body around the shaft of his spear and turned his face toward the village.

He was filled with triumph, for at last he had a badger skin for the hood of the costume in which he would celebrate his man-rite. Each clan considered a boy a child until he had faced his own clan beast and made his ceremonial headgear.

Tomorrow he would be honored by his Badger-Clan family with a chant, and E-lo-ni's family, who were Terrapin-Clan, would come. Not until he became a man would her mother consent to their marriage, though her father, a childhood companion of his own father, quietly approved. Yet disposition of a daughter was the mother's and the grandmother's right, and now they would be pleased, Do-na-ti thought, to give their consent.

For all the seasons of their lives the two of them had been friends and companions. Only when E-lo-ni became a woman, a part of the vital women's element of the clan, did they separate, he to learn the demanding techniques of weapon-making, stalking, and hunting, she to learn the multiple skills that clothed, fed, and healed the People.

Now the two of them were competent adults, fully able to form a family and begin their work of securing the continuation of their tribe. As he sped through the tall grass, Do-na-ti was thinking of the time to come, their future as a family, the children they might have to delight their parents, the work they both would do that would help the People to remain secure and well fed.

He dogtrotted through the grass, keeping an alert ear tuned to the sounds about him. Insects zipped away before his feet, chirred and creaked about him. From time to time a bird shot up, scolding, from a nest past which he ran, and rabbits fled frequently from the quiet sound of his skin-shod feet.

Those were familiar sounds, which his mind noted and dismissed without conscious thought. If the bear had been moving, he would have heard it long before he slipped through a thick growth of sunflowers and found himself face-to-face with the long-legged beast.

Do-na-ti's heart seemed to pause before starting to race frantically. He froze for a moment, hoping the shortsighted animal would fail to notice him. But the short-faced bear, huge and supremely fast, was a predator to rival even man. Its keen nose caught the scent of prey before its eyes picked up the stocky shape of the youngster.

Instantly the boy darted aside, crashing through the tough, head-high flower stalks and then breaking through the thicket into the less resistant but still difficult terrain covered with knee-high grass and sagebrush, which disguised ridges and runnels that could mean a broken leg if one did not keep a close eye on his footing.

He was a strong runner. Indeed, all of his people were runners, for that was necessary for survival on the plains and in the edges of the mountains to the west. As toddlers, they

began racing each other, and by the time they reached
Do-na-ti's age they could hold their own with almost any
pursuer.

The short-faced bear, however, was built for running, its
long legs capable of covering ground with incredible speed.
The big strong body was also able to continue the chase
when other predators might have flagged, and to run down
exhausted prey at last.

This was foremost in Do-na-ti's thoughts as he fled
through the grass, heading toward an arroyo worn by the
sudden desert floods and the seasonal migrations of the
long-horned bison. Those gigantic beasts were moving
through the country on their way to summer grazing
grounds; if some of their number were already in the arroyo,
it would be the end of Do-na-ti, he knew.

Yet the bear was immediate and dangerous beyond any
possibility that might wait in that deep and crooked crease
leading toward the small river. If it caught him, he would
end as the bear's meal.

The badger, flopping around the shaft of his spear, was a
nuisance, but the boy did not drop it. He had waited long
and stalked carefully to kill the wary beast. It would prove
him a man, even if his people found his remains where the
bear or the bison left them. They would know, even in their
grief, that he had become a man before he died.

He leapt surely from the edge of the ravine and landed,
knees bent, at the bottom, twice his own height beneath the
level of the prairie above. He could hear the oncoming
growl of the bear, the pad of its paws as it came to the edge
and stared down at him.

Do-na-ti did not wait. He turned toward the deeper
reaches of the ravine and ran for his life, leaping over rocks
and twisting around abrupt bends. Now he listened for any
sound coming from ahead. He had no desire to plunge
straight into the curling horns of one of the big bison.

The arroyo was only one of an erratic maze of dry
washes, ravines, and other old game trails that gullied the
grassy plain. The animals that had helped to form it had
avoided big rocks and difficult passages, on their way

toward the water, and winter rains had followed the courses of the trails, digging them even deeper.

As he sprang around such a kink, Do-na-ti leapt spasmodically to avoid a snake, which had begun coiling at the sound of his pounding steps. A rattler as long as his body filled the air with its dry rustle of warning.

The boy paused at the end of his long jump, well out of range of the creature, and looked back. The rattler struck after his flying shape, lying flat on the rock for an instant. Without hesitation, Do-na-ti whirled and bent in the same motion.

Before the reptile could gather itself to coil again, the boy grabbed it behind the head, holding the tense and resistant body stretched between his hands as it tried to squirm into a coil against his grip.

He waited behind the blind corner for his pursuer to arrive. He knew he would hear no footsteps, for the bear rolled over the ground almost as silently as a cloud, but at last he heard the faint click of pebble striking pebble as the beast's great weight moved over them.

At that moment, he stretched the rattlesnake even tighter, resisting with considerable strength its attempts to coil again. As the bear's blunt face came into view, he flung the snake over its neck, the gaping fangs hanging on one side and the wriggling tail on the other side of the startled beast's head. The enraged snake began striking at anything it could reach, and the bear lost interest in his former prey and focused on the swaying head and perilous fangs threatening his face.

Do-na-ti backed away as the bear rose onto its hind legs, pawing at the snake. Before he could deal with the serpent, the rattler struck again at the side of his snout; the bear roared and flung the long body onto the ground.

The boy did not wait to see what happened afterward. Instead, he went around another bend and climbed the wall of the arroyo. Once clear of the cleft, he took off across the grassland at top speed, the badger bouncing and bobbing behind his shoulder, on the spear.

The snakebites would probably not kill that huge beast,

he understood, for he had seen the bears survive far worse things than that. He had no desire to be within sight when the animal finished his business with the snake and remembered, if he did remember, that he had been chasing two-legged prey.

Once clear of the area, the boy slowed to a jog. This time he kept his mind strictly on watching and listening to his surroundings, for the plain was alive with very large animals. Most of those would attack a man if he surprised them. One such encounter in a single day was more than any of his people wanted.

It was a long way to the village, and he climbed up and down swells, hummocks, and ravines, his instinctive sense of direction keeping his course as straight as possible, even as he avoided obstructions and perils. One such problem came into view when he stopped on the top of a hillock and gazed along his proposed route.

A small group of bison, stragglers from the great herd that had moved north several suns before, grazed in a loose clump, directly in his path. Sighing, Do-na-ti changed shoulders with his burden and turned his steps to the right, to circle the beasts.

Sometimes one could go near such a quiet group without peril, but their tempers were uncertain at best and murderous if they were suddenly roused by something they saw as a danger. The summer before, he had seen the best hunter in the clan trampled to death by four bison that had been lying down in a small valley. Seeing him pass, they had risen to charge.

Luckily, they had targeted only one of the three who had traveled with On-e-to, which had spared Do-na-ti and his friend Sem-it. Even now, the boy shivered at the memory, for all they had found of On-e-to, once the beasts had thundered away, was a crumple of blood and splintered bone and torn flesh. The two boys had borne him back to the village wrapped in a deerhide, for the rituals of death demanded that his body be present. Do-na-ti had never forgotten the lesson he learned that day.

As he moved cautiously around the quiet animals, the young man kept his mind focused on that terrible incident. When the women had wrapped On-e-ti in his best robe, binding him together with strips of hide hidden beneath the softly tanned leather, his face had been covered, for it was no longer a face.

Do-na-ti had no wish to end up so, particularly now that he was so near to beginning his life as a man. Tonight his mother and father would be quietly glad. Tomorrow they would prepare the ceremony. And then . . . and then E-lo-ni would be his wife, and they would begin their adult lives together.

TWO

THE HERD BULLS STAMPED AND SNORTED UNEASILY, FEELING A CHANGE in the density of the air, the texture of the wind. Although their minds were slow and dim, the animals sensed weather with an unerring instinct, and the entire massive group seemed to hesitate before continuing the northward movement that was normal at this time of the year.

After the noon rest, sheltering amid the scanty growths of trees that dotted the landscape, the herd did not continue moving slowly northward as they grazed. Instead, they turned back on their tracks, though the grass left behind was chewed short and fouled with dung. Driven by the threat of weather, they moved south again.

The bright morning had turned into a cloud-ridden noon. As Do-na-ti hurried across the plain toward his home village, where the circle of earthen lodges huddled against the lee of a small hill, the towering clouds moved over the country. Now the sunlight was gone, the patches of sunflowers making the only brightness in a landscape gone gray-tan and lifeless. The scrubby brush was gray and spiritless now, and the tree leaves hung limp.

The boy felt suddenly very alone, very far from the comfort of his clan's lodges, vulnerable beneath the lowering sky. In the distance there was the mutter of thunder, and lightning stitched from sky to earth at the edge of the plain.

Shivering again, Do-na-ti began to trot, taking the chance of running into some enemy, for a strange fear of the open had overtaken him.

In the shelter of the rounded lodge, protected by layers of brush and earth from the gods of the sky, he would feel safe and warm in the midst of his crowded family. There he and his mother would skin his badger. Then she would scrape the hide and rub the raw side with ash. She would be up all night, working the fur to make it dry enough, supple enough, in such a short time, to serve as his hood on the day of the ceremony.

The wind shifted uneasily, straying from south to west to north. The smell of rain was heavy as the storm approached, whirls of dust curling upward from the dry soil beneath the grasses. Tufts of dead sagebrush tumbled across the way, driven by the wind.

More and more, the boy longed to see the low huddle of houses at the edge of the sky, for when the gods quarreled and fought, it was best for humankind to be hidden from their sight. His strong young legs pumped steadily, but he was growing weary by the time the hump-shouldered straggle of homes appeared against the backdrop of a low hillock.

It was with great relief that he sped forward, now running amid gusts of rain-laden wind, toward the low doorway of his mother's house. His small brothers were standing beside the pole frame, taking down drying meat to save it from the wind and rain. Ka-shi shouted with excitement when he saw the striped shape bobbing about his older brother's lance shaft.

"Do-na-ti has killed his badger!" the child cried, and heads popped out of other lodges to see.

Now, observed by so many of his people, Do-na-ti slowed to a casual pace, holding the lance high between his hands to show the carcass of the badger. He could see E-lo-ni's face, half-hidden behind the curve of her family's lodge. She pretended not to look, but he knew she had seen and her heart must be pounding as quickly as his own.

His mother came to the low doorway of their lodge and ducked out of the opening. She said nothing, for it was not proper for a parent to boast about the achievements of her children, but her eyes were bright as she reached for the spear.

The boy lowered it into her hands, and their gazes met over the striped fur. Today a man-son dwelled in the lodge of Ash-pah and De-lo-nit. He could see the pride of that thought in the straightness of her back as she bore his prey away. She had lost two sons older than Do-na-ti, and this was a great day for her, he knew.

Ka-shi and Pe-ti-ne, his sister's son, both were still too young to hunt badger alone. The animal itself was not so dangerous, if one took proper precautions, but the trek to find its burrow and the long wait for a chance to kill it exposed the hunter to the many perils that lived on the plain. Very young boys could not be risked for such purposes, and that made the achievement enviable in their eyes.

The pair tagged at Do-na-ti's heels, awed by his sudden elevation to the status of an adult. The few seasons of difference in their ages loomed larger now than it had only yesterday. Do-na-ti found himself filled with pride at their expressions of awe, as he made his way to the lodge of the Elders.

Tu-ri-nit, who was elder of the Badger Clan, had gone inside, for now the wind had risen to wild gusts, carrying stinging grit and even small pebbles as it battered the plain and flung itself against the solid curves of the houses. The old people were huddled together inside, although even with the storm approaching the air had not cooled much, as yet.

Their smudge of fire did little more than send smoke whirling about the circle enclosed by the pole, mud, and thatch structure, as the wind pushed it back down the smoke hole. Do-na-ti stood inside the low doorway and spoke to the elders of the Badger Clan. "Today I have killed my badger. I go now to take the skin, and tonight my mother will prepare it and shape the hood that shows me to be an adult member of our clan. Grandfather, Grandmother, I come to you as a man of the People."

Tu-ri-nit gazed toward him through the swirling smoke and the dim red light. That clouded gaze saw more, the young man had always understood, than far younger and sharper eyes were able to see. The thin lips widened as if to smile, and the old man raised his hand.

"I see you, Do-na-ti, son of Ash-pah and De-lo-nit. Go and skin your prey. Send one of your kin to speak with the family of E-lo-ni. It is good that you add another man's strength and skill to our hunting."

Do-na-ti, who had been ready to turn to his own task, paused, feeling his heart race, hammering inside his chest. "They have sighted game, then?" the boy asked, barely able to keep the excitement from his voice.

"A group of the Great Tusked Ones has moved from the west. They come slowly, eating bushes and the tops of the small trees along the streams, but if nothing disturbs them they will come to the trapping place when the moon is a fingernail's width in the western sky." He waved Do-na-ti on with one withered hand.

"So prepare your hood and ready yourself for the ritual. It is a good omen that you become a man just in time to help with a Great Hunt."

Almost shivering with excitement, the boy moved into the wind between the lodges, crossing the dust-ridden space to the lodge shared by the two bands of people who were his direct kin. There was no fire inside, for most of them were young. Light came from five twisted-grass torches, whose ends were thrust into the earthen floor.

The wind whistled from the open doorway up through the smoke hole, fluttering the flames and making the family blink at the gust of grit. "Tie down the door flap," Ash-pah said, as Do-na-ti entered. "The wind will blow out the torches."

He obeyed her before going to sit beside her at her work stone. "I will skin the badger, if you would like for me to," he said. "Tu-ri-nit says there will be a Great Hunt at the time of the new moon. I will be ready."

His mother nodded, her eyes bright. "The great tusked beasts move toward the trapping place," she said. "And my son will be among those who drive them, instead of waiting with the children to help skin the huge creatures and cut their meat. That is good."

The boy hid his smile as he bent over the stiff body of the badger. Deft cuts with his flint knife opened the skin of the stomach and made a slit down each leg. He slipped the blade beneath the skin to free it from the lower jaw, taking care not to cut through the face fur. Having the snout of the animal intact, snarling above his own face, was vital to its effect.

Unconsciously Do-na-ti bared his own teeth as he worked the hide from the head, peeling it from torso and legs almost without damage, except for the main cuts. He glanced up to see Ka-shi staring at his face.

"You look funny," the child said. "Angry. Are you not happy that you have killed your badger?"

Do-na-ti relaxed into a smile. This was, after all, a child. He could not understand what it meant to reach this point in his life, the feel of the cooling blood on his hands, the anticipation of the fur hood about his neck and ears, the knowledge that E-lo-ni would be his . . .

"I was thinking like a badger," he explained patiently. "We are Badger Clan. We work hard, like the badger, gathering seeds from the grass, netting birds, digging roots from the riverbed, catching fat insects. We are fierce, like the badger, when any other people threaten our lives. We are like the badger when we hunt the great beasts, for we do not fear them. So we must think like badgers in our minds."

Ka-shi's forehead wrinkled with puzzlement. "Do you feel like a badger when you snarl like that?" he asked his brother. "Are you thinking about biting when you do it?"

Do-na-ti nodded slowly, thinking about how he had been feeling. "I smell the freshly dug earth, feel it on my paws, under my claws. I can hear things that I never heard before, feel the weather building in the sky, understand the very worms and grubs that I dig as I make that burrow."

The boy nodded slowly, as if beginning to understand. He smiled, his eyes brightening. "I will be a badger, too, when I am older. Let me hold the front legs so you can pull the skin evenly, without tearing it."

Together they freed the striped hide from the thick, powerful body of the animal. No part of that would be wasted: the flesh would go into the pot; the ligaments would be used for thread or twisted into thongs; the bones would be used for dozens of different things, from needles to stitch together hide robes and moccasins to pins that would hold the leather door flaps closed.

But it was the fate of the fur that fascinated the brothers. Ash-pah stretched the flexible skin, pinned it to the earth with bone pins, and began scraping it hard with a half-moon of chert. Blood trickled from it, to be absorbed into the dirt floor of the lodge. Fatty fragments rolled up, to be gathered carefully and added to the ever-hungry stew pot.

So skillful was she that the hide was cleaned quickly. Then she rubbed in the ash and turned to her other tasks while this first treatment dried the skin side of the fur enough to allow it to be used for the ritual. After it had, she would beat it, scrape it again, and hang it, stretched on willow hoops, to dry completely before being permanently shaped to Do-na-ti's head.

It was growing late. The heavy pot sitting beside the fire in the center of the lodge had been tended by the small girls, whose task was to keep rolling rounded stones into the fire, pulling out with wooden tongs those that were hot, and dropping them into the pot to keep the stew boiling.

The badger had been added, along with the scrapings of fat; the smell of strong meat, wild onion, and wild sage filled the rounded space where the family lived. Most of the members had been sitting quietly in the shelter of their house to avoid the storm. Now, as the single meal of the day neared readiness, those who had remained to talk with friends in other lodges drifted in to join the rest. They were not a demonstrative people, but most found a moment to pause beside the newest man among them.

Some merely smiled. Others touched his shoulder and nodded. The grandfather, oldest of this family, offered a small gift, a badger carved of bone to be the fetish beginning his bag of powerful things that would go with him all his life.

Do-na-ti took the small badger carefully, trying hard to keep his face solemn. This was an important gift, the first of the magical items that would safeguard him as an adult.

After the pot had been emptied and the family lay beside the fire, belching and talking quietly, Do-na-ti moved close to his grandfather. The old man turned to the young one and gazed at him with speculation in his rheumy eyes. "I believe that we have a new dog who will hunt the great woolly ones," he said.

Do-na-ti felt his heart leap and pound. To wear the dog skin, slipping through the herd of mammoths as one of the plains wolves, was a dangerous and wonderful thing. To begin one's manhood with a hunt in which he played the part of the dog would mean that he would acquire respect much earlier than most new-made men.

His mother glanced at him over the fire, her eyes widening, then closing. She understood the danger. She also understood the honor of the thing, and he knew she would never say a word against his taking on the role.

Ke-len-ne, his uncle, slipped away to the place where valuable items were piled. When he returned, he carried the pale pelt of a huge dog that had been skinned for the purpose of the hunt. That had been a brave dog, unafraid of man or snake or giant bison, and, for that reason, when he died he had been so honored.

Do-na-ti held out his arms, and Ke-len-ne laid the soft pelt over them. Holding the head skin high, the young man slipped his own head into the cavity where the dog's had been.

The skin slid silkily over his back, and he dropped to all fours and tried his best to walk like a dog. He let his hindquarters sink, wagging them back and forth to make the tail move. A feeling of power and warmth filled him, and Do-na-ti managed a yelp so lifelike that the other dogs belonging to his clan, who lived outside in the weather, replied in a series of shrill yelps and staccato yips. For a moment the noise was so great that the smaller children were frightened and took refuge beside their parents and older siblings.

But Do-na-ti, satisfied with his ability to play the dog, quieted. Around him his people smiled with quiet pride. He would, he could see in their eyes, make them proud when the hunt went forward.

He laid the skin reluctantly into his uncle's hands again. Being an adult, he was beginning to understand, held strange and exciting matters that as a child he had not suspected. Among those was the ritual—he could hardly contain himself as he schooled himself to wait.

THREE

‒ ‒ ‒ ‒ ‒ ‒ ‒ ‒ ‒ ‒ ‒ ‒ ‒ ‒ ‒ ‒ ‒
‒ ‒ ‒ ‒ ‒ ‒ ‒

THE DAY OF THE BADGER DANCE DRAGGED INTERMINABLY.
Do-na-ti went about his usual tasks so absentmindedly that
he lost his knife twice and himself once, which was highly
unusual for one as familiar with the intimate details of the
countryside as he.

This day was unlike yesterday. The sun shone harshly,
even as it halved itself on the horizon and sank. Night
moved up the east, and no cloud marred the blue-black vault
of the sky. The hot breath of the sun-soaked land began to
cool as drums thudded softly amid the huddle of lodges.

Do-na-ti, having found himself once and his knife twice,
returned to his lodge to find his family waiting to dress him
in the ritual attire. To no one's surprise, he brought nothing
to show for running his snares, but his family only smiled.
They understood the importance of this night to their newest
hunter and warrior.

Ka-shi was bouncing with excitement, and the younger
children were wordless with awe as Do-na-ti shrugged
about his shoulders the robe made of many badger hides.
This robe was old—older than the grandfather.

Only the badger hood was new, shaped and stitched with
care by the hands of his mother. She had used red-dyed
thongs as ties, and they were bright against the fur as he
lifted the hood over his carefully smoothed braids and
allowed his uncle to tie the bindings.

16

He stood very straight as his parents, the elders of the clan, all his uncles and aunts, and the children admired his splendor. Then the sound of a bone flute began wavering through the night breeze, and Do-na-ti dropped into a crouch, as his uncle had taught him when he was a child.

Again he put himself into the mind of the badger, and his fingers curled into claws, his lips peeled from his teeth in a snarl. A strangeness rose inside the young man, and he wondered if at this moment all the other men of the Badger Clan felt as he did.

His uncle, already resplendent in his badger costume, came to touch his shoulder. As he looked into the older man's eyes, Do-na-ti knew that he, too, had become, inside himself, the beast that was the totem of their clan.

Obeying the pressure of his uncle's hand, Do-na-ti stooped beneath the low doorway and stepped into the night. Behind came his uncle, the grandfather, all the family.

Others of the People of the village were coming from their own big lodges, led by adult men wearing hoods much like the new warrior's, all portraying the totem beasts of their clans.

The glare of fire touched the low domes of the house with orange light as they wound their way among the random clusters of lodges to the center of the village. Off to the right, the Fox Clan was emerging into the light.

On the other side of the village, the dark mass of walkers showed that the Bison Clan was on its way to the ritual. E-lo-ni's own clan, the Terrapin People, would already be in place, the boy knew.

Tu-ri-nit was already there, his wrinkled face invisible beneath the badger hood. Beside him sat Fe-ka-na, Elder of the Foxes, wearing the fox mask that was the hood of her people. Ku-lap, elder of the Bisons, wore a cap of woolly hide, for the head of the giant bison was too large to be borne by a single person. Go-eh-lit, who had been elder for the Terrapin Clan, had died the previous moon, and his replacement had not yet been chosen.

The remaining three were the anchors of the village; the collected wisdom of generations of the people of the plains

country lived in their minds, in the songs they had learned
from their ancestors. The dangers and triumphs dealt with
over centuries were the heritage their hearts and memories
preserved for their people.

Now they sat at the points of a triangle whose center was
the fire. To leave an empty space where the Terrapin elder
should have been would have left the village open to
unthinkable perils, and they had rearranged their positions
to compensate.

Facing one another, they chanted softly, telling of a
thousand seasons of rituals, a thousand young men who had
faced manhood wearing the hoods of their clan totems. The
skills and strategies that kept their kind alive among the
many perils of this country served each succeeding generation, which added its own inventions to the rest.

> "In the season of fire from the sky,
> when our people fled into the tall lands to the west,
> we built our fires in an alien place.
> The new-made men,
> their hoods all fresh killed
> and made by the hands of family
> to replace the old ones that had been lost
> in the flight of the people,
> danced in a different country.
> Yet the chants were sung,
> the steps were the same
> that we have danced for long, for long."

That was the voice of Tu-ri-nit, as his fingers drummed
lightly on a deer hide stretched over a willow hoop.

From beyond the fire the quavering voice of Fe-ka-na
took up the tale.

> "Snows fell,
> suns burned us,
> but we lived and returned
> to our own country.
> The Great Horned Ones fell before us,

and we used their flesh for our food.
Their hides wrapped our bodies from the cold
and formed door flaps for our lodges.
We of the Plains Clans
mastered the giant Tusked Ones,
slew the great bear,
as we do now and will continue to do
until the sun no longer walks the sky."

Her withered fingers moved, striking together thin bones
to make a musical clack.

Ku-lap raised his head, the woolly hood dropping away
from his broad face.

"The hunters of the People
walk the grasslands,
catch small game in their strong hands,
pursue the very winds,
if there is need.
We shall eat the wind, my brothers!
We shall eat the wind!"

His raised fist came down on the big bison-hide drum that
sat before him, adding its deep note to the music.

Do-na-ti, joining the line of hooded warriors, taking his
place for the first time with the adult men of his village, felt
the booming of the drum inside his stomach. His heart kept
time with the clacking of the bones; the throb of the finger
drum seemed to pulse inside his body, in his own bones. As
he picked up the rhythm, joining his steps to those of his
elders, he knew that this night would change him forever.

The women made a circle around the elders, and the
maidens formed another, facing the younger warriors. The
mature men stood motionless in a giant ring that enclosed
them all. The wide-eyed children sat quietly within the
protective curve of the group.

When the chant ended, the elders stood and raised their
hands in command. The women began a shuffling step,

clockwise around the fire. The girls moved in the opposite direction, and the young warriors began to move, too.

Do-na-ti found himself looking into the eyes of E-lo-ni as she moved slowly past, her feet keeping perfect time with the drum. His heart felt too large for his chest, as if it might choke off his breath and smother him.

The firelight mottled the fur hoods, the faces, the bodies of the dancers. The young man found himself dizzy as he danced, for the circling shapes blurred before his eyes, light dancing with dark, shadow with red-gold reflection.

The face of E-lo-ni floated before him, and he could not say if it might be passing him in reality or was a part of his mind, embedded in his heart. That, too, seemed to fill him, taking away his breath, stretching him to a point at which he felt that he might split like a puffball in the autumn.

But he kept his face properly expressionless, his gaze straight ahead, his shoulders straight. The already rank smell of the partially treated fur of his hood was strangely exciting, making his blood throb almost painfully through his body; his loins ached as he danced.

The drum pounded more and more loudly, more quickly, forcing the dancers to pick up their pace. The dust raised by the shuffling feet became a golden mist in the firelight, and its tickle in his nose made Do-na-ti sneeze. But others were also sneezing and coughing, and no one noticed.

He moved faster, faster still, keeping his steps in time with his companions and the demanding drum. Now he was sweating, the fur almost unbearably hot and irritating as it trapped his own sweat close to his skin.

The fire was dying as the dance reached its height. When the blaze had been reduced to a hillock of red coals, the drum crashed with a final thunderous boom.

Instantly the dancers halted. For a long moment no one moved or spoke. Then Tu-ri-nit said, "Let the new warrior of the Badger Clan come forth."

Numb with exhaustion and excitement, Do-na-ti almost glanced about to see who was meant. And then he remembered. He gave a great sigh and stepped forward, passing through the ring of maidens, the ring of women, to face the triangle of elders and the embers of the fire.

He knew the ritual, for he had seen it done many times as he grew up among the People. He untied the red thongs, removed the badger hood, and stepped forward to face the Badger elder.

Tu-ri-nit extended his arms, his hands held palm upward. Into those hands Do-na-ti laid his badger-skin hood, with the mask upward so that the teeth snarled into the lined face of the elder.

Tu-ri-nit raised it high, showing it to the moon, just rising above the eastern swells. He held it low for the Fox and the Bison elders to see. He held it to the fire, for the fire was akin to the sun and was the source of life.

"Tonight, Do-na-ti becomes a man. He has slain the badger. He has done his work as a boy among our people, and it has been well done. Now we place this symbol of manhood upon him, and from this time forward he will be in all ways considered an adult of our people.

"The child is gone.

"Welcome the man." He extended his burdened hands, and Do-na-ti bent his neck to allow the old man to fasten the hood once more. When he straightened again, he found E-lo-ni watching from the ring of maidens, her eyes bright.

Her father and her uncles stood together now, their ring broken as the people mingled together to greet this new warrior and hunter into their village. As Do-na-ti's eyes met theirs, he saw that their faces were calm and glad, and it warmed him.

Tomorrow the people would prepare for the Great Hunt. But after that there would be time to speak about marriage. One who had played the dog in the Great Hunt, if he were chosen for that role, would come to his wife as a man, indeed.

FOUR

In some way, Do-na-ti had expected to awaken on the morning after his ritual feeling entirely different. A man was not a child, it was obvious. There must be thoughts that a man held in his head and feelings in his heart that no child could grasp or endure.

Strangely, he woke feeling just as usual, his mouth tasting foul, his eyes gummy with sleep. He yawned widely and rolled away from Ka-shi, who always managed to snuggle tightly against him, no matter how hot the night might be.

He searched his mind for new thoughts, ideas he had never known before, but the foremost thing he discovered was his need to go outside and relieve his bladder. That was so urgent that he crept among the sleepers toward the door, which showed no hint of daylight as yet.

Outside a steady wind blew from the west, as usual, carrying its burden of dust and grit. He stood beside a gray-green bush, aiming his stream downwind and staring off toward the east, which was turning paler by slow degrees. Today would bring the preparations for the Great Hunt, and suddenly he felt those adult sensations he had longed for.

A blaze kindled in the pit of his stomach, and its warmth ran up through his body, filling him with excitement. Before now Do-na-ti had been one of those young ones who had helped with butchering the kill, and by the time he and his

22

companions arrived with the women, the most exciting activity would be over. Only dead animals lay in the trap into which the hunters had driven them.

This time he would not be covered in blood, slipping along the giant body while pulling the tough hide down the back of one of the dead animals so the fresh meat could be hacked free and laid upon it. This time he would be one of those hunters, the dog-player himself, who helped to herd the leaders of the Great Ones toward the chosen spot where they would die.

He turned to gaze eastward, where the line of paleness crossed the sky. Morning was coming. Already he could hear some of his family moving about inside their lodge, and he went back quickly to join them. Today would be a day to remember all his life, for never again would he live through this preparation day before the hunt that was his beginning as a killer of the great beasts that wandered the plain.

He wondered, as he pushed back the door skin and stooped to enter the lodge, if it would be the Great Horned Ones or the Great Tusked Ones that they would hunt tomorrow. Although the Tusked Ones had been moving in this direction, a small herd of Horned Ones was now nearer than the other group.

Last night they had spoken only of the Great Ones, and every sort of animal that roamed the plains was huge—the bear he had encountered was actually one of the smaller kinds. There was the sloth, as long as a lodge and strong. The wolf that roamed the grasslands was itself very large, compared to the size of a puny human being.

Do-na-ti joined the group in the center of the lodge, watching as his uncle spoke to the wide-eyed children about the shaggy dog hide in his hands. "The one who plays the dog goes into the midst of the herd, making the tail move in a lifelike way, walking as a dog walks, sniffing as he sniffs.

"If he is not skillful, one of the females will suspect this may be a threat to her young, and she will pound him to death with her hooves and horns. If she is one of the tusked ones, she will smash him with her great curving teeth and step on him with feet like flat boulders.

"Taking the part of the dog is a task for one with young nerves and great courage. Our nephew Do-na-ti has honored us all in being chosen."

The young man felt himself grow warm with pride. To honor his people was one of the most important things one could do, and he intended to play the dog better than anyone else ever had. The story singers would make songs about tomorrow's hunt, if all went well.

The day dragged, as Do-na-ti went out to check the rabbit traps along the draw beyond the edge of the village. Four fat ones jerked and flopped at his approach, and he swiftly broke their necks with the edge of his hand and put them into the net bag slung over his shoulder.

The wind was blowing briskly from the west, flattening the long reaches of grass, as he turned toward the low growth of scrub where he had some time earlier seen birds fly down as if to nest. There should be eggs there now, and those were always a welcome addition to the food supply.

He watched his step as he crossed the rough patches of grass and gravel, for in this hot weather rattlesnakes were sometimes too irritable to give fair warning to approaching feet. When he arrived at the edge of the clump of bushes, he stopped and reached to shake the nearest.

A dove shot up from one of the higher branches; he spotted the dishlike nest and moved to gather the two pale eggs there. There were three other nests along the edge of the large patch, though the hen birds were not sitting on them. One held four greenish eggs, one a single pearl-gray one, and the last was empty. Not a large haul, but every morsel of food was precious to the People.

He felt as if he were playing at being a child, now that he was officially a man. For this was children's work, though only after tomorrow would he have to give it up entirely. One last time he would gather eggs and take rabbits from the snares. Tomorrow he would begin his life as a hunter.

The day ended at last, and the family came in from gathering seeds from the grasses and rushes, and roots from the stream. When it was dark outside, they went to rest, though the youngest fidgeted and coughed and fretted, too excited to sleep.

But Do-na-ti forced his eyes to close, his heart to slow to a regular beat. *I will need all my strength tomorrow,* he told himself, as he slid quietly into sleep.

He dreamed of the moon, riding low in the west as its narrow arc went to rest. In that tenuous light, he could see a great mass of the horned ones, their backs rough and woolly and dark against the sun-bleached land. The moon-light glinted on horns here and there as they raised their heads from cropping the grass or moved to a better patch of graze.

He seemed to float above them, seeing the calves grouped with their mothers in the center of the herd, the bulls ringing them. Nothing threatened, and yet he could feel the wariness of those immense animals. They were prepared, he realized, for any danger that might approach.

Floating in his dreams, Do-na-ti thought about the hunt tomorrow. Was this a warning? Was it a promise of good hunting? He could not untangle all the possible meanings of this vision, as he moved along the wind, drifting over the mass of animals until he came to its farther side.

He looked again at the moon in the west. To use the wind to his advantage, he would have to move toward them from the north. Dressed in his dog-skin disguise, he must per-suade those shrewd old bulls that he was, indeed, only a wolf passing through the herd.

He wondered if for some reason that might not be possible when the time came. More and more he felt that this was a dream of warning, a caution to him, who must play the dog tomorrow. Why else should he be given this vision on the eve of the Great Hunt?

Do-na-ti struggled to wake, but the dream held him fast. The herd shifted restlessly, moving away toward the south . . . toward the village where his sleeping body lay.

Behind there was a distant rumble, and threads of dark cloud began moving across the declining moon. A flash interrupted the blackness to the north, and again thunder

grumbled through the sky and quivered in the earth. Was
there a storm approaching, so soon after that other one on
the day he killed the badger?

Rain and wind would delay the hunt, cause the prey to
become nervous and irritable, make the danger for both
"dog" and hunters too desperate to risk. Often storms
stampeded the creatures, sending them pounding away from
the wind, to smash anything in their path until the weather
calmed again.

Chilly disappointment filled the young man. To miss his
first hunt because of a storm . . . that would be a dismal
thing indeed.

He tried to move back toward the village and his sleeping
body. The dart of lightning was nearer now, and the thunder
louder as he circled, bodiless, against the wind. The moon
was peering through a veil of cloud, as if ready to take
shelter below the horizon, and he faced it, feeling that it
might lend him strength to stop this oncoming disaster.

"Bright One!" he tried to cry, although no sound came.
"Oh, Bright One, drive away the storm! Keep the Horned
Ones in their place until we can drive them into our trap!"

That narrowed eye of light seemed to blink slowly, as if
freeing itself of cloud. The golden glow grew brighter,
pushing against the encroaching darkness in the north. As
he watched, Do-na-ti felt the first stirrings of triumph in his
heart.

He woke, sitting upright between Ka-shi and his young
sister. Rubbing his eyes, he crept among the sleeping people
to the door flap, which was left wide open to let in the air,
though the opening was guarded by the huddle of dogs.

He stepped over their shaggy mass and moved outside. To
the west, the moon rode low, clear and steady and without
that cloudy veil. To the north, he found when he moved
around the lodge, there was a distant, dying flicker of
lightning and the dim echo of thunder.

There was no sign of the herd in the low-angled moon-
light. Was it possible that he, Do-na-ti of the Badger Clan,
had dreamed away the storm and prevented the movement
of the herd? It seemed strange, impossible, but he had a

feeling inside him that this was exactly what had happened.

Even as he waited, the last trace of that distant storm died away, and the night grew still. Even the west wind had calmed, for the moment, as he returned to the lodge and lay again between the children.

Tomorrow he would certainly play the dog!

No other dream came to him as the night wore away toward morning, and the day of the Great Hunt began.

FIVE

THE RANK SMELL OF THE WOOLLY HERD FILLED THE HOT DAY AND WAS *carried down the wind as the animals grazed and moved, grazed and moved. The bulls, alert for any danger, lifted their heads from time to time, checking for stray calves or approaching wolves.*

Though only the very young and the sick usually fell to the dire wolf, instinct ruled the great beasts. The circle of bulls kept watch over the terrain when the herd was on the move. As the grasses had been depleted in their present location, and the threat of bad weather drove them, they were making their ponderous way southward again, where their dim memories told them they would find fresh growth.

They came to a tremendous complex of prairie dog mounds, and the herd scattered, all of them taking the opportunity to roll in the loose dirt, scratching their hides pleasurably. A cow, finished with her efforts, rose awkwardly and headed toward a patch of green refreshed by the recent rains. Her calf, calling gruffly, trotted after her and chomped at the grass.

Others, seeing the bent necks as the escapees grazed, came to join them. Soon a considerable number of the bison ranged over this new area, greedily gulping quantities of grass, later to be regurgitated and chewed at leisure. As the sun rose higher and the heat shimmered over the wide sweep of land, some lay down to rest, while calves bucked and ran about them.

When the wolf-dog ambled into view, the nearest bull turned to look it over carefully, though its dim eyes were less than efficient. Still, it smelled like dog, though there was something else, alien and odd, about the odor.

The animal's tail twitched with excitement as it moved forward, nosing for rabbit scent among the chewed-over grasses. The movement of the legs was right. The angle of the tail was right. The bull turned back to a new patch of grass, accepting this newcomer at face value.

The dog sniffed and waggled and trotted and paused as it moved past this separate group of bison. Once it reached the edge of the bunch, it began to angle toward the outlying members of the herd, edging them toward the west and south. So gently and unobtrusively was this done that the giant beasts did not realize what was happening as they obeyed their impulse to avoid this intruder, who gently manipulated them into motion without alarming them.

Those lying down rose as their herd mates moved toward them, and soon some triple handful of animals was moving slowly along, guided by the persistent and subtle movements of the dog. When they were well away from the bulk of the herd, separated by a wide reach of grassy swells, there was a rush of smoke scent and strong, oily stink. Alien cries rose into the air, and small figures, holding long sticks, came running, yelling, waving, and leaping toward the startled bison.

The bulls snorted, and the cows grouped the calves in the center of their sparse ring. Then the nerve of the beasts broke, and they stampeded madly in the direction in which they could see no danger, galloping blindly across the broken country ahead. They could hear only the cries driving them forward, and no warning came to their dulled senses as they ran.

Their small minds filled with panic, they did not see the edge looming ahead. They did not hear the bellows of terror as the leaders plunged over into the hidden ravine, and only

when those behind began to fall onto their trapped fellows
below did they know what was happening.

But it was too late to stop. Not one of the bison was able
to halt its mad plunge into death. When the last was down,
struggling amid a heap of broken and bellowing companions, the dog came lolloping to the ravine's rim and stared
down.

Do-na-ti rose onto his legs and removed the stinking dog
hide, for his work was done; he had played the dog to good
effect. But his quarry did not know and could not see how
they had been manipulated, for already the hunters were
among them with spears, the beautifully chipped spear
points reddening with the blood of their victims.

Do-na-ti dropped the dog skin over a bush, where it
would be safe, and ran along the ravine to a path leading
downward. His uncle came out of the draw, holding his arm
close against his side, and the young man stopped to help
him along.

"A bull turned his head and caught my arm against the
horns of the one beneath him. I think the bone is broken,
Nephew," he said. "Take my spear and go to help your
kinsmen."

Do-na-ti took the spear from Ke-len-ne's hand and helped
the older man to find a place to wait beneath another bush.
Then he turned toward the bellowing, thrashing, blood-
stinking tangle that was the slaughter pen. The wild odor
filled his nostrils, and excitement tingled in his heart.

He plunged toward the mess ahead, avoiding hunters who
were busy with their own prey while he looked for a suitable
kill. A young cow, eyes rolled back, elongated horns
glinting in the sun, which was now overhead, raised her
head to moan.

No one was near, and Do-na-ti thrust the spear deep into
her neck. Blood gushed over him, bathing him in its hot
flood, but he was busy trying to catch the haft of the spear,
which had jerked free when the cow reacted to the stroke.
The wood was lashing up and down as the animal died.

Do-na-ti got a hand on the thing, then another, and after

bearing down with his entire weight, he forced the cow's head down; the eyes dulled and went blank as her struggles stopped. Jerking free the spear, Do-na-ti turned to find other prey.

Blood now ran down the gully behind the mass of trapped animals. Flies already buzzed in great numbers, gathering along the edges of the scarlet runnel and on the hands and faces of the men engaged in further slaughter.

It was almost impossible to recognize individuals—between the blood and the dark masses of insects, the features of individuals were lost. Only shapes and distinctive bits of clothing allowed the young man to locate the men of his aunts and other sisters.

He shifted his position, finding a calf that he dispatched before moving on to other game. As the sun cooked the rocks and the slimy men in the ravine, he killed and killed, intoxicated now with the stink of death and the excitement of danger.

Already two lifeless bodies of the People lay behind him, pulled from the tangle where they had been gored by the terrible horns or crushed by the giant weight of some beast that had half risen to fight before being felled permanently. On Do-na-ti's chest there was a hot line of pain where a horn had raked across him in its owner's death throes. He was bruised from head to foot, for he had moved onto the pile of broken bodies, and more than once he had been kicked or bashed with a thrashing head.

Almost all of the giant bison were now dead. From deep within the pile of hulks there came an occasional grunt or moan, but the surface was now still except for the swarming flies.

Already there was the mutter of voices as the butchers came up the ravine. Women and older children arrived, armed with skinning knives and ready to secure the meat and hides, the tendon and gut and horn and bone that formed the materials that allowed the People to exist in this harsh country.

Do-na-ti leapt down from the shoulders of a great bull and staggered as he landed. Suddenly he was exhausted;

excitement and fear, the labor of playing the dog, and the peril of killing the trapped bison came together to make his head reel and his eyes dim.

He leaned against the wall of the ravine, his chest heaving under its wild pattern of drying blood. His eyes closed as he tried to control his dizziness.

There came a soft touch at his elbow. A gourd of water touched his lips, and he opened his eyes and drank greedily. He was thirsty and hot, and the water settled his vertigo and cooled his fevered skin.

E-lo-ni smiled up at him, holding the gourd steady as he drank. When he stopped at last, he smiled back, knowing that he must look terrible in his grim mask of red and brown and shimmering black-green, but she didn't seem to mind.

"Did you find the uncle?" he asked her, finding to his relief that he could again stand steady on his feet. "He had a broken arm." His voice sounded funny, but thirst would do that, he knew.

"They have taken him back to the village with the other injured men," she said. "I think he is not badly hurt. It was only the lower arm bone, and that broke cleanly and did not shatter."

That was a relief. Corruption from the ugly wounds made when shattered bone pushed through the surrounding flesh was what killed most of those suffering from broken bones.

She gave him a push. "Go and rest. Your work is done, and it is time for us to do ours. I heard Tu-ri-nit say that you played the dog better than any has ever done in his lifetime. You may be proud of that, Do-na-ti of the Badger Clan!"

He touched her shoulder with a filthy finger. Then he turned, taking up his spear, and started toward the path that would take him back up onto the plain. Then as something occurred to him, he turned again to her.

"That calf over there . . . try to save its hide, complete, instead of opening it down the backbone and peeling it away. I have a thought; we might have someone play a calf, rather than a dog. It is an interesting idea, and if we have a complete calf hide, I may be able to persuade the elders to consider trying it."

She stared at him, eyes wide as if she wondered at this unusual idea. Then she nodded. "I shall skin it myself," she said. "And I will bring it to your lodge, so that your own clan may dress and preserve it. You are, indeed, a wise warrior, Do-na-ti."

Flushed with triumph and dripping with sweat, he made his way out of the draw and stood again on the lip of the cut, looking down onto the scene below. Now the butchers swarmed over the carcasses as thickly as the flies had, and already great knobs of red-streaked bone marked the bare spines of many of the giant beasts.

There would be meat to dry for winter, meat to gorge on at a great feast. They might send a runner to nearby villages of other clans, inviting them to share this bounty, for there was more here than Do-na-ti's own small group could eat or dry. Those who had made this hunt would be honored when the work was done and the workers rested from their labors.

Do-na-ti knew that he would be honored with them. The thought sent him toward home at a trot, the wind and the air of his passing whipping away the flies that still tried to settle on his streaked and dappled body. Inside, his heart settled again to its old rhythms, as the last of the killing-fever left him.

SIX

THE CHILDREN HAD SCAVENGED FAR AND WIDE AFTER DEADWOOD
for a great fire, while their elders rested from their labors.
On the second evening after the kill, members of nearby
clans began to straggle into the village, guided by the tall
column of smoke before nightfall and by the red glow of the
blaze once it grew dark.

Many rhythms throbbed around that fire, as drummers
and players of the flute expressed their pleasure through
music. Children danced in the firelight, their small faces
smeared with grease, their hands clutching stringy fragments of meat or chunks of fat. Their elders were not yet
ready to appear, for the triumphal feast after such a hunt was
always carefully choreographed.

Watching the activity from the shelter of a lodge, Do-na-ti
felt the scratchiness of his hood against his neck, the
too-warm weight of the robe over his shoulders. All his
people would be clad in their ritual finery tonight, but he
was still boy enough to wish for the bare chest and skimpy
loincloth that allowed the air to circulate about his skin.

He wondered where E-lo-ni was. There was no activity
yet near her lodge, though the Fox Clan was already
beginning to move toward the fire. As the other Badger Clan
people joined him, Do-na-ti straightened his robe, brushed
the fur of his hood flat, and stepped out behind the Uncle to
lead the family toward the fire.

In the pride of that procession, he forgot the sweat sticking his skin to his robes, for keeping pace with the older men required great control. He wanted to run and leap into the firelight, brandishing a spear and shouting his hunting cry.

Smoke billowed upward in a column, for the wind had died at nightfall. The heat was stifling, but no one paid any heed to that, for the fire was central to their rituals. It gave life and warmth, like the sun.

The hunters reached its bright circle and filed off, half to the right, half to the left, until they stood in a long line, whose ends trailed away into the darkness. Tu-ri-nit, at the middle of the file, remained there, for he was the oldest of the Elders, the most seasoned in battle and the finest hunter the village had ever produced.

He beckoned to Do-na-ti, who stood near the end of the line to his right. The young man turned, his heart warming with delight, to join the clan leader at the center of the row.

"Our newest hunter has played the dog!" Tu-ri-nit cried, and his voice rolled away across the plain like thunder.

The circle of many clans from many villages clapped their hands to their mouths and warbled with wonder, "Oo-wo-wo-wo-wooo!"

"He has killed the Great Horned One, after helping to drive the herd into the trap!" the elder shouted, his old voice wavering with the strain of it.

Again the gathered people saluted him, and the boy felt his entire being swell, as if he might float away into the sky, among the ranks of brilliant stars. He stood erect, eyes fixed on the face of his mother, who stood among the other Badger people. He kept his face under control, though he felt a great smile growing inside him.

Tu-ri-nit swirled his cloak dramatically, his face dark beneath the badger hood. "The daughter of the Terrapin Clan has agreed for this new hunter to visit her lodge and speak with her grandmother."

Everyone understood what that meant. After several moons of such visits, while he learned to know the Terrapin Clan people as intimately as he could manage to do, the

ceremony would take place. Then he would move into that
strange lodge as part of E-lo-ni's family, leaving behind his
own familiar people.

The thought was exciting and somehow daunting.
Changes were both good and bad, he understood, and this
one was so drastic that it frightened him. As he returned to
his place in the line, he caught E-lo-ni's glance. Her eyes
seemed to burn into his as he resumed his place and stood
still with the other hunters.

He understood at that moment that this was the turning of
his life, even more than the Badger Dance had been. All
people must grow up. Every person married, if he lived to
be an adult. He would be near enough to visit his own clan
often, and he would not lose sight of Ka-shi and the other
children.

The elders took their turns, praising the hunters, mourn-
ing those who had died, commiserating with those who had
been injured. Such things happened always, when one
hunted the Great Horned Ones, and were to be expected, but
to be lauded made those still suffering the effects of their
experience feel braver and happier.

He was too far away to hear the words as the elders
spoke, but he knew what they would say, for Do-na-ti had
attended many such celebrations. Sitting in his mother's lap,
a round-eyed baby, he had learned the words of the ritual
laments and songs of praise. Now he could hear them inside
his head, though they were only a blur of sound to his ears.

Then the line in which he stood stirred, the ends moving
to join each other as the hunters formed another circle,
larger than that of the Badger Dance. Ku-lap took his place
in its center, wearing the headpiece that signified the bison
head, and the hunters began to dance, their steps intricate
and timed to the pounding of the drums.

Do-na-ti darted from his place in the circle, shaking his
hips to imitate the wagging tail of the dog skin he had worn.
He angled into the farther arc of the circle, moving those
there out of his way. Individually the hunters acted out the
parts of both prey and predators, until at last the wild dance
turned into a charge across the firelit space.

Those in the lead fell flat, and those behind tumbled onto them. The rear guard pantomimed jabbing with spears and shooting with bows, as their quarry plunged and quivered and rolled back their eyes in death throes almost as convincing as the real ones had been. All the while, the women and old men and children kept up a chant timed to the drumbeats, while the wandering notes of the bone flutes wove in and out of the cacophony that filled the village.

Do-na-ti stood, his chest heaving almost as strongly as it had when he stood above the ravine where the Horned Ones lay dying. Then, his feet stamping out the rhythms of the instruments, he leapt high in the air and came down with a shriek that cut through the noise and stilled every voice, every drum, every flute.

The hunters straightened and stared about as if returning from a trance. Those who had lain flat rose and brushed the dust from their finery and their faces. They, too, seemed strange, as if they had been in another place and had only just returned to the living world of their fellows.

But Do-na-ti, carried out of himself by the strong emotions of the dance, seemed to float above the village, seeing the fire make its patterns of light and shadow over the bodies of the people gathered there. He could distinguish individuals: Ke-len-ne held his arm close to his side, wrapped in a fold of his best robe. His mother, Ash-pah, stood beside his father and the smaller children.

Tu-ri-nit moved into the center of the disorganized group of hunters and clapped his hands twice, the sound sharp in the still air. All faces turned toward him. Even so high above them, Do-na-ti could see that their eyes were glazed, dreaming still with the power of the hunt and the intoxication of the ritual.

The fire, dotted about with dark figures, seemed to expand, growing upward like some red-gold mountain and swallowing the shapes that stood about it.

Do-na-ti had never had so strong a vision before. Now he found himself in the grip of a powerful one, for he saw that fire grow into a burning mountain, spouting flame from its top, spilling burning stuff that rolled away in fiery floods to cover the land about it. Ash spewed into the sky, but it did not blind him as he watched the lava cool into ridges and runnels, marking the land below.

The moon spun above him, casting weird shadows behind new mountains, strange canyons that he did not know, though he had lived on the plain all his life. He felt dizzy, as if he had seen many seasons pass within the space of a few heartbeats, and he closed his eyes. When he opened them again, he was in his body once more, and around him the people were stirring and sighing, as if they had just awakened from a dream.

Do-na-ti shivered, feeling he had traveled a very long distance since he joined the hunters for this celebration. He turned to gaze across the crowd of people, who were beginning to speak softly with one another, turning their steps toward their clan lodges. The smallest of the children had begun to whimper for their blankets, and even the older ones looked sleepy and confused.

He felt a touch at his elbow, and when he looked E-lo-ni stood behind him, smiling. "You will come to my grand-mother tomorrow night," she said, "if you would like that."

He felt a great smile growing inside him. "I would very much like that," he said, as she turned away toward her retreating family.

SEVEN

ALTHOUGH HE HAD THOUGHT BECOMING A MAN AND TAKING PART in a Great Hunt would mean his life would change completely, Do-na-ti found that the memories of those great events soon faded into the past. The people were busy with the matters that kept them alive and healthy. Trapping, netting birds, gathering seeds and roots and leaves from the plants growing on the plain and along the streams must go on, for the meat from the Horned Ones was soon eaten or dried for the winter.

Only in songs and tales around the fires in the evenings were individual stories of the hunt preserved. Those in the Terrapin Clan, to Do-na-ti's surprise, included his own story of playing the dog, along with the stories of those Terrapin hunters who had taken part in the hunt. That, more than anything else, told him that the grandmother was ready to accept him into her family.

Yet during the long days of setting, moving, and running his traps he found himself thinking like a child again, letting his imagination wander. When he caught himself doing that, he chided himself. He had slain the giant bison—he no longer needed to pretend to hunt or to play at casting his spear at shadows. Adults had no need for such play.

Yet it was hard to break the habits of a lifetime, for the land was filled with fascinating things. Small animals scuttered along the ravines, where snakes rattled and coiled.

Flowers bloomed their short lives and left behind seed heads
that provided medicines and foodstuffs.

Insects exploded from the grass about his feet with
buzzes and flutterings. The shadows of tall ranks of cloud
drifted across the rolling landscape, making patterns of
plum-blue against the golden-tan swells and the upthrust
darks of the mountains at the edge of the sky.

Despite himself, the young man danced along stony
ridges, waving his knobstick spear and singing a hunter's
chant, for his heart was joyful. In a hand of suns, he and
E-lo-ni would be paired, and he would be a man in all ways.
Happiness swept him up, and he sprang down at the end of
the ridge onto a grassy knoll.

His heart paused for an instant in its beating. Facing him,
its head low, ears back, skin crinkling into threatening
ridges at the back of its neck, was one of the huge wolves
that roamed the plains. Long-legged, as tall at the shoulder
as the boy's chest, it stood its ground, unafraid of this puny
man-thing that had landed before it.

The bear he had met on the day he killed the badger had
been danger. This might well be death.

Do-na-ti stood still, drawing his breath deep into his
lungs, calming himself into that concentrated center that
could mean survival. If he ran, he would end this day in the
direwolf's belly, for the animal was used to taking fleeing
prey.

No, he must attack. But he had to do it in a manner that
would allow him some chance of survival. His mind darted
about like a trapped ground squirrel, trying to find alterna-
tives for every possible action.

If he moved straight forward, lunging with the fluted
chert spear point at the other end of his knobstick, the agile
beast would sidestep and grab him in its terrible jaws while
he was off-balance. If he eased about sideways, not retreating, keeping the same distance . . . perhaps that might
puzzle the wolf just enough to give him a chance for life.

There was no time to work it out, for the wolf was
shifting its weight, preparing to move. Do-na-ti edged to his
left, keeping the sharp point ready to counter any attack.

The animal cocked its head, watching, sniffing, trying to understand what Do-na-ti was doing. The green eyes focused on him, and the animal turned its head to keep him in view.

Again the boy moved sideways. Now the wolf backed a step, in order to turn with Do-na-ti's movements. Something strange and compelling caught Do-na-ti in its grasp, and he raised his head and shook the knob-ended spear in his hand. He began to dance in a circle about the wolf, chanting as if he were in the ritual circle in the village, dancing with his kindred about the council fire.

> "Ho-he-ho! Ho-he-ho!
> The Great Horned Ones
> flee from the warrior.
> The woolly ones, large as mountains,
> run into our traps.
> The bear and the sloth,
> the wolf and the great cat
> fall to our spears.
> We are the People!
> We eat your flesh!"

The wolf growled deep in his throat and his ears flicked forward, trying to understand this strange sort of howl. Do-na-ti could see unease in his eyes, and he knew that Those Who Went Before and the Old Spirit Ones had guided him as he faced this enemy.

He danced still, chanting, circling the bewildered animal. At last the direwolf gave a shrill cry and turned to flee from this strange one who did not behave like normal prey. As it disappeared over the long swells, in and out of the purple shadow patches, Do-na-ti chanted still, his voice triumphant.

> "I have faced the great wolf!
> He has looked into my eyes
> and felt fear!
> He has listened to my song
> and it has filled his heart with terror!"

But now the wolf was gone, and Do-na-ti stood alone on the grassy hummock, his hands sweating, his heart pounding with the aftereffects of danger. It would have been sad to die before his marriage day, he thought, as he turned to check the next trap down in the adjacent ravine.

His triumph had come too soon. Standing behind him was another wolf, head low, neck ridged, ears flattened. The mate of the first? He had no time to wonder, for this wolf did not wait to see what he would do. It sprang, and he dropped and rolled away before it landed.

Yet it had the preternatural swiftness of the wild creature it was. The wolf turned and caught his leg between deadly teeth; he felt his flesh rip and his bone grate between the pitiless jaws. Yet the pain worked as a stimulus.

Do-na-ti wriggled his weight off his spear and slid it up as far as he could manage, while the wolf growled and chewed on his leg. With all his desperation and more than his natural strength, Do-na-ti plunged the spear down the length of his body, into the top of the direwolf's skull.

That point, smaller than those designed for spearing the great beasts in the hunt, was still deadly. Its fluted edges made it very sharp, and its clever design made it strong.

It plunged into the brain beneath that relatively thin skull; the wolf's jaws clenched agonizingly before relaxing into death. Do-na-ti drew his leg free and sat, watching the twitching, jerking death throes of his attacker.

When the wolf lay still, the young man bound a thong about his leg at the knee to slow the bleeding. Then he crawled to that great body and began skinning it out.

The meat was rank, even for his meat-hungry kind, but the hide was a mark of valor that not one of his people would ever waste. With his flint knife from the sling at his side, Do-na-ti slit the body down the belly, up each leg, peeling it away from the hot flesh beneath.

He felt very faint by the time he had worked the hide free of the entire body, but he had this precious thing in his hands. Now his problem was that of getting it back to the village, for it was very heavy and he was extremely weak.

He rolled it easily, for it was still flexible with the life that had so recently left it. The roll was as thick as the boy's body, and when he tried to lift it he found that beyond his depleted strength.

Do-na-ti sank onto the ground, lay flat, his chest heaving with effort. He must return to the village, and he must take this with him. How could it be done? He felt as if merely taking himself home might be impossible now.

Perhaps he might pull it behind him as he hobbled, using the spear stick for a crutch. He cut a long, thin strip from the side of the pelt and bound it around the bundle. Then he forced himself upright, using the spear to manage that.

Sweat slicked his skin, even the dry plains air being incapable of evaporating it as fast as it ran from his pores. His leg was such torment that it became something too large to perceive, and he pushed it out of his mind.

That way lay the village. He turned his face toward the invisible shelter of his home and began to move, with great effort and more pain, toward his family and E-lo-ni.

Behind him, as he moved through the long slant of the afternoon light, he could hear growls. Some scavenger had come to feast on the body of the direwolf. Perhaps its own mate was even now slavering over its bones.

The sky blurred before him, and he felt as if he might drop into darkness. Yet Do-na-ti of the Badger Clan went forward without stopping until he fell, facedown, and knew nothing more.

EIGHT

============

THE DIREWOLF'S FLIGHT SLOWED, STOPPED. HE RAISED HIS HEAD AND stared at the sky, bewildered by the sudden panic that had sent him running. What had that hairless thing done to him? What kind of howl was it that had filled his heart with terror?

The wolf dropped to his belly, his tongue lolling, saliva dripping from its red tip. He panted, resting, allowing his heart to regain its usual rhythm. Few animals on the plain threatened his kind; even the lions left them strictly alone, and the greater beasts that walked on hooves and huge pads hardly noticed the wolves at all.

In his own experience, only the bear and the snake had posed any threat, and that only when he walked in the ways they held as their own. That thing that had frightened him was helpless, small, without fangs, though the single claw it possessed was a long one with a sharp tip. Why had he run?

The wolf rose and shook himself, scratched a flea under his belly, and turned his head to stare back across the swells toward the place he had left. Something in his dim animal mind drew him back, now that this sudden panic had subsided. He smelled his mate's odor on the wind, back there where he had left that succulent bit of flesh.

He turned and trotted upwind, keeping the scent of his mate in his nostrils. Something changed, even as he moved, and he flung up his head and howled. Blood tainted the

44

wind! The stink of death made him break into a run that ate up the miles he had covered since fleeing that mad thing with the long claw.

Head down, tail streaming behind him, the direwolf returned even more quickly than he had fled. But when he reached the spot where he had faced that mad animal, there was nothing there. Yet he knew that he smelled the blood of his mate. Sniffing, he moved over a small ridge and came to a halt beside a red tumble that was her lifeless body, now recognizable only by the smell of her urine, for the rest was a ruin, red and shapeless.

Her eyes were there, but no head fur surrounded them. Her tongue trailed out of her skinless jaws onto the dust. Flies buzzed about the bloody mess that was her body. He licked awkwardly at the remnants, but he knew in his deepest instinct that she would never move again.

She was dead, the mother of the cubs, and her killer's stink still hung on the wind. The scent of his mate's hide traveled along his track!

Growling again, his ears back, his ruff ridged, the direwolf crept along in the steps of that thing. When he caught it, he would tear out its throat, eat its meat, and leave its bones for the buzzards that were already wheeling overhead.

E-lo-ni smiled often these days, for she knew that soon Do-na-ti would move into her family's house as her mate. Even when she was doing the worst of her tasks—gutting rabbits, grubbing for roots, skinning her knees as she crawled through the rocks hunting lizards—that bubble of warmth was always within her. Soon, it told her . . . soon she and he would be together.

The afternoon began to wane as she worked with her digging stick, searching for cattail roots in the muddy edge of the stream that ran out from distant mountains. Tonight she would bake those and pound them flat on stones, and the family would eat until their bellies rounded.

She liked to gather food—she felt that to be much more worthy than killing animals, though she never mentioned it.

She smiled more widely, remembering Do-na-ti's pride in his kill. Her grandmother had explained to her the ways of men, and the foremost, the old woman insisted, was that men had to play games.

Hunting and war were their favorites, and both posed some danger to their women and children, but it was something every woman understood. That must be endured and dealt with, when the time came.

E-lo-ni felt the truth of it. Yet she was also certain that she would never mind Do-na-ti's posing and gesturing among his fellows. Meat was, after all, very good to eat fresh. When dried, it sustained warmth and energy through the winter. If he wanted to play man games while getting it, and even afterward, that was fine with her.

The day had passed noon, and her shadow began to lengthen as she turned toward the village with her string bags filled with an odd accumulation of foodstuff. Roots bulged damply. Bird eggs were fitted carefully among leaves to avoid breakage. A smaller bag squirmed with its burden of lizards, which, while scrawny and not much substance between the teeth, made excellent additions to clay-lined basket pots of soup or stew.

She came within sight of the huddle of lodges. Hides from the recent hunt were stretched along frames, drying in the sun. Those would make moccasins and bedskins, linings for new lodges, leather for thongs when they were cured at last. The furry shoulder parts would make warm cloaks for those who must venture out into the winter blizzards. Stacks of bones were piled haphazardly at intervals, for they, too, were useful parts of her people's economy.

Her small brother Su-ni came running to meet her, his fat stomach bouncing and his round cheeks scarlet as he hurried. He was too small to go with the children who ranged the plain after food, but he did his best to be useful. She handed him her bag and smiled as he turned to race back toward the lodge. He would arrive, panting and gabbling his baby talk, and her mother would know at once that E-lo-ni was back from her morning's work.

Before she reached the home lodge, however, the girl

paused and raised her head. Far away, almost beyond her range of hearing, there came a long howl. Faint though it was, it held such fury and grief that it chilled her heart. She had heard many a direwolf cry in the night, but never before had she heard such a sound by day.

Do-na-ti had gone in that direction when they parted that morning!

Some instinct as sure as the wolf's told E-lo-ni that she must go. Without pausing to do anything except catch up her grandfather's spear that leaned beside the lodge, she began to run, her feet sure on the rough ground, her strong legs pounding steadily toward the source of that terrible howl.

Focused upon that unseen goal, she ran until her heart drummed in her throat, her pulse threatened to burst her veins. Yet she was a woman of the People, honed by the plains and toughened by their dangers. She did not pause to rest or take a moment to think of what she might meet when she arrived. She would know what to do when she came to the spot where she would meet the direwolf.

The sun slipped down as she sped over the undulating ground, up and down ravines, through patches of brush and over the mounded villages of the Small Brothers who lived beneath the ground. Long before she arrived, she could see a darker brown lump lying flat against the pale tan of the ridge behind it.

As she drew nearer, E-lo-ni knew that it was a person. Whether it was Do-na-ti or anther of the People, she felt grim triumph that she had realized his danger and come so quickly. Whoever it might be was in need of help.

Her steps were loud, crunching into the dry and pebbly soil, and as she came very near she heard a raucous squawk. Heavy wings flapped, and buzzards rose beyond the ridge, as if interrupted as they surrounded carrion. To her relief, none seemed, as yet, to have attacked the prone body that was, without any doubt, that of her man.

As she slowed, from beyond that ridge there came a silent, snarling shape. A direwolf topped the stony outcrop and moved toward Do-na-ti, its neck hair erect, its eyes blazing with hatred and deadly intent. The stink of it shocked E-lo-ni into caution.

A spear was all very well when one was surrounded by hunters, all intent upon distracting a beast while getting a good chance to kill it. One person alone, faced with a creature whose shoulder reached higher than her head, must think before acting, if she wanted to live to see another sunrise.

Strangely, the wolf had not seemed to notice her, all its attention being concentrated upon the unconscious man. That gave her the chance to drop behind a shelf of rock and slither around it into the protection of the curving ridge itself. The stone layers were stepped, with a shallow ditch between them for most of the way, offering concealment as she crept along.

That held its own dangers, of course. She moved quickly, but each hand or knee went down only after a searching glance that would spot any snake within striking distance. A rustle off to her right froze her in position as E-lo-ni tried to locate its source.

A mottled brown shape slithered out of a cranny, its scales whispering against the hot stone, and looped across the way ahead of her. When it had flowed into a crack in the next ledge, she breathed out at last, sweat beading her body. She did not fear death, but she had seen people die in convulsions after being bitten by one of the reptiles, and she had a healthy fear of them.

Then she went on, following the ridge until she was behind the wolf. Always she was watching for rattlers while keeping an eye on the buzzards as they settled again onto whatever dead thing lay behind the ridge. If they came on this side and went for the eyes of her mate, she must attack them, direwolf or no.

When she peered out between two angles of rock, she could see that the wolf was approaching Do-na-ti very slowly, as if it feared him. Its ears were laid back, and its belly almost touched the ground as it slunk cautiously toward its motionless prey.

From this angle she could see on the other side of the

limp body a bundle about which flies buzzed frantically. A hide? It had to be, fresh-killed, already beginning to stink. The direwolf paused beside that and sniffed at it. Then it sat back on its haunches and raised its muzzle toward the sky.

This howl was even more mournful than that other which had set E-lo-ni on the trail. It held pain and anger and blood lust. Understanding that from her own experience and that of her people, the girl knew that if she did not distract the beast it would kill her mate-to-be. Retribution, whatever one's kind, was something built into the plains creatures.

She reached into the edge of the ditch, where shards of stone had weathered away from the parent rock, and took up several sharp-edged missiles. The wolf rose, and she threw with the accuracy of one whose life has often depended upon the power of her arm. The shard struck the beast on the side of the neck; it flinched and yipped, turning to see where the attack came from.

Before it could gather its wits, E-lo-ni rose onto her knees and sent a bombardment of rocks to batter her opponent. The wolf snarled, its lips crinkling to reveal its terrible fangs. Then it leapt upward into the shelter of the farther ridge that curved behind it.

Now she knew what the animal intended. It was the thing she would have chosen for it to do, and she felt that one of the Old Spirit Ones might be nearby, bolstering her efforts. Backing into a nook in the rock, she watched the higher ledge beyond which the wolf had disappeared.

It would spring upon her from above—that was the hunting technique of its kind. It suited her very well.

Holding the spear slanted upward, she wedged the knob at its butt between two melon-sized stones and placed her knees at either side of those. With both hands on the haft, she knew her position would allow her to shift her aim if the wolf came from an unexpected angle. Then she waited, her ears straining to hear the click of claws against rock, as well as the hoarse breathing of her enemy.

When the wolf sprang, she heard the change in its breathing before it came over the ledge. E-lo-ni raised the spear a fraction and clung with both hands as the heavy

body leapt down and the fluted point impaled it between
throat and chest. Hot blood gushed over her hands and arms
before she could drop the haft and let the struggling body
fall to the ground.

Those furious eyes stared into hers, even as the creature
died. E-lo-ni, remembering her grandmother's teaching,
whispered, "Oh, beast that must die that I may live, I send
your spirit to the Ones Beyond. Do not hate me that I have
killed you!"

But as the last breaths panted from that ruined body,
she knew that the animal had died hating her and Do-na-ti.
The feel of its hatred surrounded her as she set her foot upon
the still form and jerked the spear free.

Then she turned toward her mate-to-be and sank to her
knees at his side. He was breathing, she could feel as she
laid her hand on his back, but his leg, she saw, was bitten to
the bone. He had lost a lot of blood, she could see from its
livid color, though the thong he had bound around his knee
was holding it to some extent.

How might she go for help without leaving him to the
mercy of any predator that might come? Then she saw that
bundle again. Unrolling it, she found it to be most of the
hide of another direwolf . . . the mate of the one she had
killed? It was likely.

Then, with her nose wrinkling in distaste, she pulled the
bloody hide over the body of Do-na-ti and weighted its
edges with rocks. Few creatures would venture near the
stink of a direwolf. It should keep him safe until she could
return with someone to help carry him home again to the
village.

NINE

THE DREAMS, LACED WITH FEAR AND PAIN, WERE STRANGE AND terrifying. Do-na-ti stood amid a pack of direwolves, all facing him in a circle, their teeth gleaming in the pale light of a half-moon. His spear hung in his hand, its tip shrinking as he watched it, until it was as small as those the children used with their tiny bows to shoot birds.

The haft itself seemed to be melting, drooping like a withered leaf. How could he defend himself with such a useless weapon? His own teeth and nails were no match for those of the beasts that now began to move around him in a circle like that of one of the rituals.

Did they chant, those wolves, as they watched him, echoing his own song that had sent the other beast flying away across the swells?

There lies the hunter of the Great Horned Ones.

He seemed to hear those words among the growls and snarls.

Watch as he faces us,
trying to think how to run.
We shall eat his flesh and crunch his bones.
We shall feed our cubs
upon his entrails

and leave his hide for the vultures.
Watch the hunter,
with his pitiful spear!

Do-na-ti knew those words to be true. His muscles felt as weak and useless as his weapon, and terror filled his heart. Even as he realized that, his senses drifted into a fog that hid the circling wolves. He was sinking into death, he thought, and that was something he understood and might even welcome, young as he was.

Darkness enveloped him, and then agony worse than any he had ever known wrenched him out of that awareness. Someone had lifted him and was carrying him away, but he could not rouse enough to open his eyes. Who had come to him, there on the plain that ended only at the feet of the distant mountains?

When he woke again to consciousness, he was lying on his back. His leg was on fire, cuts and scratches all over him were twinging, and he could feel tight bindings in many places on his body. But he was of the Badger Clan, and he did not groan as he fought to loosen his eyelids, which were stuck fast.

A hand touched his cheek. "You are in the village," said a quiet voice. "You are with your mother, Do-na-ti. Do you not recognize my touch?"

He sighed. Of course he did. But still he knew that he must see, must fight to bring himself back from the edge of death, where he had heard the wolves singing.

"Eyes," he managed to croak. "Open eyes."

Wetness touched his eyelids. Moss soaked in water, he knew at once, was being rubbed lightly to loosen the gummed lids. When he suffered from a fever, many seasons ago, when he was a child, his mother had done the same.

He tried to smile, but his face threatened to crack. Still, he knew she understood that inside he was smiling for her.

Then the wavering voice of the grandfather came to his ears. "How is the boy?" it asked, and a finger touched his hair. "Do-na-ti, hunter, how is it with you?"

"It is well, Grandfather," he said. "I thought I would

die . . ." His voice dwindled, for his mouth was dry, his throat parched.

A horn cup touched his lips, and he felt a strong arm beneath his shoulders. The water was cool, welcome, and he sipped slowly, knowing that he must not drink too much all at once.

He tried to sit, but he was too weak, and the arms laid him back. Now that he was more alert, he realized that he was in his own bed place . . . He could tell by the smell and the feel of the fur blankets beneath him. The familiar smoky meat and sweat smell of his own family's lodge was reassuring.

"Hide. Did you bring the . . . hide?" he asked.

His grandfather's voice was gruff with pride. "We did, indeed. E-lo-ni covered you with it while she came for help, and it kept the vultures and other scavengers away for long enough for your uncle and the other men to arrive." He paused for a long moment, and Do-na-ti knew he was trying to find words that were not too flattering to offer a very young hunter, yet were true and admiring.

Then he went on, "Few men have killed the direwolf without help. Fewer women have done that thing. Yet on a single day, both you and your mate-to-be slew a direwolf. That is an omen so strong, a thing so rare and unexpected that the Elders are sitting in the Council Lodge at this moment, reading its meaning."

The boy heard his mother sigh. Though men relished strong omens achieved with blood and anguish, women preferred their lives to go by without danger or heroism. They liked their days to be the same, passing in safety for their children. He had learned from watching his mother and sisters that they desired a life that did not make their constant labors any more difficult than they already were.

But his grandfather was talking again, and he strained to hear his words. "The village is filled with pride. E-lo-ni is honored greatly for her courage, and you are held up as a model for the young ones. Our clan is proud, though do not allow that to make you reckless, Grandson."

Now his eyes opened a slit. His mother rubbed again with

the wet moss, and he forced his eyelids apart completely. Her face, bending over him, was a mixture of pride and concern, and his grandfather, just behind her, watched him closely, his wrinkle-tracked face expressionless.

"I can see," the boy murmured. "E-lo-ni—will she come?"

"She has come twice, while you slept. I will call her," his grandfather said. He moved out of sight toward the door flap, and Do-na-ti listened to the sound of his halting steps as he went outside. There was a glad cry, and light footsteps pattered toward the lodge.

Then E-lo-ni was there, touching his cheek softly with a timid finger. He could not see her face, for she stood against the light at the doorway, but it was her shape, her warm salty smell. He smiled. "You came," he murmured.

On the next day he sat and put his feet to the dirt floor of the lodge. Though he had been dried by the sun, drained of much blood, worried by the fangs of the wolf, he was Badger Clan. If there had been need, he would have risen and fought beside his family, or run before a stampeding herd of Horned Ones, or battled a devil wind itself.

Though E-lo-ni was busy with her own tasks, she found time to help him as he returned to his round of traps. Now Ka-shi accompanied his brother, for Do-na-ti's strength had not yet returned, and she seemed to worry when he was not beneath her eyes. That amused Do-na-ti and warmed his heart.

Before the first cold wind swept down from the north, he was himself again, taking part in rituals and grasshopper hunts. The last of those took place at the tag end of summer, when the high tan grasses rasped with the creatures.

Do-na-ti, feeling that this was a pale imitation of the Great Hunt he had known, circled with his clan, sweeping the insects forward with brooms of brush, while the children clattered sticks together to frighten their prey.

This was the most pleasurable sort of hunt, for everyone could take part without any danger, other than the chance of encountering rattlesnakes or scorpions or bad-tempered badgers. Whoops and laughter accompanied the hunters as they gathered up the nets and bags and baskets of insects.

When the nets were filled with wiggling grasshoppers, there were enough to feast everyone to the point of bursting. But that was the last such hunt of the season, and all knew it. Winter would come soon, and the insects would go away, to return with spring.

The People would hide from the sharp winds in their lodges, keeping warm with the stores of brush and dried dung the children had gathered all summer. When the sun shone, they would tend traps and dig for roots in the edges of the streams, but for most of the cold season they rested and talked together.

Before that time came, the grandmother of the Terrapin Clan visited Do-na-ti's lodge and invited him, with all formal ritual, to share her home with her granddaughter.

He took the basket of pollen she had brought for him, and he gave it to his mother. This was the first step, and he thanked old Na-tah and dipped his finger into the yellow powder. With it he drew a circle upon his forehead and another on that of Na-tah.

His uncle brought to him a bowl filled with red paint, and he thanked his uncle as solemnly as he had the old woman. Another finger went into the bowl, and he drew red rays around the sun mark. The sun brought all good things, and it was the best omen for beginning a marriage.

When the decorations were done, marking everyone in his family as well as his grandmother-to-be, he rose and offered her his hand. Together they left the lodge and moved toward that of the Terrapin Clan, chanting together the ritual of marriage.

Behind came his mother and her daughters and sisters, his uncle and the grandfather, all carrying gifts of well-cured skins, basket pots for cooking, and string bags, intricately woven and brightly dyed. They sent their young hunter to his new life with every convenience they had created in their spare moments, over the past months.

When the family group came to the big lodge where the Terrapin Clan lived, they stopped politely well before they reached the door flap. E-lo-ni stood there with her mother, her uncle, and her mother's sister, and the grandmother joined their huddle.

Do-na-ti stepped forward and reached for her hand. The girl raised her head proudly and moved to meet him, their hands meeting solidly between them. Behind the young man the chant began again, as his family wished them well.

Then the Badger Clan turned away from Do-na-ti, who was now a member of another clan, and began moving toward their own lodge again. As they went, they sang:

> "Two walk together,
>   Ai! Ai!
> Two sing together
>   Ai! Ai!
> Two make another,
>   Ai! Ai!
> Three walk together,
>   Ai! Ai!"

Do-na-ti smiled. Although his children would belong to the Terrapin Clan, he knew that his own family would take secret pride in them. They would make shy gifts to and solemn conversation with their grandchildren, when they chanced to meet about their work or in the Ritual. He had seen this with the children of his older kinsmen, who were now counted as Fox and Bison and other clans, and he knew it would hold true for his children even as it did with everyone's.

But as he turned with E-lo-ni to enter the Terrapin Lodge, he forgot such distant musings. Her hand was warm in his, and when she glanced aside at him her eyes were very bright.

His heart was tripping with excitement as he followed the grandmother, leading E-lo-ni by the hand still, into the back of the lodge, where a blanket of hides had been stretched to surround a capacious bed place.

As he stooped beneath it, he realized that the direwolf skins had been used to make their marriage room. That was a good thought, surely an excellent omen for their future together.

But he lost the thought as his new wife turned to him and smiled, her eyes shining in the dim light. "I welcome my husband to our home," she whispered.

And then he forgot to think or even to dream.

TEN

THE WOOLLY MAMMOTH SHIFTED UNEASILY, TURNING HIS GREAT TUSKED head toward the wind, which had changed and changed again, whipping from north to west to northwest. A lifetime of experience warned the huge bull that a storm was on its way, one of the blizzards that came with blinding intensity to lap the plain and the mountains beyond it in a thick layer of snow.

His huge bulk and thick coat made excellent insulation against the cold, but the mammoth hated the wind, the ice that coated his woolly hide, the sting of sleet in his eyes. The small herd, all that was left of the much larger ones he could dimly recall, were also snuffling through their trunks and trumpeting warnings to one another. Without waiting for him to make the first move, they turned toward the south.

Now the wind was at their backs, and the big bull pushed his way to the front of the herd and moved ahead, his great bulk traveling almost silently over the rolling lands. The long legs of the beasts carried the herd faster then any man could run; before the first blast of snow-laden wind came sweeping down from the north, they were well on their way.

Over frosted grass, up and down ravines cut by runoff, over ledges of rock and patches of grit, the great animals sped. Now sleet bombarded their impervious backs, but their faces were turned away and they did not slow. Only when snow came blasting down the wind, hiding everything

58

in its path, did they stop in the bottom of a shallow canyon.

Three hand counts of mammoths huddled in groups, heads together, their great bodies touching for warmth, their eyes closed now against the stinging snow. Drifting into a dreamlike state, they began to sway from one front pad to the other, as if dancing. Self-hypnotized, each group moved quietly in unison, as the storm intensified above them.

The sun, hidden so deeply in snow clouds that its light was almost invisible, slid down the west; blackness so deep that it held nothing except flying snow enveloped the plain and the canyon. The lead bull realized, in time, that he was being buried in the drifts accumulating in their shelter. He heaved himself out and trumpeted, making himself heard even above the shrilling wind.

Groaning and snorting and trumpeting, the herd moved off into the night, keeping the wind at their backs, oblivious of whatever obstacle might lie before their huge, trampling feet. They could not see bushes, and they trampled them down. They did not recognize boulders or lava ledges left from the formation of the distant mountains, and they rolled over them without slowing. They could not see the huddle of lodges that lay ahead, hidden in the blast of snowy wind that scoured the plain.

The wind was whipping around the lodge, audible even through its thick earthen walls. Do-na-ti listened without concern. He was snug beneath layers of furs as he curled against E-lo-ni's back, his arms wrapped around her warm shape.

The lodge of the Terrapin Clan was larger than that of the Badger People, its domed roof-walls even thicker. No chill reached the People, whose body heat kept the space relatively warm, even when no fire was lit beneath the smoke hole. Only the creaking of the thongs that held the layered leather flap tight across the doorway could be heard above the wind.

He had long ago grown used to the individual snorts and snores of the sleepers in his new family. The soft moan was the grandmother, whose knotted hands and painful legs troubled her badly when the wind blew cold. The regular grunt-snort was the grandfather, and it was a reassuring sound, for it never varied.

Do-na-ti was thinking how very comfortable and well provided for his new family was when he realized that he must get up and use the jar the men kept near the door. That was a convenient thing, for it meant he did not have to go out into terrible weather in the night. Nevertheless, getting up to use that meant leaving his warm nest behind the direwolf hides.

He turned and stood. Then he froze in place, feeling with his feet rather than listening, for the wind blanked out any sound beyond the walls. Something was vibrating the dirt floor—something huge and terrible, maddened by the wind and the snow, was coming toward the lodges.

Bison? It was not the season when they ranged to the north. The Great Tusked Ones? He gasped with shock. Only they, pounding over the land with their huge bulks and their swift pads, could shake the ground so strongly.

"Rise," he yelled. "Hurry! Something is coming!"

There was a sputter of grunts and groans, of questions and comments, as the family woke. The first to stand understood at once, and with incredible swiftness the People gathered furs and pots and foodstuffs together, as the vibration became a continual pounding that shook dust down from the roof.

Which way should we run? Do-na-ti wondered, as he reached to help E-lo-ni with her burden of wolf skins. Those precious things must not be lost, for they were the totem of this new little family and the omen for their future.

He peered around the curve of the lodge, into the snow-laden wind, but no one could see into that blast. "The ravine!" he yelled to his wife. "It is too narrow for them to get into."

She nodded and passed the word to her mother, putting her lips to the older woman's ear, for only so could the words be heard at all. The group struggled toward the narrow cleft leading to the stream that provided their water;

only when Do-na-ti had seen the last safely into its stony depths did he turn toward the lodge of his birth family.

E-lo-ni did not put out her hand to stop him, for she understood what he must do. Yet he felt her gaze on his back as he pushed against the terrible wind, trying to reach that other lodge, which seemed too distant to find in the tumult of the storm and the noise of the approaching animals.

Before he neared the doorway, he saw dark shadows that were his people coming out. His mother, the grandfather, the uncles and sisters and aunts were burdened as the Terrapins had been, and he caught his mother's attention and gestured toward the ravine. She started after him, and he went to help her with her load of furs.

The grandfather came close beside them. "No," he shouted. "Too small, if the Terrapin are there. The hillock with the great boulder. That will shelter us! Go to your own wife, Grandson."

Do-na-ti knew the old man was right, but he turned reluctantly. Now the wind pushed him almost off his feet and sped him to the cleft where his new family waited. When he reached it, they were already well blanketed with snow; he burrowed down until he found E-lo-ni, who had spread the wolf skins to make a place for all the smallest children.

The ground quivered beneath the hides, and snow shook down more layers from the walls of the ravine onto the shivering people, as the herd of mammoths drew near. Even above the noise of the wind, Do-na-ti heard cries shriller than the trumpeting of the beasts, accompanied by crunching sounds that filled his heart with dread. They were trampling straight through the village, and those who had not received a warning might well die beneath those terrible padded feet.

He held E-lo-ni tightly, and she in turn held as many of the small ones as she could manage. Around them the children whimpered, too frightened to cry aloud, and even older people shivered against Do-na-ti's back. This was a thing more terrifying than the devil winds, more uncontrollable than his encounter with the direwolf.

The people beneath the wolf hides quaked as the great animals thundered forward, their route taking them very near the narrow slit in the rocky soil. Pebbles and grit and snow pelted down from the edges and sides of the cleft, and Do-na-ti spread the upper hide as far as it would stretch to protect all those he could cover.

It seemed to take a very long while for the herd to pass, and before they were gone one of the Tusked Ones passed so close to the ravine that it seemed ready to plunge into its narrow gap. Though the opening was too small to admit that huge body, Do-na-ti knew that the beast might well kill them all in its death throes.

The trampling and trumpeting passed at last, and in their wake the voice of the wind seemed almost peaceful. But E-lo-ni stirred in his arms and wriggled free. "We must see to the other clans," she said. "The young and the weak will be safe here, sheltered from the worst of the wind and covered with the furs. We must go and see to our village."

He knew that to be true. He had heard cries that rose even above the sounds of the mammoths and the shrilling of the wind, and his people did not cry out without cause. So Do-na-ti slithered after his wife from the shelter of the direwolf hides and climbed after her up the treacherous wall of the ravine.

The wind seemed to slice through the thick antelope-hide robe he wore, but he ignored his shivering and tried to peer through the darkness and the snow toward the place where the lodges stood. It was impossible to see even E-lo-ni now, though she stood within arm's reach and held his hand.

Do-na-ti faced into the wind. There lay the village, and only by his keeping the blast full on his face would they find it. Together the pair struggled along the short distance between the ravine and the spot where their lodge had stood. They found it when E-lo-ni fell into the edge of the pit house. The domed roof had been crushed and pushed to one side, leaving a shoulder-deep drop.

When he felt her fall, Do-na-ti held fast to her hand, going to his knees but never losing his grip. "They have destroyed our house," he heard her cry as she scrambled back up the dirt wall.

The remnant of the soil-reinforced roof held off the wind a bit as they huddled together, wondering how to reach any who needed their help. Another shout gave them direction, and they rose and, hands linked, moved into the wind toward the next lodge, that of the Bison Clan.

The cries came from the ruins of the Bison lodge. The stampeding beasts had moved over the top of it, crushing the roof into the pit, burying the clan alive beneath layers of earth and wood and snow. The voice crying for help was a young man's—it was too hoarse to recognize, but Do-na-ti knew it must be one of his boyhood companions.

Frantically the pair began to dig into the rubble, throwing behind them broken support poles and clods of frozen dirt. They tunneled like dogs into the heap, and in time they came to a foot, a leg, a body that lay alarmingly still and was cooler than it should have been. Do-na-ti pulled as E-lo-ni dug along it, and after a moment he tugged free the shape of a woman.

They laid her carefully out of the way and went on with their digging. Now others were appearing from the direction of the ravine, and Do-na-ti realized that the wind had lessened, enough to allow him to see the shapes of these other people, coming from those lodges that had escaped damage.

He sighed with relief. Hands joined his amid the broken bits that had been the Bison lodge. The rubble began flying faster, and more people were unearthed. Three were dead, broken and crushed, but the living began to emerge, as well.

When dawn paled the sky, the land appeared as unbroken layers of snow from horizon to horizon. The remaining lodges were black shapes against the white blanket, though even the unbroken ones showed signs of the close passing of the Great Tusked Ones in the night.

The Badger Clan lodge was flattened. Once there was time for Do-na-ti to search the knoll with the big boulder, he found most of his former family alive. But his mother was dead, crushed when a boulder had been pushed aside by one of the animals.

Near the lodge of the Elders, Tu-ri-nit was also dead, lying in the open as if defying to the death the invasion of those terrible visitors. Staring down at the misshapen body that had belonged to the Elder of his clan, Do-na-ti felt wrath build inside him. He looked up at the edge of the sun, just visible above the eastern horizon.

"There is blood between us, Tusked Ones!" he shouted toward the snow-laden south. "I will hunt you! I will kill you! The rest of my life will be devoted to slaying you and taking your flesh and your bones, your tusks and your hides!"

The words did not ease the pain he felt as he returned to the knoll and crouched beside his mother's body. He could feel the silent anguish that filled the hearts of those who still lived among the Badger Clan.

Never, even though he might live long, would he lose this flame of fury that devoured his spirit. Until he went into the Other Place, he would be the enemy of the mammoth clan, wherever they ranged, whatever they might do.

If he must hunt the terrible creatures alone with a single spear, he would do it whenever they came near. If he must die in the doing, that suited him well. This would be the work of his life. If there were children to come, he would teach them to hate as he did.

ELEVEN

T̲ʜᴇ ʙʟɪᴢᴢᴀʀᴅ sᴡᴇᴘᴛ ᴏᴠᴇʀ ᴛʜᴇ ᴄᴏᴜɴᴛʀʏsɪᴅᴇ, ʟᴇᴀᴠɪɴɢ ᴘᴇᴏᴘʟᴇ ᴀɴᴅ animals alike to dig themselves out of snowdrifts and to repair the damages of wind and rampaging mammoths. Although the People were not numerous enough to spare any life among them, they had lost fewer than they might have in the dangers of the night.

While the Terrapin Clan had lain safely in the shelter of the ravine, the Badger Clan had lost three. One of the children had been trampled and lay beside Tu-ri-nit and Ash-pah on a pile of skins at the center of the ritual space, where the fire usually burned. Around their silent shapes the rest of the village worked to help those who were injured and to save what might be salvaged from those lodges that had been damaged or crushed entirely.

E-lo-ni kept glancing aside at her man, for Do-na-ti seemed sunk in gloom. His mother had been close to his heart, she knew from their childhood together. And even though he was now officially a member of the Terrapin Clan, he had looked up to Tu-ri-nit, Elder of the Badgers, with respect and affection.

She ached for him, but she knew that grief must be worked through alone. She had lost an infant sister who had been like her own child. As the young one sickened and died last summer, E-lo-ni had known the despair that

shadowed the sun and made the inside of one's own mind a
place of darkness.

Beside her husband, she dug into the flattened remnants
of the Bison Clan's lodge. Hides emerged from the heap of
earth and broken poles, some in usable condition, once they
could be cleaned. The pots had been smashed; hafts of
spears and bows, and arrow shafts had been snapped when
that weight fell onto them.

E-lo-ni thrust her hands deep into a pile of debris, sifting
unseen items through her fingers. At elbow depth, she felt
sharp edges, cold hard surfaces; the store of new spear
points, she was sure, had been placed in this spot.

"Do-na-ti, come! I have found the Bison Clan's points."
She withdrew her hands and moved to allow Do-na-ti to
kneel beside the hole she left. Together they pushed aside
debris until a rosy glint of chert and the dark shine of flint
could be seen at the bottom of the depression.

E-lo-ni watched with interest as Do-na-ti withdrew a
handful of points and held them out in the brilliance of sun
on snow. Then he sighed and let them drop, a shatter of
fragments in muted colors. The spear points were broken.
Only one seemed to be intact, and it split into two unequal
parts when it hit the trampled snow.

Ke-lo-ti, the Bison flint knapper, had spent most of the
past year in making the new supply, for he was the best
maker of large spear points in all the village. No one could
equal his sharp edges, fluted elegantly and capable of being
reshaped if the tips were broken in use.

Those ruined points would have tipped the spears of the
best hunters in the village when spring came again. As more
handfuls came to light, it became plain that, with random
exceptions, all were lost. Only those left from the year
before remained to use in hunting the largest beasts on the
plain.

The flint from the canyon where the point-makers gathered their supply had been depleted as Ke-lo-ti painfully
chipped away through the grim days of winter. If the hunters
were to replace those points lost in hunts of the past year, the
long journey to that canyon would have to be made again,

this time in the season of storms and cold. Ke-lo-ti would have to begin his winter's work all over, with little time left before spring warmed the plain and the herds began moving again.

E-lo-ni leaned forward and touched Do-na-ti's arm. "We might make the journey to gather flint. We could bring back enough to replace the spear points that were lost or broken last year."

He looked up into her eyes, and she saw the thought take root in his mind. "There is nothing left to do except sit in the lodges and wait for warmer weather," he said softly. "I must continue to grieve, if I do that, for all is sadness inside. But if we went, we would go eastward, toward country that will take all our strength and cleverness to cross safely.

"That is a good notion, E-lo-ni. I will ask the grandmother and Ku-lap. He will, I think, become Chief Elder now. He may approve such a venture." To her relief his expression had lightened and there was a spark of interest in his eyes.

E-lo-ni kept digging in a different spot. If she smiled now it would be a harsh thing, for her man was, as yet, unable to smile. But she nodded, knowing that the journey, however perilous, would be good for them both.

The Terrapin lodge had been crowded with other people, and even with their wolf-hide screen, their lovemaking had been hesitant and cautious. Out in the clean vastness of the plain, they might find more closeness and warmth than they had so far in their life together.

They worked hard, along with others from various clans, until everything usable was dug free and carried away to shelter in one of the more scantily tenanted lodges. Finding space for those whose houses were unlivable occupied their thoughts after that.

The Moose Clan had dwindled over the past generation until only a handful now lived in the great lodge that their numbers used to fill. They offered space to those whose lodges had been destroyed, and soon the homeless Badger and Bison people were sheltered once more.

Other lodges, only partly destroyed, were quickly shored

up with poles scavenged from the devastated ones. The soil was frozen, but hides went over the poles to keep out the cold, and soon the damp leather was frozen to iron hardness.

As soon as that task was done, E-lo-ni turned back to help her Terrapin Clan repair the broken places in the dome of their own lodge. All the while she worked she thought about the journey she would make with Do-na-ti. Even a stampede of mammoths, it seemed, could have a few happy side effects.

They worked long after the sun set, but the snow light made the world bright. When they fell into their newly arranged blankets behind the rehung wolf hides at last, E-lo-ni slept at once, exhausted with terror and cold and hard work. At her side, Do-na-ti twitched and moaned, waking her from time to time as he dreamed again of his loss and his grief.

She woke early and went to the door flap, pushing open a crack and looking out into the black bowl of the sky and the snow-whitened softness of the land beneath it. Again the sun was going to rise without any threat of another storm, for there was no cloud to obscure the brilliance of the stars.

Perhaps today her people would complete their work of restoring the village so that life could continue. Tonight they could make the ritual of departure for the dead who waited so patiently to be released from this place.

Once all those things were done, Do-na-ti might find an opportunity to speak with Ku-lap. Before another storm rode in on the north winds, they might be well away to the east, following the winding canyon that held the river. It would not be comfortable, surviving another blizzard outside the warmth of the lodge, but E-lo-ni knew that Do-na-ti needed something very difficult, very dangerous and demanding to do, or he would spend a winter of misery.

She had seen people die of such depression, withering away in their narrow segments of the communal lodge and dying for lack of any will to live. Some had been old, like the aged aunt whose man had died and who afterward looked always inward, with seemingly no life in her eyes, even before she closed them for the last time.

Others had been young. Her cousin Na-pi-li had injured his arm in a hunt, and the right hand shrank and curled until it was unusable. Though he still had a good, quick brain and another hand capable of doing many tasks about the village, the young man seemed to lose interest in life. If he could not hunt with his companions, he seemed to shun doing anything else.

He had died, and E-lo-ni had a cold feeling in her heart that her husband might do the same for grief, if something drastic were not done at once. So she willingly faced the risks inherent in winter travel, craving the change that might bring his eyes to life again. They would go, even if they could not find young men foolish enough to go with them.

By making travois of poles and hides, they could haul in enough rough-chipped flint to supply the knapper for the time he would have at his disposal before spring came again. It was easier to pull the travois over snow than over rough rock and dirt, and together they might well supply enough flint to keep the hunters from running short of points.

The People managed to finish their work before the sun moved down behind the horizon. Broken lodge poles and other debris were piled in the space where the ritual fire must burn, near the bodies of the waiting dead. Even the injured, wrapped in layers of furs and hides, were brought out into the night, once that blaze was kindled and roaring into the black sky.

The People circled again, their feet silent on the frozen ground, and their chant was one of sadness and hope, as the bodies of the dead burned on the pyre. They sang:

"Go free, go free, brothers and sister!
You will hunt in the Other Place
where it is always summer,
where streams are fat with fish
and the plain is thick with moose,
antelope, and bison.
Your eyes will be glad,
for they will see our lost kindred.

Your mouths will smile,
for they will greet
those who went before you.

Go free! Go free,
brothers and sister!"

In two more suns the village was returned to its winter condition as well as could be done. Summer would free the frozen soil to layer on the roofs again, and until then no more could be accomplished. Ku-lap, when asked, gave his consent for the expedition after fresh flint, but none of the clans provided anyone foolhardy enough to go with the couple to that distant canyon where the flint was to be found.

For some reason, that seemed good to E-lo-ni. She felt that her husband would be best alone; even she must be silent and allow him to do the same. He needed cold and quiet and hardship, she felt, more than any comfort she could offer.

As she packed bedrolls, extra winter moccasins, dried berries pounded into fat, strips of jerky, and flat cakes of seed bread into her string bags, he remained outside the repaired lodge, pacing nervously and staring eastward across wide stretches of snow and shadow. When she peeped out, she could see that he was impatient to start their journey.

They left before the sun was overhead; around them the world was frozen to stillness, for not even the bright sunlight was able to melt free the blizzard's handiwork. They wore knee-high moccasins made from double layers of fur, which had the last layer facing outward for traction on the frozen snow. Thongs bound the furry tops about their legs, protecting the knees from frostbite. Heavy fur cloaks and hoods protected their bodies; as long as no wind blew, they should travel in fair comfort, at least for now.

The pair made fair speed across the white surface, dropping, from time to time, into soft sinkholes where existing hollows had filled with snow. Until there was a thaw, this was no great problem. Only if they got wet was there danger of freezing.

As the sun sank, however, a keen wind came out of the west, and then the intensity of the cold was serious. They must find shelter soon, both knew, and E-lo-ni kept watching the land ahead, hoping to see a ravine with some niche in its wall that would shelter them for the night.

There would be no fire, of course, but that was to be expected. Any bushes were thickly buried; dried dung of bison or wild horse was well hidden under the snow. Yet with the two of them rolled into their sleeping furs, their bodies sharing warmth, they would be safe from freezing, if they found some barrier sufficient to knock off the wind.

E-lo-ni did not worry. Death came when it came, and if she froze in the night, along with Do-na-ti, then she would be well content. The Other Place was always waiting for the People, and she had no fear of the passage between this life and that other one, where winter never came and the hunting was always fine.

TWELVE

IT SEEMED TO DO-NA-TI THAT HE HAD AWAKENED FROM A SLEEP, LIKE that after his encounter with the direwolf. For days after the disaster, he had moved in a dream, thinking of his mother and of Tu-ri-nit, grieving in a way that the People considered foolish. Death was nothing to his kind, and yet it pained him incredibly that he would never see his kindred again.

He had worked hard but automatically, helping to put the village back into some kind of order, but his hands had moved without involving his mind. His thoughts kept spinning with possibilities: If he had taken his mother back to the Terrapins' hiding place after delivering his warning, she would have been safe. If he had insisted that the Badger people come to the ravine, crowded as it was, no one of his original family might have died.

Yet, though that was true, he knew he could never have persuaded his mother to leave those who were her responsibility. And Tu-ri-nit would have been insulted even to be asked to crowd another clan in its refuge. Both would have chosen to die rather than to leave their clan. The questions and objections and the awful finality of that night had kept running around in Do-na-ti's head, tormenting him.

When E-lo-ni discovered the broken spear points, it was as if he woke from a nightmare and saw clearly. The expedition she proposed was something that would keep him wakeful, he knew, preventing him from drifting back into that dreamlike state. This would be of great benefit to the People, if he and his wife succeeded in returning.

He had endured the farewell ritual, though the smell of burning human bodies, the crackle of the flames, the thought of Ash-pah there on that bed of red-white coals tormented him. Yet there had been the promise of a winter journey to keep him focused and alert, and now they were on their way.

He wondered if E-lo-ni feared the dangers of this trip. He did not—indeed, he might welcome death in the snow, if it came. The Other Place had opened its door flap a crack, allowing him to see the warmth, the fat game animals, the throng of hunters who had already gone through into its welcoming plains and mountains.

All his people who had died over the generations waited there for their mortal kindred. How could one help longing to go through into it?

Thoroughly aroused from his depression, he broke trail ahead of his wife, feeling his thickly clad feet crunch through the frozen crust as he plowed ahead. Without the trail he made, E-lo-ni, with her shorter legs, would have been exhausted long before they reached this downslope into a ravine. An arroyo led off to the south, and once they were beyond the first bend, Do-na-ti spotted a nook well up on the rocky wall.

"That will knock off the wind," E-lo-ni said, moving up beside him. "And there is a way to climb—see?" She pointed off to one side, where a slanting ledge led almost to the end of the cleft they had located. The ravine angled; no snow had collected on that cliff side, which promised secure footing.

Once Do-na-ti struggled onto the ledge, he was able to lift E-lo-ni up beside him fairly easily. They adjusted their bundles of food and fur so as to help them balance on the narrow lip of rock, and then he tested the first step along the way leading toward the waiting shelter. The rock was lightly coated with ice, but the furry soles of his moccasins clung to that securely, as he edged ahead.

Behind him he could hear his wife moving steadily. Before sunset left the sky entirely, they reached a spot where he had to leap onto the out-thrust lip of the little cave. Now Do-na-ti was fully alive, all his wits and his strength dedicated to making certain the two of them survived this night.

He judged the distance carefully, noting the slight downward slope of the stone onto which he had to spring. Then he unslung his pack, letting it rest against the wall of the cliff so that E-lo-ni could hold it in place, and bent his knees many times. The cold had stiffened them, but he must land with the soft security of a cat. That waiting stone was also thinly iced over; if he came down off-balance, he would fall many man-heights onto the snow-covered rocks below.

When he felt ready, he looked again, calculated once more the length and strength of his leap, and sprang without thinking. His feet came down, his knees bent. One foot slid minimally on the slick stone, but the furry moccasin adhered to the ice, and he rose and turned toward his wife.

She flung the packs into his arms, one at a time, and he laid them far back in the cave before going again to the edge of the apron of stone fronting the shelter. When E-lo-ni leapt toward him, he reached out to catch her tightly, and they stood for a moment on that perilous edge, clasped together in triumph.

Then they moved together under the overhang and into the deep crack that offered better shelter than Do-na-ti had hoped to find. They opened their packs and spread heavy strips of rawhide over the cold stone. Over that went the supple furs of smaller animals. Then Do-na-ti laid a thick layer of furs over all and the pair of them crawled under it.

There, huddled together in darkness, they shared out the dried meat and the seed bread from the food supply, eating just enough to keep them warm and able to move with energy when they rose the next morning. The People gauged such matters closely, for there was never food to waste.

He lay flat, at last, and E-lo-ni curled into his arm, her head on his shoulder. Their shared warmth filled the space beneath the furs, and Do-na-ti relaxed, drowsy and content.

Before he could remember his mother, he slept; exhaustion made his sleep dreamless and deep.

He woke as the sun rose, though in his shelter and beneath the bedding it was impossible to see it; only his instinct told him the time. E-lo-ni was awake as well, and before he could rise he felt her hands on his body.

He smiled, and they turned together and made love gently and without haste. For the first time there were no interested ears listening to their movements, no curious eyes fixed on the wolf hide that had hidden their nook in the lodge. Never had he felt so close to her. When they were done, they lay for a time in silence, relishing the memory of the past moments.

But they must go. Both knew it, and they acted as one when the time came, to roll their bedding, restore the food to its bison-bladder container, and move again to look out over the ravine and the sky. The weather today would be very important.

Again wrapped in thick cloaks and with their moccasins retied tightly from ankle to knee to shut out the chill, they stood on the apron of rock. Below them the ravine was in deep shadow, the snow blue-purple and the protruding rocks still dark, though as the sun rose higher, they would turn to sandy gold.

The sky was still almost clear, though streaks of mare's tail marked the northern part they could see from the canyon. Without speaking, Do-na-ti sprang once more over the space and landed on the ledge. This time he faltered, and only the weathered finger holds in the rocky cliff allowed him to cling fast and recover his balance.

Once the packs and his wife were beside him, he led the way down again, and this time he followed the ravine until its walls dwindled, allowing them to walk easily up onto the plain. Do-na-ti paused for a moment, squinting between the folds of his furry hood over the blinding field of snow.

The canyon they sought was perhaps another day's march to the east, if all went well. It offered shelter from the worst weather, for its walls were pitted with old diggings where their people and others had chipped out supplies of new flint for generations. Brush from shelters built in past summers would be piled there, making fires possible and creation of another shelter easy.

E-lo-ni pushed him from behind. "Go quickly, husband. The sky to the north is thickening. We must push hard, if we are to reach the canyon before another storm comes down."

When he turned and looked where she pointed, he saw that she was right. The north was now dark blue, where it lay against the edge of the land. He hitched his pack more comfortably on his shoulders and headed toward their goal, his feet sinking into the snow, slowing his passage more and more as the warmth of the sun now began to soften the last layer.

His moccasins grew heavy with snowmelt, and his legs ached with effort. Behind him Do-na-ti could hear his wife breathing hard, her shorter legs laboring even more than his. As the sun moved overhead, he knew they must find another shelter before the storm overtook them in this exposed country, for it was now a dark line moving higher into the north and west.

Off to the south, he remembered from past journeys after flint, there was broken ground; mazes of small canyons offered protection from the wind and thickets of brush provided something to burn. He gestured in that direction, and E-lo-ni nodded. Together, with Do-na-ti breaking trail, they trudged toward a line of irregularities on the horizon.

The wind had been quiet when they left the shelter of the last night. Now light puffs of breeze stirred loose patches of snow into pale mist, chilling Do-na-ti's face. Shifting from the east, from the west, even at times from the south, it promised bad weather to come, and he pushed himself hard to reach the first outcrop of rock, dark against the white plain.

Beyond that the arroyos were visible as streaks of purple shadow on the snow. The sun was now going down, and half the sky was shadowed. Without pause to rest or eat, Do-na-ti led his wife toward safety, while behind them the sky grew darker and the wind began to gust fitfully.

Now his heart thudded as if to break out through his ribs.

His legs wavered, feeling as if they were made of water instead of tough muscle and bone. He knew his wife must be suffering, too, yet it was better to suffer than to die.

That was what the first long sighing breaths from the north promised, if he did not find the blind canyon he remembered. The brush growing along its bottom, where an irregular stream offered water, would supply fuel, and that might allow the pair of them to weather this new storm.

"It is . . . a bitter . . . winter," E-lo-ni panted, coming up beside him as he paused to look down into the canyon that had appeared in their path. "This looks . . . deep enough. Do you want . . . to go on?"

"Last night we had a cave that would have sheltered us from wind and snow, yet there was no fuel. Tonight it seems that there will be fuel, but I see no cave, as yet." He gestured downward, where a dark line of bushes followed the frozen stream that nourished them in summer.

Do-na-ti laid his pack on the gentle slope that flowed over snowdrifts to the bottom of the ravine. E-lo-ni positioned hers beside it. Then together they slid down the incline, saving themselves the stress of climbing down through deep snow, which hid any treacherous holes beneath its smooth blanket.

They halted abruptly against a thicket, which tumbled both of them off their packs into the drifts that had collected against its brittle gray wall. Do-na-ti struggled to his feet and helped his wife to rise. Looking about, he saw that farther along the twisting arroyo a knee of rock thrust out over a narrow bend. If nothing else, they could pile brush there against the wind and burn more to keep them warm.

"Come," he urged. "We may find a good place there. The wind is rising, though we are now protected by the cliffs. Can you see the snow blowing like smoke toward the south?"

She turned her gaze toward the cliff top they had left. Just since they moved from that edge, the breeze had risen and was now hard enough to sweep up gusts of snow and send it flying before it. They had found a windbreak just in time.

The two moved toward the bend, gathering dead branches

into bundles for fuel and walls as they went. This ridge of
brush was going to save them, Do-na-ti thought, if they
could be saved at all.

But the mutter of wind across the top of the canyon grew
still more threatening, and random currents whipped down
the cut where they sheltered. The cold was even more
intense. By the time they reached the spot Do-na-ti had
chosen, their hands were almost too cold to pile the dead
branches against the worst of the wind and to arrange the
fire. E-lo-ni drew the fire pot from her pack and spilled red
coals to kindle their blaze, and they crouched over the tiny
flame as it began to crackle among the snow-damp wood.

She poked fresh fuel into the vessel to feed the remaining
coals and replaced its top; in winter it was necessary to carry
fire when traveling. If they had used a fire drill, feeding
tinder into any spark they managed to ignite, they would
have frozen where they crouched.

Now, the crook of the cliff wall curved on three sides and
their barrier of branches on the fourth. With fire to ward off
the chill, there was a chance that tomorrow would find them
still among the living, instead of rejoicing with their kindred
in the Other Place.

There was no way to keep the fire burning through the
night. Both Do-na-ti and his wife were exhausted, for one
thing, and for another the supply of dry wood was limited.
Going out to gather more would have been risking death by
freezing.

The two melted snow in a horn cup and drank water. They
roasted strips of dried meat to help warm their bellies. They
hugged the blaze until both glowed with warmth; then
they went again into their pile of furs, their bodies sharing
heat as they slept.

Do-na-ti was weary, and yet he dreamed. When he woke,
staring into the darkness under the furs, he knew a tremendous secret, and he waited impatiently until E-lo-ni woke.

"There will be a child," he said, there in the warmth of
their nest. "There will be a man-child in the summer."

He felt her head turn against his chest, and her breath

riffled against his throat as she asked, "How did you know? I am not really certain, myself!"

Triumph filled him. Not all the blizzards in the north could chill him now! His mother was gone into the Other Place, but there would be another among the People to stand where she had stood.

"I dreamed," he said.

E-lo-ni had been his wife long enough to understand. Do-na-ti's dreams had often held danger and death, but this time he foretold life and joy. He hugged her close and felt her giggle. What a piece of fine flint was his wife! She did not fear what others held in awe, and she stood beside him, true and firm, even when he spoke of strange matters.

THIRTEEN

THE LIFTING OF HIS SPIRIT SENT DO-NA-TI ONWARD, ONCE THE SUN
rose and turned the snow into a glittering plain that soon
became slushy and difficult. When they came to the flint
quarry in the river canyon, built their fire against another
rocky cliff, and began chipping out fresh slabs of flint, he
did not feel the effort or the cold. His mind was warm with
a new wonder.

The colorful splits broke free easily, made brittle by the
cold, and E-lo-ni snapped the segments into manageable
sizes that she loaded into the bags they had brought.
Do-na-ti did not dig out too much—it would be wasteful to
leave good flint lying on the ground, for it was the newly
dug stuff that was best suited for knapping. Old, weathered
rock was all but useless.

The arduous journey back to the village did not exhaust
him, though dragging the bags over the snow was difficult
for both of them. Do-na-ti was borne up by the joy of his
dream. There would be a son! As soon as the weather broke,
he knew that he must go on a spirit journey in order to make
himself and the guardian totem ready for that great event.

The birth of a child was a momentous thing, and those
who shared the responsibility must seek the best and
strongest spirits to guide and protect the life that would
come. He found himself looking forward with anticipation
to the time when he must travel west toward the setting

sun—for that was the direction his clan favored—in order to secure the future well-being of his son.

The snow melted and fell again. Blizzards raged down from the north while the sun reached its greatest distance to the south and began its long trek northward again. When it was clear that winter was broken, though spring had not yet begun, the young man bundled into a long roll his spear, his pouch with flint and hammer stone for making extra points, and his fur robe that also served as bedding.

E-lo-ni, already showing a pleasing roundness, watched him, her face serious. "It will be midsummer when the child is born," she said. "Could you not wait for a while longer and let the weather warm? I will worry that you might become sick, if there is a late storm."

"I am not one to sicken," he said. "You know that. Only the direwolf has injured me badly, and that was a battle to remember."

She smiled, lowering her chin to conceal it, but he knew her all too well.

"I know—you killed that wolf who injured me. That sealed our bond, E-lo-ni. Now the child welds our blood together, and I must make certain that all is well with him.

"The time has come when I must go. You must care for yourself and for him while I travel. Speak to the spirits for me, asking that I be shown the proper places, the correct chants, the powerful animals that must guard our son. It is not an easy thing to prepare the way for the one who comes."

She rose and put her arms about him, her head against his shoulder. "I will pray for your success. I will pray that you meet no enemy people, for the Long-Heads live among the mountains to the west. Do pray for my welfare as well, my husband, for there are times when birth goes hard and neither child nor mother survives."

The thought chilled him to his heart. "Your grandmother is here, your sisters, my own people. The healers of all the clans share skills. They know much, and they will be at hand if there is need.

"But I had not thought of the danger. I will pray, indeed, as I go, E-lo-ni. Both of us must hold good thoughts and strong hearts. I will return in late summer, when you hold our son in your arms."

Despite his brave words, the memory haunted him as he moved away from the village across the rolling plain. Ahead the mountains made dark smudges against the sky, and underfoot, from time to time, the ground groaned and shook. To the south, he knew, fresh mountains had risen in the time of his grandfather. Now he wondered if the earth itself were trying to give birth.

"Will there be a new mountain born to make a companion for my son?" he asked the sun, now growing almost warm on his face. But that, too, was a frightening thought. What payment would be demanded of a man whose son was brother to a mountain?

He walked for three days, without hurry but also without tarrying. From time to time he paused to eat dried meat or seed bread, but he made no fire. He rested only as much as required to keep himself strong and alert, as the mountains began to take shape ahead of him.

Now there were trees—pines and junipers and, along the lowlands and the occasional creeks, willow and cotton-wood. Following such a stream, he came at last upon the first of the series of great cliffs, thrust upward into the sky and outward in rugged angles that pushed into the flanking valley. Those were striped with ochre, brown, rose, and white.

Moving between two ranks of cliffs, he traveled forward, seeing no human being and few animals. The roughness of the land through which he traveled was something that did not trouble him, for it was all he knew. His dogtrot pace covered ground for hours without tiring him, for instead of thinking of his body, he was thinking about his son-to-be and the quest for a dream or a totem that might safeguard that child in his life to come.

It was midday on the third day of his journey when Do-na-ti became aware that there were other men on his trail. Someone was stalking him, and only the Long-Heads hunted this land.

They had raided eastward before this, rampaging into the villages of all of the tribes of people on the plain, taking women and stores of dried meat. If they were on his trail, it was for no good purpose.

He had reached an area flanked by cliffs at some distance on each side. Between ran a shallow river, and a dependable source of water was always a good thing to have at hand, though there was still snow to melt as needed. The trackers were behind him, and to his left that series of angular cliffs jutted into the valley along which he traveled.

To the west the other line of cliffs seemed to veer away, but the country was fairly level and offered too little cover for one pursued by the Long-Heads. Making a swift decision, Do-na-ti began to run steadily, keeping close to the nearer heights. There were many ravines cutting between the prowlike promontories, as well as tumbles of boulders fallen from above, offering places for concealment.

He needed no conflict, for his was a sacred duty and a journey that posed no threat to anyone. However, the ones who followed were persistent. They were also trackers who seemed able to follow even the wind through the sky. He used every trick he had learned in his short lifetime, yet before dark he knew that he would not shake those who came upon his track.

They would not hunt him in the dark, he knew, for all men understood that the night held terrible beasts that devoured men and one another without distinguishing between them. And there were stranger things, spirits that howled in the darkness and devoured anyone who risked himself to the night.

Do-na-ti took shelter under a boulder, high on the side of a narrow slot beyond a sharply thrusting cliff. A cluster of rattlesnakes that also occupied the hole beneath the great rock rattled irritably, but the day had been cool and the night was almost cold. The snakes were too stiff and slow to trouble Do-na-ti, and he knew they would give warning if anyone peered into the crevice through which he had crept.

With a small prayer of thanks and apology, he caught one of the reptiles for his nightly meal. Eaten raw, it was not tasty meat, but it would give him the strength he needed.

Below, in the rough-bottomed valley, great creatures howled and grunted and sang their spring mating songs to the half-moon. In his cranny, Do-na-ti snugged his knees to his chest and slept soundly, knowing that no one would move across the arroyo-cut land until dawn touched the sky.

Do-na-ti woke, as he had determined to do, the moment the first pale streak touched the eastern sky, even though that sky was hidden from him by the cliffs among which he hid. Without pausing to chew any more of the snake, he put the remnant and the rolled skin into his supply bag and shook the stiffness from his limbs.

Then he climbed onto the top of the cliff, using the ravine as his stair for most of that way. Lying between two slabs of rock, he peered down into the long valley he had left, his quick eyes searching for his pursuers.

The sky was now filled with light, though from the northwest a line of cloud was billowing high. A spring storm was coming, and it might well conceal his tracks, if he could find a way to hide himself from the Long-Heads.

Do-na-ti did not tarry. Before the light had reached those dark masses of cloud, he was on his way, running lightly through the scrubby bushes and sunflower clumps, leaping runnels and rocks as he made his way around the long curve of heights edging the valley.

When he had to stop for rest, he again hid himself, lying flat and peering through a bush at the lowlands where his enemies might appear. He saw a pair of lions, tawny dots in the distance that were stalking prey of their own, raise their huge heads and stare up the long valley. That told him his own pursuers were there, and he kept his gaze focused on the spot the lions watched.

When the tiny shapes of men came into sight, his heart sank. There had never been communication between his kind and the Long-Heads. Those the People captured in past years had told the Elders nothing they could understand. One, who had killed a clan leader, the Badger Clan had punished cruelly, inventing even worse tortures than they had used in the past.

Do-na-ti could still remember the smell of scorching hair and flesh, the grim lines marking the face of the man who was bound to the post; his skin was removed in strips and his flesh was burned before his eyes. Even then, the captive had not spoken or even moaned. So brave was his death that the Elders of the People ate his heart in order to share in his strength and courage.

Do-na-ti had hidden his tracks as carefully as possible when he left the valley. They would not locate his trail easily, when they took up the chase, but he realized that they would have trackers searching the edges of the low country.

Unless the storm came quickly, they would find some trace that he had not seen . . . some betraying sign. He knew they would find where he had gone upward.

It was almost impossible to escape the Long-Heads, as some of his kind had learned with pain and effort. Sliding backward until he was clear of the edge, he rose and ran, crouching, still following the edges of the successive surges of cliff.

From time to time he approached the verge of the height, looking for some way in which he might leap down to some trackless area without leaving any sign above his goal. At last he came to a sheer edge that dropped for many man-heights.

Below that, a slope of snow-white sand stretched at a steep angle along a wide space between the rocky crown where Do-na-ti stood and the gray ridges that formed the toes of the mesa. Those thrust themselves into growths of juniper and pine that would provide cover, if he made it so far.

A dwarfed juniper, rooted among the cap rocks, leaned over the drop. He carefully worked his way toward it, checking for any mark, any dislodged stone or bruised plant that might betray his passing.

Now he was far ahead of his trackers, and this buttress faced away from the valley toward an indentation in the line of heights. No one in the valley could see him when he moved. He held onto the scratchy trunk of the juniper and let his body slip over the edge, holding for a moment before he allowed himself to drop into breathless space.

Do-na-ti landed feet-first in deep sand. His knees took up some of the shock; he flung himself sideways and dug his elbows into the resisting stuff. When he got his breath, he turned and sat, examining the spot where he had landed. Only the holes made by his feet and the mark where he had rolled showed the impact of his landing.

Anxiously he looked up at the sky, where the black clouds now loomed almost overhead. Already a chilly wind brushed riffles of sand into his eyes, and he nodded with satisfaction. If he could dig himself in, rain and wind and even snow might well hide him completely.

He felt fairly secure as he dug into the sand, covering his entire body and most of his face, after smoothing out the track where he had landed. There, wrapped in his fur blanket and comforted by the sun warmth held by the sand, he slept, resting up for another desperate dash, if it might be needed.

FOURTEEN

IT WAS A WHEELING HAWK THAT WARNED HIM THAT THE LONG-Heads were nearby. Its *skree,* drifting down the wind to his ear, brought him out of sleep, though he made no motion to disturb his covering of sand.

He wondered if it had rained or snowed—he had been too weary to think of that once he was hidden and at rest. His heavy cloak held away moisture, and it was impossible to know. He found himself hoping desperately that it had done both.

No matter what track the scouts might have found, with rain or snow there could be no mark showing that he had descended onto this apron of sand. If the small disturbance he had so carefully smoothed away was washed clear or coated with snow, they would never know where their quarry had gone.

Yet he did not become foolishly confident. No man ever covered his trail perfectly, and the Long-Heads possessed scouts who could trace the passage of the wind over the plain. He must behave, when he emerged from hiding, as if the enemies were behind him, determined to catch and kill him.

His own people seldom had a human enemy to avoid. With the bear and the wolf and the lion to deal with, not to mention the huge tusked or horned beasts that might trample

a man without knowing he was there at all, there was
enough peril to make any of the real People cautious.

They did not fear to travel alone, as he was doing, when
there was sufficient reason. It made him wonder if still other
men lived beyond the Long-Heads . . . men who made
even those fierce fighters feel the need to go in groups.

It was a strange notion, though the People had known
contact with others, who had once come into the area around
the village. They had been starving, and so the People had
found it easy to drive them away, southward and eastward,
until no sign of them remained on the land.

Now Do-na-ti found himself wondering who they were
and what terrible thing had sent them wandering out of the
country where they had lived before. Had they come from
the north, as his own kind had done in the days of the
greatest of grandfathers?

Moving alone as he now did, he thought of things like
that; even as he crept out of his sandy burrow at last, hearing
the hawk still circling at greater and greater distances as it
watched those who traveled through its country, he felt as
those men must have felt.

They were few, hungry, and afraid. Had they known chill
knots in their stomachs as he did while he listened to the
passing of the hawk?

Patterns of runoff from rain marked the slope of sand,
rippled into tiny runnels. He would disturb it, and he must
minimize that disturbance, brushing away any mark he
might make. He stood on a steep slope, staring down into a
dark canyon, which still held impenetrable shadows.

Trees rose there, their needled branches stiff against pale
remnants of snow and sand. If he could get down among
them, those who now walked above would not be able to see
him.

It was hard to see a path downward, and he must not leave
an obvious trail behind him. He edged along the sand,
brushing out the marks as best he could with the edge of his
robe. As the slope eased, he was able to do a better job of
it, and by the time he reached the rough soil below the lip

of sand, he was encouraged. This might be possible, after all.

Before the sky had entirely filled with light, he was halfway down, reaching with cautious toes for chinks in the rock, clinging with desperate fingers to tiny ledges that offered handholds. As the sky turned silver-gold, he heard a distant yapping . . . a fox?

A totem awaited his son, and any animal might prove to be the one destined to guide the child through his life. The world was too dangerous to allow a young one to go out on his own to find that spirit guide, and the People understood that.

It was the task of the father to make that journey. The danger was no less, but the seeker was better able to survive the search.

Even if he did not live to take the name of his totem to his child, it would not matter. A totemic beast, once discovered, found its object and kept watch over him as long as he lived. If some bear or lion, some fox or dog or wolf, or even some giant bison was the one Do-na-ti sought, its spirit would accompany his and E-lo-ni's young one to his final end.

It was a goal worth dying for, but it was one that he intended to live to accomplish, whatever the Long-Heads might do. As he slid down the last steep angle into the midst of a group of junipers, the young man braked with his feet in a mat of duff that was damp with the night's rain.

There he rested for some time, digging a bit of meat from his pouch and gnawing on it as he felt his pulse ease and his heart steady. It was high country here, and he had traveled to such heights before, as a child following his uncle. The breathing of one used to lower places became difficult, and even young hearts often fluttered and drummed uncomfortably.

After a bit he ventured to climb into one of the prickly junipers until he could look up at the edge of the looming cliff. That bib of sand now gleamed with sunlight, reflected from a layer of high cloud, and the ragged edge above it was stark against the sky.

No rounded shape of a head showed there, although he

understood how difficult it was to pick out even a standing man from such a distance. The rocks and the mountains dwarfed anything as puny as a human being.

He would have no better chance. Do-na-ti checked the thong holding his pouch and caught up his spear, the tip catching the light and gleaming dark red and pale rose. Then he moved through the trees toward the distant slope that was the next cliff, now catching early sunlight at its top.

The arctic fox, now beginning to shed his white winter coat, loped easily along the canyon floor, his agile body slipping between tumbled rocks and over obstructions as silently as the breeze that whispered among the juniper boughs.

He was not fearful. The wind brought no taint of a predator to his keen nose, and the human scents it carried were so unfamiliar as to be disregarded.

Familiar enemies lived in his mind, in scent, sound, shape, and color, but there was no experience marking these new odors as those of enemies to his kind. He was young, yet, and did not know the peril posed by Man.

The fox knew that another animal came behind him, at a distance, its great feet crunching and crumbling among the stones and the juniper needles. Such a clumsy creature could pose no threat to one of his kind, he knew without worrying about it. He could outrun most of those who lived here.

No, his blood danced with spring, and his feet were light where they pranced and leapt, and pounced at times upon an unwary mouse or rabbit. Every kind of creature was stirring now, coming out of a burrow in search of food and sun and exercise. It was a fat time for those who lived by hunting smaller game, and the fox was satisfied with his life.

Filled with youth and energy, he headed west and north, toward the ranges that still held snow. He did not worry about his destination, depending upon his instinct for guidance. He was following its urging as it moved him through the morning to find a snug den.

When twilight came, still early at this time of year, he

moved again, dancing through lingering patches of snow, always toward the west and the north, moving around obstacles, over forested slopes, up into the ranges. From time to time, as he rested on some quiet promontory, his nose detected every scent that moved on the wind. At one such pause, he caught a distant hint of that animal he had heard in the lower country.

It seemed to be following the course he had set, but that did not worry the animal. He was concerned now with grooming himself, for he was shedding his winter coat of frosty white, leaving tufts of snowy fuzz wherever he stopped to scratch or lick himself. The dull brown of his summer coat would be invisible among the trees ahead, although it was not a thing he was aware of knowing.

For now he was carefree, too young, by a bit, to have any concern for mating or hunting to feed hungry pups. He was busy following the urge that took him high among the mountains and along the small rivers that cut this intoxicating country.

Spring was a time for following the call of the blood. The fox danced onward, making a trail that the man behind him could find easily.

Do-na-ti saw the spoor of the fox as soon as he emerged from the scatter of junipers and small pines. Was that the one that had yelped before? Was this the animal he was to seek? But it was soon, still, to think of that.

He must follow his heart, which led him up and down heights, through canyons overgrown with bushes and trees filled with the buds of new leaves. He crossed rough country, cut and tumbled by the heaving and washing of the land, to go up at last into a range of mountains that promised to provide both food and rest.

When he slept, he dreamed of strange things that he could not recall upon waking. When he traveled, he seemed to move in a dream, though he did not miss any sign of the animal that went ahead of him.

The mountains into which he came at last were wooded, their tops still snowy, their slopes beginning to sprout grass on the sunward sides. There he made a camp, for he was worn with hard travel. He must hunt and cook food, if his strength was to last.

Now the tumbled mountains that bordered the plain were to the east of him, and he sat on a high ridge from which he could see the last sunlight touching the tops of that more familiar range. Even as he smothered his small cook fire and buried the bones of the rabbit he had killed for his supper, he felt the ground beneath him quiver.

The Old Spirit Ones were fighting beneath the earth, he knew, heaving the covering of soil and rock with their struggling bodies as they created new mountains. He lay flat, holding onto the ground, feeling the mountain surge and grind beneath his body.

There was a groaning mutter from all the country around him, as the Old Ones settled their ancient differences. When he pulled himself up to sit against the tree behind him, he could see at the edge of the darkening sky a red glow, where the blood of the Ancients drooled from the peaks their rage had raised over the generations.

There were songs among the People that told of those underground wars, and as he rested, Do-na-ti chanted softly:

> "Oldest of Mothers, Oldest of Fathers,
> you rose out of the ground
> to shape the animals and the People
> to carve the rocks
> and plant the grass
> in the Time of Beginning."

He drummed softly on his knee, recalling the rhythms pounded out by the drummers in his village when that song was sung. The familiar words were comforting, here in this alien place where no kinsman's voice could be heard, no friendly lodge held welcome and shelter.

He leaned back comfortably and sang on.

> "Oldest of Mothers, Oldest of Fathers,
> why did you return below the earth,

when the sun was warm upon your heads,
the soil dark and rich under your feet,
game ran freely before your spears,
and plants offering food
were plentiful?"

In the distance, a shrill yip joined in, as if even the fox enjoyed his song. Grinning, Do-na-ti set his feet on the still-warm earth covering the coals of his cook fire, for night was coming, and the spring wind, so high, was cold.

He shrugged his cloak about his shoulders and over his knees, but he did not lie down to sleep.

"Oldest of Mothers, Oldest of Fathers,
what quarrel did you find
there beneath the ground when you returned?
Now the earth shakes,
the rocks groan and shiver,
as you struggle there in the darkness
and your fiery blood
runs red across the land.

"Oldest of Mothers, Oldest of Fathers
who trouble the plain,
why do you raise mountains
where the land was level
and the grass was green?"

Yip-yip-yeee! shrilled the fox in the growing darkness. Do-na-ti rolled himself closely in his robe and lay on the spot where his fire had burned. Warmed and comforted, he closed his eyes. Not since his mother's mother's grandfather had anyone seen a new mountain grow from the earth.

FIFTEEN

E-LO-NI SLEPT BADLY NOW, FOR HER BODY WAS ENLARGING WITH the coming child, and it was hard to find a comfortable position. As well, she missed Do-na-ti's warm shape beside her, his comforting hand on her shoulder when she tucked her head against him in the night.

The weather was warming now, and the sun beat down by day, heating the earth. After dark, the breath of the soil was still warm, and the People removed the covering of earth from the walls of some lodges on the windward sides so that the breeze might blow between their supporting poles and cool the sleepers inside.

On such a night, E-lo-ni rose, her stomach queasy, her mind ill at ease. There was a subtle vibration in the soil beneath her bed skins that troubled her heart, and she went outside to gaze westward, in the direction where Do-na-ti had gone to find their son's totem.

The new moon had already set, but the stars shone bright and clear in the distant dome of the black sky. She leaned against a frame holding stretched hides and stood gazing toward the mountains that loomed invisible below the horizon.

A warm glow shone there, and she knew that the angry mountain was spilling its burning blood down its side to harden in rippling ridges that spread farther and farther about its base.

She had traveled there once, when she was small. Her clan had gone farther westward than usual to hunt, in a time of drought on the plain. She still recalled the terror of the smoking cone down whose side rivers of burning stuff flowed. She could almost see the Ancient Ones of whom the old tale spoke, rolling and wrestling down there in the dark soil beneath the mountain.

The clan had killed enough deer and moose to carry them through the winter. They had even slain a young bison, which supplied much meat to dry. Yet the child E-lo-ni had never forgotten passing near to that smoking mountain. She could see, when she closed her eyes, the ragged slant of black rock down which the red-gold fire spilled very slowly.

The brittle ridges arcing away below the height stopped those bright rivers, building higher and higher layers, but she had thought with dread about being caught in such a flood. Even seen from the top of another mountain, it was a terrifying sight.

Indeed, she had seen the result of such entrapment, hardened into an older dike of lava, where one of the Tusked Ones had evidently been overtaken and engulfed. Its gigantic tusk thrust out of the rock, and a bit of blackened skull as well. The eye socket, filled with black as it was, still seemed to stare at her in agony as she passed among her kinspeople. What could destroy such a beast would certainly leave nothing of a small girl-child of the People.

Now she stared at the faint red glare against the sky. The mountain was vomiting its molten bile into the night, and somewhere out there her husband rested.

He lived—she would have known if he were dead, E-lo-ni was certain, but was he in good health? Did he eat well and sleep warmly?

Her heart thudded, and the child kicked sharply against her ribs. It would have been better to have her man here beside her, she was sure, than out there alone. A child was a child, and it lived or died as the Old Spirit Ones willed.

She had little confidence in totems of any kind. People prospered or perished, she had observed, mostly by their

own efforts. Searching for mystical helpers seemed to her a
waste of energy.

Yet she said nothing. All of her people, her clan and the
other clans as well, believed this to be very important and
completely necessary. Who was she, young and inexperi-
enced still, to question it?

She sighed, looked once more at the light beyond the
horizon, and turned into the lodge. The space seemed
airless, for no breeze blew, which was strange here on the
plain. The interior was heated even more by the many
bodies sleeping there. As she crept between bed places, she
felt more alone than ever before, and it troubled her.

These were her kindred, her mother and grandmother and
the men and offspring of her sisters. They cared for her,
tended her needs, when she could not, and tried to keep her
busy so that she would not worry about Do-na-ti.

But when she curled about that rounded lump in her belly
and closed her eyes, they were wet with tears.

Do-na-ti moved through the mountains, now growing
leafy with spring, still following the fox but certain that this
could not be the totem he sought. When the small prints of
the animal's feet were joined by even smaller ones, he
smiled. This one, too, was finding a mate.

He wondered fleetingly if a fox could be its own kit's
totem—then he laughed. Animals did not need totems, for
they were a part of the spirit world themselves, connected
with the Spirit Ones in ways that men could not aspire to.

By now Do-na-ti had traveled farther than any of the
People had ever gone and lived to return with tales about it.
Even the glow of the mountain was lost beyond the
intervening mountains. He shivered, feeling somehow more
alone than ever before in his life.

He was moving through thickly grown country, where
moose were traveling upward toward their summer grazing
in the high country. Do-na-ti killed a young bull, creeping
up on it and plunging his sharp-tipped spear deeply into its
side as it grazed in a thicket of aspen.

He spent a day and a night gorging on the fresh meat.

This hard journey was wearing him down to bone and tendon, and he felt the need of the bloody strips, the raw liver, and the pulpy brain. Stripping out the best of the meat, he built a fire of green wood and smoked it as thoroughly as he could in the time he could spare.

Rabbit and marmot and grouse were good to fill the belly, but that small meat did not sustain muscle as the big animals' flesh could do. It would make his journey harder, his pace slower, but he felt that he would save time by taking the moose meat with him, rather than stopping like this again too soon.

Now he climbed, through aspen and fir and spruce, into very high country indeed. He had need of the extra food, and he was glad of the meat when a late snowstorm tore down from the heights and trapped him in a thicket for several days.

He dug a shelter into the snowbank beneath a great fir tree, building his fire small but keeping it fed with deadwood that he retrieved from a fallen giant. With his back to the tree trunk, his feet to the fire, the wind whistling past the opening beyond the blaze, he was more than glad of his earlier kill. The meat would keep him for many days, and at this time of year the snow would not last long.

It was a good time to sleep and regain energy for the rest of his journey. He ate sparingly now, dozing through the long day. When night fell, he covered his fire again with ash and soil and rolled himself into his robe, lying atop the comforting spot where it had warmed the soil beneath it.

Tomorrow the sky would clear, and he would go forward over the freshly fallen snow toward whatever goal the Old Ones held in store for him. He closed his eyes, and E-lo-ni's face appeared within his mind. The warmth of her smile sent him quickly into sleep. And into dream.

Do-na-ti stood in a place stranger than any he had ever seen. Around him, strangely shaped red-gold rocks twisted and curled, some thrusting toward the sky, others looping over to form windows through which a child might crawl.

The sun blazed down, and the colors were almost blinding as he gazed, trying to determine where he might be.

He walked forward, moving between outcrops weathered almost to the shapes of men or animals, to find beyond them a long sweep of land, at one edge of which gray folds lay in regular patterns beside tall red and ochre cliffs. There was no green, no immediate sign of game, spring though it seemed to be.

A warm wind touched his face, bringing with it a sound that made him pause, listening hard. A whimper? Was some animal, wounded or sick, lying under cover of one of these irregular ledges?

He needed no more meat, and he did not intend to hunt here. Yet something made him search the area, taking great pains to overlook no hiding place.

The vision quivered and shifted, in the manner of such dreams. He stood now under a rocky overhang, down which streaks of ochre had bled, making marks like the paint his people sometimes wore on their faces and bodies when grieving or when preparing for a Great Hunt.

When Do-na-ti looked down, his own hands were streaked with red and black and yellow, as well, and he knew that he was being shown something important to his quest. He was painted for a hunt, though he did not yet understand what he might be trying to find.

He knelt to peer into a crevice leading back under the rear of the ledge; there in the dimness he saw something move. Lying flat, he slithered forward, still staring into the cranny, though he did not reach into it. Even in dream, one did not risk disturbing some dozing rattlesnake by probing into its den.

But what he saw was a face, round and smooth. Two bright but dark eyes stared back at him, and the glisten of tears shone in the light reflected from the stony apron behind him.

Again he heard the sound, a stifled whimper, and he knew that this was a child, trying hard not to betray its position by crying. Why would a child appear in his dream? Was it his own unborn son, or some other spirit-child, sent to guide him to his goal?

Something pulled him backward, and he drifted out of the

cranny, out from under the ledge, to find himself drawn high into the air above a deep canyon. At its bottom those colorful stone shapes blurred into the distance as he moved.

Now he spun in midair, with the free-flowing power of a hawk or an eagle. The sensation was sheer joy, and he lost himself in it, longing to hold onto the feeling.

Do-na-ti opened his eyes, instantly aware that the wind was no longer crying past his shelter. The needles of the fir above were quiet, their whisper barely audible. Light penetrated the snowy dome over his burrow, and he knew that it was time to go.

West—yes, west was his direction, bearing north, as well. The totem waited there for him. The vision of the child was one of those misleading things that dreams sometimes provided, but the place, the shapes of the bright stones, the position of the canyon among the surrounding badlands were all clear in his mind.

He would eat now, only what was required to keep him moving quickly across the land. Days of hard travel lay ahead, for the sense of distance covered after that dream was great. He could not fast, but he would not gorge himself again until he stood there in the spot of which he had dreamed.

He must speed over this range, cross country that was alien to the plains where his own people roamed. Deep-canyoned rivers lay in his path, and cliffs that would challenge even his tough young muscles.

When he arrived among those contorted shapes, he would put aside his food. He would sit beneath that ledge, if he could find the right one, waiting and fasting until the totem appeared.

Now he must hurry, for there was a note of urgency in the whimper that had haunted his dreams. He must go fast and arrive as soon as possible. Something strong and terrible was compelling him, pulling and pushing at his will, to force him to move with all speed toward that goal his vision had shown him.

SIXTEEN

Now Do-na-ti traveled swiftly, though the country he had to traverse was cruel—steep slopes, deep canyons, dry stretches of desert presented obstacles that his weary body had to overcome. The elk meat was long gone, and he had killed other game along the way, always searing and quick-smoking enough to allow him to travel for days without stopping to hunt again.

The sun had moved northward, and spring was in full sway when he came over a high ridge and looked down at the canyon of his dream. There were the contorted stone cliffs, striped with earth colors from red to ochre, brown to white. There was the small river, dry in his dream but now half-full of water. Someplace down there was the ledge he had visited in his vision.

He went down quickly but carefully. Alone as he was in this vast land, far from his own people and unknown to those others who must live here, he knew he could not risk injury. A broken leg would mean his death, for even the strongest will could not force a one-legged man back across the terrain he had crossed.

The narrow valley flanking the stream was green, and he could see the distant shapes of grazing animals, elk and deer and at least one of the huge moose he knew from the plains. This was rich country . . . Surely people lived here or at least near enough to use it as a hunting ground in the season when the grass grew tall and animals gathered in such numbers.

When he stood beside the stream, he saw many tracks of beasts; hoof marks of all sizes, pads of big cats, the prints of wolves and foxes and much smaller beasts marked the game trails down to the water. Twice he had reshod his calloused feet, using the skins of the game he killed, but now his own track, marked into the soil, showed worn patches on the soles of his deer-hide sandals. Soon his toes would come through and he would be forced to make other footgear.

He smiled, wondering if any beast ever thought about the marks on the trails it followed . . . but that was a child's question. Now he had a man's work to do. He must find that ledge, settle himself beneath it, and wait for his true vision and the totem of his son.

The canyon between the bright cliffs was a long one, and he walked all day, pausing at last to climb the height he had followed. From the top he gazed up and down the stretch that he could see.

Then he caught a glimpse of a patch of shadow deeper and darker than that cast by the cliff. It was far up the canyon, in the direction he had been traveling, tucked into the angle of a sharp notch in the canyon wall.

The long yodel of a direwolf echoed along the river valley, and Do-na-ti sighed. It would not do to travel by night, particularly in this country that he didn't know. Where so much game gathered, predators would also be many and bold.

He would camp on a shallow shelf he had found on his way up the cliff face. Tomorrow he would reach the ledge and his vigil would begin. He climbed down again to the shelf, and once in place on his chosen spot, he rolled himself in his robe, for the desert night was chilly.

He did not eat. From now until he discovered what he had come to find, he would not touch food, and he would drink only sparingly from the gourd in which he carried water.

Already he was worn with his journey, his bones light, his mind filled with images that seemed real but were certainly those sent by the Old Ones. The journey had all but emptied him of self, creating a vessel into which his vision could be poured.

When he closed his eyes, he slept deeply at once, safer on his isolated shelf of stone than he had been so far. Yet the moment light touched the sky above the cliffs across the canyon, he woke, alert and ready for the climax of his journey.

The predawn was filled with sounds—shrillings of night birds, howls of wolves, anonymous growls and chirps and shrieks from predators and their prey. But day was coming, and before Do-na-ti had shaken the sleep from his mind and his bones, the stillness of dawn gripped the canyon.

He went down into quiet, interrupted only by the wind crying along the valley and whistling past broken teeth of stone. He could hear the little river's voice as it hurried over the rocks in its bed, and it made him thirsty.

He refilled his gourd, though his intake of water would be strictly limited; he would drink only enough to keep himself alive while he waited for his totem beast and its accompanying vision.

As soon as it was light enough to allow him to avoid pitfalls, he ran toward the spot that was burned into his memory. Now he could remember more of that vision, and as he moved, he found elements falling into place.

That twisted chimney of rock now looming black against the dawnlit sky—it had been a part of the dream. The broken tumble that had fallen down the breast of a cliff beyond the river was familiar. The abrupt twist in the streambed had been plain to see when he was carried so high at the end of the dream.

He nodded as he ran, breathing deeply and easily, holding his spear in a firm grip, feeling his pouch bumping against his thigh. His feet seemed to fly, touching the ground so lightly that hardly a sound followed him along the canyon.

His heart filled with joy as he found himself so near the end of his quest. Soon, he hoped, he would return to the People and to E-lo-ni. But for now all thoughts of them must be pushed from his mind. Regretfully, he turned all that he was toward the thing he had come to do.

The ledge ran more deeply beneath the cliff than the dream had indicated, but that was the way of such matters. His mother had explained that to him when he was very young: "The Spirit Ones do not make everything plain and clear, for if they did, it would make the People lazy in mind and body. We must use our own wisdom, our own hearts to learn the meanings of dreams and visions."

As a child, he had felt impatient with that explanation, but now he understood that if he had been given everything at once that he needed to know, he might have doubted the thing he would be shown. Now he was honed lean, sharp, and close to the bone; any vision the Old Ones sent, any creature they brought to him, he could accept without question.

He had reached a point at which he was open to anything, his spirit tender enough to feel the slightest touch from the hands of those who governed the lives of men and animals. This was a man-thought, he knew. It gave him hope that he would find here the thing needed to help his unborn son through the long life his father wished for him.

The cave-like space beneath the ledge was low and wide. After checking carefully for snakes and scorpions, Do-na-ti set aside his bundle and his spear. He drew out of the bundle his cloak, folding it so that he could sit for a long time without too much distracting discomfort from pebbles and grit beneath him.

Once he was in place, his legs crossed neatly before him, his gourd of water at hand—but not too near at hand—and his back straight, he began to speak to the Old Spirit Ones, though this time he did not chant any ritual. The words seemed to rise from his own spirit toward those others who waited here for him.

"I have come, following my vision, to this place. It is as you revealed it to me, and I am grateful to you for making it so clear. Now I wait for the totem that will guard and guide my son through his life. Old Spirit Ones, send me that totem, that I may go again to my people, bearing this gift for my unborn son."

He could almost hear a voice echoing the words that moved in his mind, and that, too, he thought was a good omen. He settled to wait, his only movement the occasional blink of his eyes and the motion of his breast as he breathed.

Time did not exist for him now. Hunger was a thing he had forgotten. Even thirst troubled him seldom, and his sips from the gourd were few and tiny. His body retreated from his consciousness until it was no longer any part of him, and his mind seemed blank, waiting to be filled.

Darkness came, but he did not hear the howls and grunts and shrieks so near him in the canyon valley. Dawn did not wake him with its pearly light, nor noon with its glare of red and gold and umber. He was focused upon nothingness, and if he had thought at all, he would have known that he was ready to see whatever came to him out of the Other Place.

But Do-na-ti only waited, without impatience, without feeling, as day followed night and night followed day. How many passed as he sat beneath the ledge he could never afterward say, for it was as if he were among the dead, and the earth moved through its cycles without affecting him at all. His eyes were open, but his spirit had gone away.

He did not see the small band of travelers along the river. He did not hear the cries as another band, larger and better armed, its members taller and longer-boned, attacked them and drove away those yet living down the canyon.

He did not hear the shriek of a maddened mother when she knew that her child had been left behind and could never be found again.

A sound pierced his trance at last, pulling his spirit out of the depths into which it had withdrawn. Do-na-ti blinked hard, his eyeballs feeling dry and gritty.

Had the totem come? He could not see it, and he reached for the gourd, which still held a little water, and poured out a bit into his hand so he could moisten his eyes.

Again he heard a sound, a small hiccup followed by a stifled wail. What beast made such a sound? It did not seem to be the cry of any animal he could recall.

Stiffly he rose and shook the dust from his hair and his

lap. He shook out the robe, as well, and rolled it into a bundle. Somewhere nearby was the thing he had sought, and he must find it, for it seemed clear that it was unable to come to him.

Now there came a sniff, like that of a small child who had been crying. The glare beyond the ledge blinded him for a moment, but at last his eyes adjusted and he saw a very small shape there, just beneath the shadow of the overhang.

He moved toward it cautiously, unable to believe what he was seeing. The totem sent by the Spirit Ones to his son was a human child!

This was a very young one, barely able to toddle. Do-na-ti had seen no village, not even a lone lodge, anywhere in the canyon. How had the child come here?

Then his mind, which had been dutifully recording the things that happened before his eyes while his spirit was withdrawn and waiting, gave him the information he needed.

The people who came were attacked . . . yes. He could see the turmoil, the fallen bodies, the fleeing survivors.

He saw the attackers stripping weapons and clothing and bundles from their victims before they went after those who fled before them. He heard, after so many hours, the despairing cry that must have been that of the infant's mother.

Do-na-ti felt bewildered. Never in all his life had he known of anyone who returned with a tale of a human totem. No grandparent told of such a thing happening in all the long oral history of the People.

A seeker did not bring the totem he found back with him to the village of his people. Never had Do-na-ti heard of such a case. Yet he knew he could not leave this small one—a boy, he could see, for the child was naked—to be eaten by predators.

The People valued children. They did not raid other clans or tribes to take captive women and children, as the Long-Heads did, but the dangers that were a part of their lives meant there were always too few young ones in their lodges. Sickness and snakebite and accidents constantly removed members of the village, though always the People managed to survive with the numbers that remained.

Taking a child back to the People was a good thing, whatever his clan or tribe. But was this truly a totem? The question was maddening.

The young one looked up to see this big stranger staring down at him, and he fell forward onto the ground, digging his forehead into his hands and shaking with terror.

This would never do, Do-na-ti thought. He bent and lifted the child, holding him in one arm as he had done the small brothers when they were tiny. "Come, Totem-Gift, I will not harm you. We will go together toward the rising sun, and you will become one of the Terrapin Clan. You will grow up with my son, like a brother, and you will guard and guide him through his life."

Something in his touch or his tone reassured the little one. He gave a final hiccup and opened his eyes to stare up into the dark face above him.

He looks bright and strong, Do-na-ti thought. *A fitting totem-brother for my son. But feeding him on our return journey will not be easy. I will have to stop often to kill small meat so that he can chew out the juices.*

He had hoped to speed homeward, returning before his son was due to be born in midsummer. Now he knew that would not happen. Such a little one could not be rushed across the distances between this spot and the village of the People.

Still, this was what the Old Ones had sent, and he must try to understand their purposes. He must, whatever came, work out their will, strange as it might seem to one who did not comprehend the purposes of those who lived in the Other Place.

SEVENTEEN

It was now midday, and Do-na-ti hesitated to go out into the valley and chance the return of the warriors who had driven away the child's people. Instead he took up the young one and crawled deep under the ledge, to the point at which its angle against the cliff was too shallow to admit further movement. So deep in shadow, they would be hidden when the hunters returned.

Outside the sun blazed down, turning the rocky cliffs across the valley to a haze of gold and red. Nearer at hand, the heat made strange shapes shimmer above the patches of grit beyond the shadow of the cliff forming Do-na-ti's shelter.

He arranged himself as comfortably as possible on his robe, laying the child on a fold beside him. He had replenished the gourd of water as he traveled toward this spot, and that was good. A small one needed more water than a grown-up, he had learned while helping tend the children in his clan's lodge.

There was a bit of meat left in his pouch, and he tore off a strip, chewed it to soften it, and put it into Gift's mouth. The infant sucked noisily on the juicy strip, and Do-na-ti noted with satisfaction that he had enough teeth to chew it, as well. It might not be as hard as he had thought to keep him alive on the homeward trail.

As they waited through that long afternoon, buzzards and

crows settled around the distant bodies beside the river. Coyotes slunk among the carrion birds, to run away with grisly morsels in their teeth. But death held no terror for Do-na-ti. All came to this, if they died far from those who would burn their bodies with proper rituals and mournful chants. It was not the bodies of the dead that terrified his people—it was the displaced spirits searching for someone to give them rest.

The infant slept much of the time, exhausted by his terror. When the shadow of the cliff under which he hid reached out past the river, the sound of voices woke Do-na-ti from a doze.

Without moving, he opened his eyes and watched the stretch of countryside visible from his hiding place. Eight warriors came into view, two of them youngsters not much older than Ka-shi, he thought.

They were heavily burdened with the spoils of their victory. Some carried three spears each; some bent beneath heavy bundles. Two acted as scouts and held nothing but their weapons, but when they came in sight of their earlier victims, all hurried to shoo away the carrion eaters.

Now they stripped even the loincloths and ornaments from the bodies, handling the mutilated remains with indifference. When nothing remained except remnants of flesh and bone to feed the beasts, the band set off again, and this time even the scouts were burdened.

They seemed to have no fear of enemies, which told Do-na-ti that those others now lying dead had been alien to this area, perhaps driven here by dangers in their own country. They had carried all they possessed, he felt certain.

When he closed his eyes and his mind replayed the scene of carnage that it had recorded while his spirit slept, he realized they had been trailing travois behind their dogs. The women and children had been bent beneath heavy packs. They had fled their own place before something that terrified them.

He shivered. Though his people moved about the plain and into the edges of the adjacent mountains in the appropriate seasons, they had always lived in the same area.

The thought of leaving their familiar sources of food and the animals that, though dangerous, were also understandable, was a frightening one. Do-na-ti did not like to think what sort of peril it might take to drive his own village's clans into exile.

When the last of the warriors was beyond sight around a jog in the canyon wall, he crawled slowly as a turtle toward the opening at the front of his shelter and lay flat. Peering cautiously upstream, he saw that the shadows had reached from cliff to cliff, and night was already darkening the eastern sky. No sound of man, no voice, no footfall came to his intent ears now.

In this time of twilight, before the predators began to emerge from their lairs, he and Totem-Gift might be able to cover the first small portion of their long journey.

But the child would be cold as darkness fell. Do-na-ti used his flint knife to cut a long strip from the tail of his robe. Shaping it roughly to size, he wrapped it around the plump body and tied it about the waist with one of his spare thongs.

Now the child was fully awake, after his long rest, and holding him still in order to fit his small robe was a considerable task. He wriggled between Do-na-ti's hands, and his bright, dark eyes kept turning to seek the mother he would never see again. But he had been well trained for survival, for he did not cry, though his small mouth shaped "Mmaa?"

"Your mother will not come again," Do-na-ti told him, his voice sad. "But I will be your spirit father. I will take you to E-lo-ni, who will be a mother to you. And you will have a brother, by the time we arrive."

Now Do-na-ti lifted the boy and set him into the sling he had created from more hide strips and thongs. Gift was still young enough not to forget his time on his mother's back, it was plain, for he snuggled into the contrivance, set his thumb in his mouth, and laid his head against Do-na-ti's back.

The warmth of the small body, the feel of his heartbeat and breathing were comforting in this place that held only potential enemies. They set off together in the dimming light, while coyotes sang on the cliff tops and the moon rose to help them on their way.

Do-na-ti hoped to reach the shelf where he had spent the past night before it grew too dangerous to remain afoot in the valley. He ran, now burdened with the child on his back and his pouch bumping against his side, but he held his spear and kept his other hand free. If some predator attacked, he could hope to kill it before it realized that he, too, had a very sharp tooth.

Nevertheless, he kept his gaze ranging from right to left, checking the shadows beneath boulders fallen from the cliff and under occasional junipers or pines along the way. His ears, always attuned to any sound about him, heard only the hissing of the wind across the broken stone and the raucous cry of a crow, still busy with that grisly feast behind him.

He covered ground rapidly, though not as fast as he would have before finding the child. When he came to the spot up which he had climbed the night before, he paused and looked up. A star gazed down at him from the edge above, but there was still enough reflected light from the sky to guide his hands and his feet as he climbed.

It was fully dark before he reached the refuge he sought. Even as he came within arm's reach of the flat spot, he heard the ominous rattle that told him a snake had decided to spend the night in some cranny.

He tucked his right toes into a deep crevice and braced his left foot on a protruding rock. The child was quiet, though his breath came in tiny sobs, as if he, too, understood the danger. Probably his lost mother had taught him the peril of the rattlesnake's warning.

Holding firmly to a knob of stone with his left hand, Do-na-ti slid his spear out of the looped thong holding it to his side. Then, balancing precariously on the sheer cliff side, he pushed the spear onto the flat spot and moved it from side to side.

The rattle grew harsher, more furious. He shoved the weapon until the point touched something solid beyond the apron of rock. The thing felt resistant but not hard and fixed like the stone. It moved when he jabbed at it with the weapon point. He ducked his head beneath the edge of the shelf and swished the spear harder.

The resistance eased, then disappeared, and the rattle stopped. There came the sibilant whisper of scales moving across stone toward the right end of the rocky ledge, where weathered vertical layers of the cliff must hide many lairs for more kinds of small creatures than snakes.

Do-na-ti listened intently until the sound stopped. Wherever the serpent took refuge, perhaps it would be far enough from his intended campsite to avoid contact with him or the child. Hoping he might be right, Do-na-ti heaved himself onto the ledge and unbound the small one from his back.

Side by side, the two put their backs against the rocky wall and chewed more dried meat. Gift was very hungry, and his few teeth made short work of the tiny strip Do-na-ti gave him. The man realized that he would not have to pre-chew meat for his charge; that also was a great help.

Again he arranged his robe, the extra skins from game killed along the way, now smelly, and his rolled bundle. He curled himself around the compact body of the child, finding to his surprise that instead of his warming the little one, the boy was like a fire pot, warming him instead.

He dozed, his hunter's ear still alert even in sleep. When Gift began to cry, quite silently, deep in the night, he woke at once.

One so young would grieve desperately for familiar people, familiar things. Do-na-ti could not give him either, but he could hold his quivering body close, whisper softly into his ear, and hope that this would comfort the child a bit. In time, it did.

They slept after a while, still huddled together, and night rolled silently across the sky, carrying the stars and the moon beyond the edge of the world. Asleep though he was, Do-na-ti was aware of its passing, of the rising of the morning star, the pale line that foretold dawn.

He woke quickly, finding the child sucking at a corner of the robe, hungry again. The boy was less than two summers old, and his mother would have nursed him for several seasons more if she had lived. He would have thrived more if they had had with them a woman with milk for her own infant, but that was impossible.

Perhaps blood might suffice, Do-na-ti decided. There were many long-legged rabbits in this country, and he could easily kill at least one every day. That should work well.

He re-rolled his bundle, bound Gift again to his back, and worked his way cautiously down the cliff. It was always harder going down than up, for one could not see the spots into which his feet would fit. Still, they made it without serious mishap, although Do-na-ti skinned his arm badly when one foot slipped and he had to catch awkwardly at a sharp angle of stone to keep them from falling to their deaths.

Once they were on solid ground again, he took the time to clean and bind up that wound, for the scent of blood attracted predators. They must move quickly, and he had no desire to fend off a direwolf, a big cat, or any other hungry carnivore along the way.

As he set off at last, the child once more snugly tucked against his back, he wondered if there were other people who might use this particular route at this time. It had been, he felt, very strange that Gift's kindred had chosen this time to move down the valley, for at any other time the child would have been left orphaned, his life at the mercy of the beasts.

The Old Spirit Ones were guiding him, Do-na-ti felt certain. Otherwise he would have come too late to the ledge, or the massacre would have happened farther downstream, too far for the small one to come to his notice.

No, this was his son's totem, unusual though it might be. This was the reason he had been given that dream, as he slept very far from here.

He must make use of this gift, whatever came, and for that reason he did not retrace his steps along his earlier route. Difficult as the way here had seemed, he knew that he must now take another, climbing what looked like impassable heights, leaving behind no track or trace to mark his going.

He would bring this totem, this gift, this child to E-lo-ni and his son, if it took until winter to make the journey.

EIGHTEEN

HOLASHEETA STARED ACROSS THE LOWLANDS OVERLOOKED BY THE ridge on which she sat. Behind her, the opening into the cave that served as her lodge was a black dot against golden stone. Her drying frame for hides leaned against a buttress of rock, and the outdoor fire pit where she cooked in summer was a blackened ring in front of her door hole.

This was her world.

She was alone and had been for many hands of snows, and yet somehow she had survived into old age, tough as an ancient root, weathered as the rocks, seemingly ageless as the height on which she sat. The slaughter of her people had occurred very long ago, she thought, though summer blurred into winter and winter into spring in an endless, almost seamless progression.

She had been young then, strong and skilled in many arts. She had fought when the Long-Heads descended upon her people, and her spear had been red-tipped with their blood. She had seen her father killed, her two children brained, her man skewered upon an alien spear.

Holasheeta had died then, she thought, though the withered ghost of the girl she had been still breathed and ate and thought . . .

Turning from that scene of blood, her spear still in her hand, though the flint tip had been chipped on a bone of one of her victims, she had dashed to the edge of the canyon wall, along which her people's village perched. The man behind her was large, spattered with the blood of her own children.

She whirled on the dizzying verge, braced her feet, and cast her spear. The point buried itself in his throat, and he went down, clutching at the spurting hole left when the heavy haft dragged the point from his flesh.

Holasheeta had laughed, there on the edge of death, before stepping off the cliff and feeling the rush of air as she dropped toward the rocks below. She had not seen the tangle of brush there, or the limp body draped across it, before she leapt.

When she fell, shoulder and hip first, onto a yielding surface, rolled sideways, and sank into a thorny tangle, she had a moment of panic. What had happened to her? She should have been safely dead by now, instead of struggling to escape the clutches of the prickly growth, her arm and leg useless.

She wriggled until she dropped the last short distance to the ground beneath the bushes, biting her lips to the blood to keep from crying out at the pain. The earth there was stickery with dropped thorns and twigs, but at least it did not yield as, with her left hand, she pulled her broken leg beneath the shelter of the leaves. She almost cried out again as the leg flopped to lie on the ground.

If she must live, it must be free and on her own terms, not as captive or slave to the Long-Heads. She would not betray her position with any outcry, no matter how her dislocated shoulder lanced agony through her body.

That could be fixed, and her leg might heal, if she found a hiding place and managed to snare lizards or small animals for food. For now she could only work with the shoulder, for anything more might shake the bushes and betray her to some attacker peering down from the height.

There were boulders and rocks and pebbles about the roots of the tangle, dropped from the face of the cliff over the years. She pushed herself painfully toward the largest, against which a fairly large bush had grown. Its trunk was the thickness of her arm, and the huge mass of branches that cupped overhead to shelter the space beneath it told her that it should be deeply rooted and strong enough to do the task she wanted.

Holasheeta reached that spot and lay panting for some moments. Then she pushed herself up on her left hand and leaned against the wood. Using her left hand again, she caught her right hand and tucked it firmly into the angle between rock and wood. She closed her eyes, bit down on her lower lip, and heaved her weight against the trapped arm.

With an audible crack and a flash of agony, the shoulder shot into place again. She could again move the fingers on her right hand. The pain she ignored. It was unbearable, but she must bear it, so it was better to disregard it entirely.

In fact, so battered and painful was her entire body that it somewhat diluted the agony of the shoulder and of her broken leg. When she got her breath again, she managed to straighten the leg, although it almost brought a shriek from between her clenched teeth. When she could see again, through the blur that momentarily clouded her vision, Holasheeta was relieved to find no bits of shattered bone sticking out through the flesh.

She had seen many broken bones, and those that sent shards outside the skin usually putrefied and killed the person suffering from the break. This was broken, yes, but it seemed to be a clean break.

She might be able to straighten the leg and bind it, but for now she must rest. It would help nothing if she fainted while trying, or betrayed her position with an outcry. She must close her eyes, breathe deeply, and gather her strength for what must come.

She was sure, all these many seasons later, that she must have become unconscious, for when she opened her eyes again, there was darkness in the sky above the leaves. No sound broke the silence except breeze rustling the growth about her.

Not even a wolf howled. She had the bitter thought that those who ate meat were probably busy above, devouring the people who had died in her village.

My children, she thought, and her heart grieved, but she did not allow herself to think of them for more than a heartbeat. "I will live," she said aloud. "I will find those Long-Heads and kill them, one by one, if I can. And if I cannot, if my leg heals crooked and prevents any long travel, I will sit on some height for as long as I live and call down curses upon them from the most ancient of spirits."

And so she had. The leg, though usable, was shorter than the other, crooked, with the toes turning inward, which made walking very awkward and slow. Yet she had made her way here, once it healed enough for moving. The journey had been terrible, hungry, painful, but she had succeeded.

She had caught lizards with her hands, killed chipmunks with skillfully flung rocks, eaten roots and rose hips and even beetles and earthworms. To the hungry, any food is good, and she had lived despite her injuries and the difficulty of moving about.

The thought of the Long-Heads kept her going when she would have preferred to die, until at last she had crept and crawled and inched her way up this series of great slopes to the ridge where she now lived. Though she was unable to hunt larger game, she had developed a technique for finding the runs of rabbits, which she snared in the meadows that lay lower on the steps of the mountains.

Antelope sometimes ranged her way; she had made many generations of spears with which she skewered them. Sometimes she lay flat and waited, often all night long, beside the brook where they came to drink. The hides of all her kills became clothing, blankets, the door flap of her cave that kept out the cold winds of winter.

If Holasheeta was lonely, she was no longer aware of it, so used was she to listening only to the wind over the rocks, the calls of hawks and eagles, the howls of the great wolves, or her own heartbeat. The world had shrunk to this mountain ridge, the valley flanking it around the curve of the height, the meadows below, and the spring that had cut a channel down the ridge to form the stream where she hunted.

When one morning she saw something tiny moving in the

long valley below her ridge, she thought it must be an antelope or a deer or perhaps one of the huge bears that sometimes ranged down from the forested heights. But it was not any of those, she realized very soon.

It walked on two legs. It carried dead game, a child, or perhaps a bundle on its back. Its hunched position told her that it carried a burden.

Down there, almost too far away to see, walked a man or a woman. Long-Head? Not alone, for those fierce people hunted only in packs.

Interest stirred dimly in Holasheeta's mind. It had been so long since she'd spoken with another human being . . . but this might well be an enemy, even though he was alone. And she had grown too old, her ill-healed bones too filled with misery, to go out of her way to provoke a fight.

The single time the Long-Heads had climbed onto her ridge, they had found a terrible surprise, she thought, grinning her toothless grin. They had thought her a mad old woman, there to be used as a slave while they camped on the ridge.

They ordered her to cook the moose they carried in bloody chunks on their backs. They used her fire to warm their evil buttocks, and she obeyed them, thinking all the while of the curses she'd spent her life raining upon their heads.

When they slept, she cut their throats, one by one, moving silently from one unconscious form to the next, while their sentinel looked afar from the tallest rock, guarding against nonexistent enemies. When he descended to take his turn at rest, she met him with a spear in the gut.

The look in his eyes had repaid her for much suffering.

Their bodies were a nuisance, after she stripped them of weapons, tools, loincloths, and ornaments. At last she rolled them over the edge of a handy ravine, and she supposed their bones must lie there still. She had never gone to see.

Now she bent forward, staring down at the toiling figure. Though her teeth were gone, her bones painful, her hands bent with the aching sickness, her eyes were still keen. As the shape moved closer, she recognized that he was, indeed, a man, and he carried a double burden.

Even as she watched, he paused in a cut between two ridges of stone. Junipers shaded his chosen resting place, and he placed one of his bundles against the trunk of the tallest. The bundle moved, and she knew it to be a child.

Holasheeta settled herself to observe what he might do there. A lone man, carrying a small one—what could his errand be? Had he, too, suffered the loss of his clan and did he flee from the Long-Heads as she had done?

Or was he some enemy she had not yet met, intent upon wickedness? Whichever he might be, she intended to learn his direction and his purpose, if that were possible. She had not lived so long in her solitary aerie by ignoring the few unusual things that happened below her perch.

She knew herself to be invisible, her dark skin melting into the red-brown and gold shadings of the rocks among which she sat. He might look directly at her without seeing her, for the distance was great. It was only his motion that had caught her attention as he toiled across the slope below.

Once she concentrated her gaze upon the shadowy spot beneath the juniper, Holasheeta could follow his actions as easily as if he had been beside her. First he drank from a gourd and cupped his hand so that the child could drink, too. Then he dug into his pouch, and she knew that it must contain food.

He lay flat on a skin beside the young one, once they had finished their food, and the two of them obviously slept, midday though it was. That told her what a hard journey this one had known. She also guessed that he still had a long and difficult one ahead, else he would have pushed onward to his goal.

She dozed, too, shaded by the boulder beside her, as the sun slanted westward. When its golden warmth touched her knee, she woke again, to find the man behaving very oddly indeed. He lifted the child to his shoulder, patted his back, took him down, and rocked him in his arms.

The man poured water into his hand and washed the small

body from head to heels. That was what one did when an
infant had a high fever, Holasheeta knew at once.

Was the child ill? All her oldest instincts returned,
bringing her upright.

She had tended her own young, back in that other life.
She had known the correct plants, the right methods of
dosing with them, the ways to bring down fevers or to draw
the corruption from wounds.

Down there was a sick child. Those children whom she
had put from her mind so long ago called to her heart again,
and the memory urged her toward the secret path she had
discovered among the tumbled boulders.

She could reach the man and the child before night fell.
But he must not move on while she came down to him. She
looked about, found a round pebble, and squinted toward
the pair below her.

They were so nearly beneath her ridge that it would not
take a long cast to carry the pebble to their feet. Gauging
from the angle of the slope, she figured the drop would take
skill, but she had been killing small game with rocks for
most of her life.

Holasheeta stepped away from the boulder, into the full
glare of the westering sun. She drew back her arm and flung
the pebble with great accuracy.

It landed almost beside the man holding the child. The
puff of dust was invisible from her height, but she saw him
start and look down. She drew off her loincloth and waved
the dark leather over her head in an arc, and when he looked
up again, he caught the motion.

She took another pebble and flung it down, hoping he would
understand that she meant for him to wait. Evidently he did,
for he sat again beneath the juniper, the young one in his arms,
the man's feet drawn up to support the small body.

And Holasheeta, feeling young again, a mother again, a
healer again, hobbled, as quickly as her crooked leg could
manage, to find her path down the ridge. She would speak
again with human beings, although they could not be the
real People she had known.

Yet they were alive, intelligent, and, she hoped with great
fervor, no enemies of hers.

NINETEEN

GIFT WAS HOT, HIS BODY DRY, HIS LIPS CRACKING. DO-NA-TI HAD tended the small ones in his clan's lodge when he was a boy. Never had he been expected to care for one who was as sick as this tiny child whom the Spirit Ones had sent to him. The feverish feel of his skin was frightening.

Do-na-ti was beginning to have a cold certainty that Totem-Gift was going to die and leave his own son without a guardian spirit. The water he gave the boy, the rest in the shade of the juniper, the bathing to reduce the fever had not helped, though Gift managed to chew and swallow a bit of fresh rabbit meat.

Many suns of travel remained before Do-na-ti might find the summer village of his people, near the toes of the mountains he had crossed on his quest westward. The child might well die long before he reached that goal.

When Gift began to cry, Do-na-ti felt helpless, lost, and alone as he had seldom felt before. If only his mother or his grandmother were here, with their stored years of healing knowledge! Even E-lo-ni, young as she was, knew far more than he, for she had learned about caring for children as part of her training once she reached womanhood.

He knew about making willow-bark tea to reduce fever, and he had passed willows along the way, but he had not gathered bark for the purpose. Sometimes that bitter tea caused those dosed with it to vomit blood, and he was afraid to try it with one so young.

He was about to begin walking again, hoping for the best, praying to the Old Spirit Ones for their help, when a falling pebble kicked up a puff of dust at his feet. He glanced down, puzzled, then up to see if the steep cliff above him was about to come down upon his head.

Nothing stirred among the rocks that rose almost straight up near the spot where he had rested. Then he saw something move on the very top of the ridge. A long strip waved in an arc; obviously someone was trying to attract his attention.

The shape was so far away, the glare of sun off rock so blinding that he couldn't identify what sort of person might stand there. Even as he wondered, another pebble landed near the first. Someone was there. Someone wanted him to remain where he was.

He had prayed long and earnestly to the Old Spirit Ones for help in saving this child. Had they answered in this unusual way? He could only wait to find out. Their answers to his prayers had so far been unorthodox. Why should this one be different?

He settled himself against the juniper again, holding Gift on his lap. As if somehow comforted, the little one hiccupped and closed his eyes, falling into a doze, though he still felt terribly hot to the touch.

Do-na-ti had rested, had even slept for a short while, but he was worn with travel and worry. He closed his eyes, and when he opened them again, it was to see an ancient woman standing nearby and staring down, as if assessing him.

"Grandmother, this child is sick," he said, holding up the little one. "I hope you understand healing, for he needs care that I cannot give him."

She shook her head, not understanding his words. Yet her hands came out and took Gift from him. She examined the child closely, feeling his skin, sniffing at his mouth, pulling back an eyelid to look at his eye.

While she checked the child, Do-na-ti stared at her. He had never seen so old or so crippled a person in all his short life. Even the oldest of the People seemed much younger than this ancient woman who had come down the ridge.

Her skin was the color of juniper bark and almost as creased and scored by time. She wore only a loincloth, and her breasts were mere flaps of skin. One leg was bent, the foot turned inward in a manner that must make walking a misery to her. Her face was tracked with wrinkles, her hair a grizzled tangle about her shoulders. She gave off a wild and alien smell compounded of dust and pine needles and very old woman.

Though at any other time he would have thought her ugly, now she seemed almost beautiful. She was old, she was a woman, and she should surely know how to cure his small charge.

When she was through with her examination, she looked down at Do-na-ti and jerked her head toward the cliff down which she must have come, though he had been asleep and missed her journey. He rose, took up his bundle, and held out his hands to take the child again.

She shook her head, her hair flopping wildly, and set off toward what looked like a sheer rock face. He hurried after her, marveling at her speed over rough ground with a crippled leg and carrying a rather hefty baby. She was a very strong and determined woman, he began to understand.

It was best to obey her as he would his own or E-lo-ni's grandmother. Indeed, all men understood the need for obeying old women, for the grandmothers held both the past and the future in their wrinkled hands. The Spirit Ones had produced this one magically from rock and air in answer to Do-na-ti's need, and he was too grateful to question their choice.

She moved abruptly around a buttress of rock, and he saw her hidden stair, a series of ledges weathered into a square-backed crack in the steep face. Softer stone had worn away under wind and water, leaving harder layers to form steps at irregular and perilous intervals. She went up them as surely as someone half her age might have done.

Challenged by that, Do-na-ti went after her, making certain that his footing was secure. He felt that falling,

where she climbed so securely, would be a disgrace. Yet it
was a long climb, and he was weary to begin with. He was
more glad than he could say when his guide disappeared
over the edge above him, and he knew they were all but
done with the ascent.

When his own head rose above the worn rocks, into the
shade of other junipers, Do-na-ti was surprised to find
himself on a fairly level surface that was backed, where it
pushed against an adjacent height, by another sheer cliff.
The woman did not pause, and he hurried after her as she
made for a dark opening in that second wall of stone.

Though the sun glared onto the stones and scanty grasses
of the ridge, blazing down between occasional clumps of
pine and juniper, the inside of the cave was cool—almost
too cool, after the heat of the sun-baked rock. It was dark,
as well, and Do-na-ti's vision required some time to adjust
before he could see clearly.

As he studied the place, he realized that this had been the
woman's home for a long time. The rough walls were
almost covered with blankets made of rabbit skins pieced
together, and her bed was a very thick pile of hides, dried
grass, and bundles of pine needles.

It had taken many seasons just to trap or kill all the
varieties of fur; seeds and grasses and roots filled the
baskets along the walls. She was a wise and thrifty gatherer
of all that would sustain life, it was clear.

A row of spears leaned against the curve of stone near the
door hole, all solid and serviceable weapons. One had a
chipped flint point, though it was not so finely done as those
Do-na-ti's own people made.

A pile of rocks had been assembled near the door, as well,
and he understood that the old woman had enemies she
intended to repel if they approached her home. He wondered
why she had decided that he was not one of them.

She paid no attention to him, however. She put the child
on her bed pile and turned to find a stone bowl, something
like those Do-na-ti's own people pounded into shape using
handily rounded rocks. She poured water from a skin

hanging on a stony knob, and into that she put a wad of something gray—moss, Do-na-ti thought.

With that she bathed the little one from head to toe. When Do-na-ti ventured to touch him, his skin had lost the worst of the burning quality that had been so disturbing.

The woman's fire, out there before her door, had been covered with ash. She left Gift for Do-na-ti to watch and went out to build up the blaze, setting stones in its edges to heat. From a bundle of twiglike material she took a handful of shoots; when the stones were hot enough, she dropped them into her stone bowl along with the woody bits of herb.

She boiled the stuff for a long time, dropping in newly heated rocks as the others cooled, before dipping up a small amount in one of her gourds. Setting it aside to cool, she returned to the cave and took the infant from Do-na-ti.

She turned to him and said something he didn't understand. Impatiently, she gestured toward a shelf of rock at the back of her cave, and he saw that she had an array of small items there. One was a thin, pale shell, deeply cupped, like those he had seen in the sand on the side of mountains in the country where his people hunted.

When he touched it, she nodded, and he took it to her. Then, hobbling along on her bad leg, she moved back to the bowl holding the decoction and dipped the shell into the dark mixture. Crouching beside the bowl, she settled the child in the crook of her arm and put the shell to his lips.

Gift made a terrible face at first. Then, as the warm liquid went into his mouth, he relaxed, as if finding the taste pleasant; his lips moved in a sucking motion. Most of the shell-full went down without any problem, and she gave him a second.

Very soon the child's eyes closed, and he fell deeply asleep. When the woman put him on a rabbit-skin pad beside her bed pile, he looked better than he had for days. The fever broke before the wolves began to howl on surrounding heights, and Gift turned on his side and began to snore gently.

Do-na-ti examined with interest the bundled shoots she had used. He had seen this stemmy plant, with dark green,

grooved stalks and scale-like leaves, as he crossed the dry
country toward the setting sun. Some grew in the country
across which he must travel, and he found himself determined to gather a bit to take home to the healers in the
village. Anything that could break a fever so quickly was
worth traveling far to find.

It was dark now, and the new moon had gone down in the
west, leaving the sky thickly studded with brilliant stars.
Here in this higher country, he found himself almost afraid
of those points of light that seemed so much closer above
his head than those he was used to. They might well be
holes through which the Old Spirit Ones peered down from
the Other Place to see what the People were doing, as some
tales claimed.

He turned toward the fire, where the old woman hunkered
down, holding a bit of rabbit on a pointed stick over the
coals. He dug into his bundle, which he had dropped beside
the cave door, and found a strip of his own from the rabbit.
He crouched beside her, while the meat roasted and drops of
juice fell sizzling into the fire.

He realized that she was studying him closely, and he
suddenly knew she did not understand that it was rude to
stare at a stranger before the proper ritual words were
spoken. Then he came to the realization that they shared no
words. The ritual would be meaningless. It was a strange
notion, shaking the foundation of all his people's customs.

How did one deal with a stranger who was not an enemy?
All of the strangers he had encountered before had been
intruders into the People's hunting and gathering country, to
be sent running away. Otherwise they were enemies to be
fought off, if possible, or fled from if they were too strong
to send fleeing back where they came from.

Sitting with a person who was not one of the People, yet
who was no enemy, was something Do-na-ti had never
heard of his kind doing in all the history the Elders recited
in the different ritual ceremonies. He, Do-na-ti, once of the
Badger Clan, now of the Terrapin Clan, was making new
history to go into the ancient tales.

Excited by the thought, he smiled at the old woman. She

looked startled. Then, slowly, with difficulty, as if she had not used the expression for so long that the way of it was forgotten, she smiled back.

She laid her hand on her withered breast. "Holasheeta," she said, and he knew it was her name.

Afire with interest, he did the same. "Do-na-ti," he said. "Of the People of the Plain."

"Do-na-ti . . . ," she said, slowly and with an odd intonation. She sighed and gestured toward the cave in a way that had to mean sleep.

Very well. Tomorrow he might learn more than her name, Do-na-ti thought as he followed her into the dark shelter.

TWENTY

THE BABY WAS VERY SICK. WHEN HE WOKE, HE DIRTIED HIMSELF and his pad with a stinking flood of fecal matter; this could kill such a small child quickly. Holasheeta strained to remember all the things that she had done when her own young ones fell ill, far back when she was young and strong and uncrippled.

She had accumulated a considerable store of medicinal herbs, spending part of each summer making her way to lower elevations after plants that did not grow high on the slopes. Now her increasing trouble with her bad leg told her that when this batch was gone, there would probably be no more.

It was as well, she thought, digging into her bag of herbs mild enough to give to an infant. She had lived too long already; if she had been amid her own people, she would have walked away at the end of the first bad winter that threatened to use up all the food supplies and leave the small ones hungry.

She found in the pouch a bit of alder bark, a few rose hips gathered from a wild patch along a stream far below her ridge. She had all the juniper berries she would ever need, of course, and those she could add to the mixture as she boiled another decoction.

Sighing, Holasheeta carried a gourd containing the ingredients back out to the fire. She had started stones heating as soon as the sun rose, feeling certain that the child would need more medicine. Now they were glowing hot, and the young man who had brought the baby was bringing more dead juniper wood to add to the blaze.

He puzzled her. She had known only the men of her own tribe, before the Long-Heads drove her into exile. It had seemed reasonable to assume that any man not of her own kind must be an enemy. Yet this one seemed both unthreatening and thoughtful, though she saw determination in his eyes and the set of his chin.

While the water boiled again in her stone bowl, she decided to try to share more words. Perhaps they might learn to communicate, though his babble was almost completely unintelligible to her ear. Yet he spoke a word, now and then, that had a familiar ring, as if their two languages might have been kindred at one time.

"*Cososh*," she said, pointing to the fire.

He looked up from poking fresh wood into the coals. "*Cososh*," he repeated, his eyes fixed on the blaze. "*Kosho*." He pointed again to the fire. The sounds were very like.

He straightened his back and pointed in turn to the stone bowl. "*Seret*."

So a bowl was *seret*, was it? Her own word for the thing was *sert*. Was there a kinship between their languages, then?

She leaned forward and took his spear from its place against the drying rack. The point had caught her eye much earlier, but she had been so busy with the child that she had not taken the time to examine it closely. The delicately fluted edges of the rosy chert point were much like the beautiful work her uncle had done, when she was small.

"*Tsit*," she said, indicating the point. Then she set aside the weapon and added more heated stones to the bowl of boiling liquid.

"*Satit*," he said. Now his eyes kindled with interest. He went into the cave and brought out her own spear, whose point she had chipped painfully from flint she had dug out of a canyon wall.

He ran his fingers along the rude edges. She had tried very hard to duplicate her uncle's technique, but she did not have the hand for it. The resemblance was there, of course, but the fine quality was certainly not. Yet hers was obviously made by one using the same knapping technique as had the maker of the chert spear point.

Was this some lost kinsman, a descendant of one of the clans that had moved away, back in the times of the grandmothers? She sighed, thinking of her joy if such a one had come when she was younger and cared for living.

These years of solitude would not have been. Perhaps she might have traveled with him to his own village. There she might have found another husband and produced children to fill the vast emptiness left in her heart after her escape from the Long-Heads.

"Too late," she murmured.

He looked up and caught her gaze, almost as if reading her thoughts. Setting her spear back in its proper place, he returned to roasting his rabbit, saving tender bits that she knew at once must be meant for the child.

She rose painfully and went into the cave, returning with one of her clay-lined baskets. She had fired it, upside down over a slow blaze, and it held liquid. She could boil the rabbit into broth, and it would be good for the small one when he woke.

The sun was overhead, making the task of tending the fire uncomfortable. The man motioned for her to go into the cave with the sick child. *I will tend the fire and heat the stones,* his gestures said to her.

This was one used to cooperating with people, and she found that she had forgotten much of that ability. Groaning to her feet, she did as he suggested. Once lying on her bed pile in the chill of the cave, she closed her eyes.

"I will save this little one," she murmured to the smoke-stained vault above her. "I will send him, with his uncle—or whatever that man is to him—to live a long life. Perhaps they will remember Holasheeta on her mountain ridge."

She almost chuckled at the thought. "But if they do not, my spirit will remember them, when I sit with my kin in the Other Place."

* * *

For six suns Do-na-ti rested on the ridge with the ancient woman, watching carefully as she dosed and tended the living totem for his own child. He learned a great deal from her, and he particularly noted the plants she used, the roots, the leaves, the woody stalks and bark.

Patience was hard, for he knew that E-lo-ni would soon bear his son, and he wanted desperately to be there when the women came out of the birth hut to give him that news. It was a pain in his heart to be so far away; yet if this was the thing he must do, then he would not allow himself to fret.

A hunter must cultivate his ability to wait, and this was good training, even though he had already killed his badger and played the dog in the Great Hunt. He would find it easy now to lie amid the tules beside a stream, waiting for game to come down to drink.

He must tell himself that the child's health was the game he hunted. He must keep his heart from yearning toward the summer village, where E-lo-ni might even now be in labor.

It would have helped if he could talk with the old woman, but the few words they managed to share referred only to tools and work to be done. Discussing anything more complex was impossible.

So he gathered deadwood along the ridge and down the slopes on the side away from the cliff. He went down to find Holasheeta's stream and killed an antelope, after a long wait. Scraping that hide, rubbing it thoroughly with sand and ash, beating it until it softened—all took days of work and diverted his mind from his impatience.

Small Gift grew sicker, his skin turning grayish, his fragile ribs showing plainly, where before he had been solidly plump. Worry gnawed at Do-na-ti's mind, and he found himself driven to find even more work to distract him.

He made a new door flap for Holasheeta, one that would keep out even the most blustery of winter winds. He ranged far down the ridge, gathering all the fallen deadwood he could find and even breaking down branches that had been damaged but that had not yet lost their grip on the parent trees. Higher and higher beside the cavern door and along its

rear wall, where it would not get wet, he piled pine and
juniper and alder and, from lower down, oak.

He mended the woman's old sandals which she had
woven from juniper bark and yucca fiber. He found broken
rock and lined her winter fire pit inside the cave, digging out
a large enough hole so that she could set her cooking
utensils very near the blaze. He cleaned away the debris that
had accumulated around her living area—bones and sticks
and terrapin shells from meals that she must have eaten
years before.

Staying busy was the only way he could hold himself in
check, he knew, and by the time he understood that the
infant had reached a desperate point in his fight for life,
Do-na-ti had Holasheeta's home in better order than it had
ever been.

All that time, he had kept an eye on the condition of
Totem-Gift. Now the child was thin, his body dry and hot.
His eyes seemed gummed shut, and he hadn't the strength to
whimper.

When Do-na-ti looked into Holasheeta's eyes, trying to
question her, she shook her head. He didn't understand her
words, but the meaning was clear. Unless something happened soon, the little one would die.

He sank onto the stony floor beside Gift's bed pad, gently
touching the dark down on his head. The boy squirmed, as
if the touch disturbed him, and Do-na-ti followed the old
woman outside.

He found her sitting cross-legged, her back straight, her
face still, her eyes turned inward. The fire had burned to
coals, which she had covered with ash.

So medicine was no longer the way. She was sending a
silent plea to the Old Spirit Ones, and he could only imitate
her position and turn his thoughts also in that direction.

"Why have you sent this child to me, only to have him
sicken and die? Spirit Ones, find help for him. Find a totem
for Totem-Gift, for it is clear that he lacks a spirit guide of
his own. Send healing, as you sent the healer, to keep him,
so young, from making the long journey to the Other Place."

The words moved in his heart, though his lips did not

move. Then, sitting there beside the cooling ashes, he closed his eyes and felt along the courses of his dreaming self.

Where was there an answer to his dilemma? Surely he could find again the ability to reach beyond his flesh, into the world of the spirit.

There was a blur of motion on the mountainside, as a small, swift animal leapt and danced there, followed by its mate. The two pounced upon chipmunks, caught field mice, dared rattlesnakes to do their worst as they darted and snapped and retreated. Foxes. Yes, foxes.

Arctic foxes, wearing their summer fur, played and fed, mated and rested in the trees on that slope. The fox Don-na-ti had followed, so long before, had led him in the right direction. Had he something more to contribute to Do-na-ti's quest?

Even as he had the thought, the fox raised his pointed face, as if looking across the distance toward the unseen presence who watched him. His pointed ears pricked upward, and he turned his head still more, his sharp gaze seeming to focus on the invisible one who observed him.

His mate, slightly smaller, her fur longer, came up beside him and sniffed at his neck, his nose, then looked in the direction toward which his nose pointed. She whimpered softly and tugged at his neck fur with her teeth, trying to distract him from this strange mood.

But the fox started off toward Do-na-ti, as if pulled by the force of his will. He scampered down the slope, disappearing among trees and clumps of alder, appearing again on stretches of grass or scree. He, or the spirit that he carried within him, was on his way, Do-na-ti knew, to answer this summons sent to him by the Old Spirit Ones. When that impulse came, whether or not it was accompanied by the furry body, Totem-Gift would surely live.

Do-na-ti opened his eyes. The sun was sinking behind the mountains to the west. Holasheeta still sat, eyes closed, in whatever trance she used for finding answers to hard questions.

From the top of the cliff into which the cave opened there came a sharp yip—the bark of a fox. From the cave came

a querulous cry, and Do-na-ti sprang up and ran to stand
beside the infant.

Gift looked up at him, eyes huge in his shrunken face. His
lips puckered in a sucking motion, and the man felt his heart
fill with gladness. If the child was hungry, he was better.

Do-na-ti caught him up and hurried out into the sunset
light. The basket pot of broth was sitting beside the ashes of
the fire, cool enough for the child to drink. The first
shell-full went down almost in a single gulp. Then Gift
steadied and swallowed several, pausing to rest between but
always showing that he wanted more.

Holasheeta opened her eyes. When she saw what was
happening, she smiled, her toothless mouth stretching wide.
Had she, in some way, pushed Do-na-ti's own vision to
completion?

It was very possible, for he would not have sought a
vision of his own if she had not done it first. The world was
so strange, Do-na-ti thought, that nothing he found in his
journeying would ever surprise him again.

Holding the child, he felt his heart ease, and the thought
of E-lo-ni was a cheerful one, not a worry. It would be all
right, he felt strongly.

The Spirit Ones had designed this quest, and he had
fulfilled it to the best of his ability. Surely they would not
allow him to fail now, so close to the completion of his task.

TWENTY-ONE

To-NAH-YE WOKE, HIS HEAD RAGING WITH PAIN. AGAIN HE HAD lost time from his life, he knew, for he lay in a tumble of rocks, without even a robe or a rabbit-fur blanket to warm his bones. Never before had he done anything so bad, during his time of darkness, that the Elders had driven him out naked.

What had happened now? His people did not drive out their own for less than terrible crimes. He shivered to think what this latest one might be, after those increasingly serious ones that had plagued him for much of his life.

He did not, when he was truly himself, hate children. Why did he mistreat them when he lost himself in the blackness that sometimes overtook him? Every time he went into that black and empty condition, some small one suffered.

He rolled over and pushed himself up, feeling bruises on his forearms, his back, his neck, his legs. Had they beaten him this time? He dimly recalled the last time he had lost consciousness. It had been a terrible thing that his body had done while his spirit was absent.

His brother told him afterward that he had thrown a small boy off a ledge into a thorn thicket. The child survived, else the beating the furious mother had given him might well have killed him. It almost did, as it was.

He remembered clearly the hands of the men who had held him to be beaten. His brother had been one of them, and the thought rankled in his spirit. When even the son of one's mother assisted in such punishment, it was a thing to cause despair.

That memory pushed him upright, to gaze about him. The People had not driven him away for that crime, though harming a child was the most terrible thing one of the People could possibly do. He strained to form some picture of what he might have done, in the past few days when his spirit was absent, to deserve such treatment. Nothing appeared in his muddled mind.

He leaned against a curve of wind-carved stone and stared down across the lower country that edged the heights. To his right stretched green-gray patches of trees, the silvery runnels that marked streams running down from the mountains, and the hazy distances where his village lay.

Some hidden instinct told him that he must not go there, for this time he might well die for something he could not remember doing. No, he must go south along the mountains instead.

He would cross the raw ridges of lava, the deep grass and thick bushes grown in the rich soil where older flows had rotted. Others of his own kind, though not of any closely kindred clans, lived there, the old tales claimed. He would search for some clan that lacked numbers and might welcome him as one of its own.

He could not bear to remain alone, as he was now, without anything to show that he was a man. He did not even have a weapon, he found, when he looked around the spot where he had lain.

No knife, no spear, no loincloth, no robe—he had been cast out to survive as the animals did, without help from anything men had made. His hands were the only tools his people had left him. Those and his mind—but his mind often deserted him, so how could he depend upon doing the right things to survive?

He looked at the sky, feeling the misery of his bruises all over his body. The sun was moving down behind the peaks, casting their long shadows eastward across the lava-looped grasslands.

Beneath his feet, the ground trembled slightly, and he knew that the fiery mountain was again belching its hot guts out into the world of air and light. He did not like moving in that direction, but the cone rose well to the west and he could stay out of its reach, if he were careful.

Almost sobbing, though that was something that not even the children among his people ever did, To-nah-ye scrambled down the rough slope, to find himself standing knee deep in grass. It was dry, for summer had drawn the moisture from the stems, but he was glad of that.

He twisted hanks of grass, tying them into bundles. When he found shelter, he would make a loincloth of the grasses, weaving them as he had watched his sisters do, since he was small.

The resulting fabric would be stiff and scratchy, but that would be better than risking his manhood being torn against brush and thorns, if he should be forced to run from man or beast. Every boy learned that before he reached puberty.

As well, he would break a long, straight branch from a tree to haft a spear. If nothing better could be found, he would make a fire drill, build a blaze, and harden the spear point with flame. He had killed game with worse weapons, when he was a boy learning to hunt.

A fire-hardened point could pierce a man, as well; he had seen it happen when the Long-Heads attacked a hunting camp when he was very young. He could still smell the blood and the stench of his victim's ruptured guts. That had been the first man he had ever killed.

He wondered now if he had also killed a child. That would be dreadful enough to earn him death, and if so, banishment was kinder treatment than he deserved. Yet he could not, even in his occasional nightmares, find any source for his cruelty to young ones in his black times.

Cheered at having a plan, he shouldered his bundles of grass, picked up a suitable rock to throw if he should need defense, and started down into the tongue of grass extending between the knees of two mountain ridges. As he walked, old thoughts crept into his mind.

He saw a picture, as if he were back in that time and

place. A Tusked One was down, spears sticking out of its hide like quills, but it still thrashed with its thick legs and round feet, still tossed its great head from side to side, the tusks moving in arcs along the ground.

The boys of the clan were excited, waiting for the hunters to complete the animal's death. When the movement of the tusks became regular, right to left and back again, the youngsters took turns running out to leap over the great prongs of ivory.

To-nah-ye ran, in turn. He leapt, but the Tusked One gave a great tremor and died; the right tusk, instead of moving as expected, came up as the head rolled sideways, catching the boy on the side of his skull. To-nah-ye could still see the strange spangle of colors and light he had known before everything went dark.

Since that day, he had had occasional periods of losing himself. He must find himself again, or he would die alone in the vast stretches of plain and brush, with nothing but snakes or wolves or bears to sing his death ritual.

The way was long. Night found him following a stream down from the height where he had awakened. Summer though it was, it grew chilly after dark, and he covered himself with his bundles of dried grass and huddled against a downed willow log.

If it had been colder, he might have made a fire drill, using twisted grass as its string, and kindled a blaze to warm himself. However, that would have been a lot of work, and he was both weary and dizzy, as he always was after a time of blackness.

So he drifted into a doze, roused from time to time by a roar from some distant hunting lion or a cry from some smaller beast caught by a predator. When the sky paled, he shook himself and stood cautiously. Nothing threatened, so he dug into the soft underbelly of the log, searching for grubs.

Those satisfied his hunger, to some extent, although he found himself wanting heavier fare. His bones felt light, and his head still seemed to float above the rest of him, which told him that he needed meat. How long had it been since he ate last? He could not remember.

An incautious rabbit leapt from the brush as he moved downstream, and he dived onto it, dropping his bundles but catching the animal. He tore loose the furry hide of its belly with his eyeteeth; then he drank the hot blood and chewed the rubbery flesh. It seemed to renew his strength, and he set off again with greater vigor than he had known since coming to himself as he lay amid the rocks high above.

The stream dived deeply between shelves of rock, falling into a pool below before running away along a gentler slope toward the grasslands. As he descended the perilous way, To-nah-ye realized that he could smell smoke. Thinned by distance, it was still unmistakable.

There must be a village somewhere down there, hidden by trees and folds of land and sweeping ridges of old lava. He must approach it with extreme caution, for he had no desire to die on the point of some hasty warrior's spear.

When he came to the level grassland, he kept to the stream, hiding among the willows, cottonwoods, and other thick growth that lined its course. He must see what was there, when he came within sight, must judge those who lived there before attempting to speak with them.

Surely these were people of his own kind, for the Long-Heads did not live in this country. They came here to hunt or to raid for women, but always they went back to the north and west. No, these were his own kind, divided though they might be by many generations of separation.

He spent another night hidden in a thicket, warmed by his dried grasses. When he woke, it was to the dizziness, the headache, the faint nausea that told him he was about to lose himself again.

He wanted to wail, to run, to weep, but instead he crawled into thick cover and shivered as he sank into unconsciousness. He did not hear with his conscious mind the soft footsteps that traveled along the path beside the water.

He did not know when the soft sounds roused him, for he had again lost himself in the darkness. He rose, his eyes glazed and his mouth agape like that of a madman, and moved toward the source of the small noises that had woken him.

A woman lay on the ground, her body heaving strangely. He stooped to peer into her face, but she was not a child and did not interest him. He drifted into a haze of darkness again, and only when he found himself facing that—or another?—woman did he know what he must do.

For this one held an infant in her arms.

TWENTY-TWO

The summer seemed long already, although it was only half over. E-lo-nik felt heavy, awkward, her legs swelling badly before her days were well begun. The child had dropped, shifting the unwieldy weight in her stomach even further and throwing her out of balance.

Her grandmother, watching her closely, had dosed her with a tea made of bitter herbs, made her drink boiled agave, and urged her to rest more than it was her habit to do. Often now her grandmother talked quietly with other old women, and E-lo-ni knew they were discussing her and the child who was so near to birth.

As spring turned to summer, the herbs had seemed to help for a time. But now that the sun was burning down and turning the tall grasses tan and umber, E-lo-ni did not seem to benefit from the medicines as she had before. Even more aware of her mother and grandmother watching her and speaking in low voices, she suspected that they saw some problem with her pregnancy that she did not know enough to recognize.

Yet it was not her way to rest while others worked. She continued to garner useful things along the streams running down on either side of the summer camp, which was set between the toes of two mountains. It made her feel normal and useful to bring back roots and shoots of useful reeds, as

well as crayfish, birds' eggs, and stores of willow bark for
fever and switches for making baskets.

She found herself stopping often to rest in the shade,
feeling a strange, empty whiteness behind her eyes. Dizziness was not a thing with which she was familiar, and she
found herself resenting the times when she had to pause to
rest.

Sitting so after a morning of searching the bank of the
stream, she leaned against a cottonwood, watching a white
heron wading in the shallow edge of the little river. Its long
legs scissored with angular grace, as it bent its snaky neck
to catch some small swimmer about its feet.

Suddenly she felt a stab of discomfort—not physically,
this time, but in those instincts that warned her people of
danger. *Do-na-ti,* she thought. *Is all well with him?*

She closed her eyes, and now she felt another stab, this
one deep inside her body. It was not really painful, but it
seemed as if some warning had sounded within her.

Was it time? Would the infant come now, beyond sight of
the village, out of earshot of the old women who were the
midwives? Normally, that would not be a thing of great
concern. She had known many women who'd gone out on
their errands as one and returned carrying another in their
arms. Yet she had a feeling that in her case there might be
difficulties.

It seemed that labor was beginning; she pulled herself up
painfully and moved toward the huddle of brush and hide
shelters that formed the summer village. Those were well
out of sight, beyond a bend in the wooded stream.

Walking, her grandmother told her, was the best way to
bring a child to birth. If he must be born now, it would be
as near to the village as she could possibly manage to go, for
someone would come looking for her before darkness fell.

Pushing her way among the thickly grown brush and trees
along the stream, she drew deep breaths, holding on and
trying to keep her body from tensing. As she paused,
holding onto a tree trunk, bending to ease the pressure in her
torso, another large bird, this one gray, flew up from the
water downstream, beyond the next bend in the river. Its

wings beat heavily as it rose through the air, startled from its fishing.

Had she frightened it? No, it had just come into sight. Even the heron she had watched earlier had not been frightened into flight by her movements. And she had made no noise, for even as heavy as she was, she knew her steps were too soft to be heard at such a distance.

Whatever had frightened the gray heron, it had been downstream, toward the village. Perhaps one of the youngsters was netting for fish there—but some inner warning kept her from calling out. It might be something else entirely.

Now she tensed in earnest, straining her ears toward every sound rising from water—vegetation, birds, and insects. If this was a beast coming down to drink, it should pose no problem; she would remain silent and hidden. Yet something told her that this was no antlered one, no wolf or lion or sloth. The day was moving well into afternoon, and such animals drank at dawn and twilight.

If something human hid there, it was not one of the People. When her own kind moved through this country, it was not with such stealth and secrecy, for this was their summer gathering and hunting place and had been for more seasons than even the tale tellers could recall.

Her gut told her that this was an intruder into the country of the People. But the Long-Heads hunted in large parties and raided in numbers sufficient to assure their own success.

They did not skulk and hide, as this one did. They attacked quickly and fiercely, took what they wanted, or died in the attempt, and then ran back into their own country.

Now she could see a quiver among the leaves of the waterside bushes. A person was there, not a beast. There was no doubt of that, for all her instincts were certain of it.

She sank cautiously to her knees. If she were herself, fleet of foot, strong, and agile as she had been when she killed the direwolf, she would have crept wide of the spot where the intruder lurked and attacked him from the other side. Armed with her spear and her keen flint knife, she would have taken him by surprise and killed him before he could harm any of her people.

That was impossible at this point. Not only was she awkward, heavy, almost unable to walk on her swollen legs, but now the warning pain inside her was becoming insistent.

A cramp spasmed through her belly, and she drew up her knees, holding in the gasp that threatened to escape. The strange weakness that had become a part of her in the past few days swept over her.

E-lo-ni drew a deep, silent breath and held it, trying to control the process that now threatened to claim her totally. When the pain eased, she let out that breath with agonizing slowness, hoping to keep it from the ears of whoever or whatever was hiding so near her.

Even as she dealt with her labor, her hand gripped the haft of her spear. She was not entirely helpless, as long as she held her weapon. Whatever happened inside her, she had control of her thought and her hand. She must retain that control, dividing her mind between the stresses devouring her body and the dangers that might be approaching from the stream.

If some enemy leapt from the brush to try to subdue her, he would be met with the fluted point that Do-na-ti's uncle had chipped from the flint she helped to bring from the distant canyon back in midwinter. E-lo-ni refused to leave herself at the mercy of some refugee who chanced to be traveling through her own place.

Biting her lip until she tasted blood, she squeezed the wooden haft. Her fingers went numb before the next pain eased. There was no time for rest between the contractions, no chance to catch her breath or ease her body.

She had helped at many births since reaching womanhood. A few mothers had died of hemorrhage, bleeding beyond the abilities of the midwives to stop it, until their bleached faces set in death. Some had become infected, and not even packings of plantain had helped them to live.

E-lo-ni had not seen anyone, in her short experience, whose labor started in such a powerful and unstoppable rush as this had done. It continued, contraction building upon contraction without pause or letup, until she forgot about whoever hid in the bushes. She was too busy to know or care, for now her entire inside attempted to expel itself from her body, along with a rush of warm liquid.

She closed her eyes, feeling the world heave beneath her. The contractions changed, though the sun was not yet halfway down the sky. It should have been a long while yet before the pains changed direction, but now they were longitudinal, pushing down and down as if to split her in half.

With hardly a moment to rest between them, the long movements pushed the baby toward the light of day. When E-lo-ni opened her eyes, for a moment the leaves above her blurred into the patch of sky framed within their pattern.

Then they swam into focus. Interrupting the swirl of gold and green and blue was an oval; dark against the glare of the afternoon, a face bent above her. Not a face she recognized. A face so strange that she pushed it from her mind. Faces did not look like that—not human faces!

She gasped for breath as another long convulsion ran down her. The child was almost there, coming so quickly that she knew she would be torn, but others had been and had still lived to produce other babies.

The face moved as the bending man stood, his head blending with the green-gold-blue of the tree and the sky. Between breaths she felt the spear in her hand, half-concealed beneath her loose robe of hide.

This was no friend. Therefore he must be an enemy. If he bent again, she would thrust as hard as she could, and perhaps, if the Old Spirit Ones were nearby, she would succeed in killing him.

He disappeared from the small circle of her awareness. Now, intent upon ridding herself of the child, she bore down, compelled by the demands of her own muscles. There was terrible effort involved, horrendous pressure, and a tearing pain that ended in a gush of blood and easing of effort. For the moment, she forgot the stranger who had looked down at her.

She went limp, taking in deep drafts of air, relaxing every

muscle for what must come after. In a few moments the afterbirth came, with almost as much effort as the child had taken. Then she heaved herself to sit and looked at the bloody man-child lying on the leaves between her knees.

Her flint knife severed the umbilical cord easily, and she tied it off with a strip cut from her robe. Shaking with reaction and blood loss, she took her son into her left arm and got her feet under her, using the tree trunk to brace herself as she stood upright.

She must wash her child in the stream. She wondered if she had really seen that face or if it had been some picture formed by her mind in the delirium of labor. But when she moved around the clump of willows to reach the water, she found herself facing a man. He looked thin and weathered, though when he moved, it was with the ease of relative youthfulness.

Weakened and confused, E-lo-ni had left the spear behind, but her flint knife hung in its loop at her waist, beneath the robe. She reached through the side slit and set her right hand on its bone hilt, holding the infant close in her left arm.

"Who are you?" she asked.

To her astonishment, he replied in the tongue of her own People. He must be from one of the groups of clans that lived to the north and west.

"I am To-nah-ye." He grinned, and his look was not a good one to see. His lined cheeks creased, and his uneven teeth seemed as fierce as those of the wolf she had killed so long ago. This was not a man to trust for an instant.

"I must wash my child," she said. But she did not turn away downstream toward the village. She moved straight toward him, as if to walk through his body if he did not move.

No sane man meddled with a woman and her child. What happened next proved that this one was not sane, for he leapt at E-lo-ni, caught the child out of her arm, and turned to run toward the stream.

She ran, though her legs wobbled beneath her; before she could reach him again, there came a splash as something went into the water. When she glimpsed him, standing knee deep in the river, he turned to her with a look of triumph.

"I have drowned your child," he crowed.

She did not pause, did not think, did not consider anything but her fury and her loss. E-lo-ni dived at him across a distance the length of her own body and sank her teeth into his scrawny neck, while her hand brought out the knife and set it between the ribs of his back.

He fell into the water, clawing at her, struggling to remove her weight, her knife, her teeth, but she was on top of him, still chewing at the tough hide of his throat, her knife digging deeper into his body.

When her teeth found blood, she bit still harder, tasting the foul coppery flavor of him as his life bled into the stream. Her jaws set in his jugular, and time seemed to pause, as if even the sun and the water ceased to move in their usual ways.

She hardly knew when Ka-shi, searching for her, came onto the scene and yelled for help to the young people who came behind him. They lifted her from the water and carried her back to the village and the old women. Yet E-lo-ni was caught in a terrible circle of labor, triumph, and despair that did not lift, even when she knew that she was safe again in the village.

She wanted to put that one to death with her own hands, peeling back his skin, pushing sharp twigs into the raw wounds, and lighting them from the ritual fire. But he was dead. She had killed him too quickly, and nothing was left to fill the empty places in her arms and in her spirit.

Pale and thin, she sat by day staring into the fire in front of her clan's lodge. At night she went silently to her bed pile and lay wide-eyed, staring into some terrible place that held neither life nor hope.

I am dead, she thought, in those rare moments when her mind woke from its trance. *I am dead, and Do-na-ti will return to find neither wife nor child to greet him.*

TWENTY-THREE

THE LITTLE ONE RECOVERED SLOWLY, THOUGH HOLASHEETA hovered over him almost obsessively, seeming to resent Do-na-ti's attempts to help her with the child. At last he backed away and left her to her chosen task, though he kept a close watch on everything she did. There was a great distance to cover still, and he must know what to do if Gift fell ill again.

Holasheeta did not object when he brought grouse or marmots or rabbits for her pot. So he contented himself with hunting and with taking care of everyday necessities, although his heart yearned to go east again, toward E-lo-ni and their child, who must now have come to birth.

The days passed slowly, though Gift began to sit again, to try to stand, his small legs unsteady at first but getting stronger and stronger all the while. His body filled out, becoming plumper, and he laughed, as if the fever had wiped from his young mind the memory of losing his mother.

It seemed that Holasheeta could not admit that her patient was healed. When Do-na-ti gestured eastward, making signs for taking up the child and his now considerably heavier bundle, she shook her head vigorously. At first he thought there must still be some vestige of sickness in the baby that he could not see, but in time he realized that the old woman

148

lived in terror of losing her small patient and of being left alone again on her mountain ridge.

Though gratitude was not a thing his kind put into words, Do-na-ti had a feeling of kindness for her. She had saved his son's totem, when he would have lost the boy to death without her assistance.

To leave her, taking the baby with him, he knew he must strike her unconscious . . . or even kill her. He could not bring himself to do that, although he had become almost wild with impatience to go home again.

Torn between opposing needs, he began to dream intensely again. On the night he had chosen for making his decision, he sank into a deep sleep instead.

The land swept away at his feet, ending in a long line of cliffs, and Do-na-ti knew he was looking down on the slopes and grasslands that would lead to the summer village. He could feel on his back the warm weight of the child. His spear haft was firm in his hand, and wind riffled through his long hair. It was real—no dream at all, he thought with sudden joy. He would soon see E-lo-ni!

Then he rose, lightly as a feather on the wind, and in rising he turned to see where he had been. There, toiling along the terrible way he had traveled, was a solitary figure, hunched, barely moving, yet still following his trail. Holasheeta.

A voice spoke in his mind, saying, "There are words. Do-na-ti, find the pictures. Find the signs! There is work for her still, before she goes into the Other Place."

He woke suddenly, his entire body jerking as if he had fallen from a great height. Sitting quietly, he listened to the rasp of Holasheeta's breathing, the baby's light breaths, the faint shifting sounds from the coals of the fire, echoing in the stone vault of the cave. Nothing was amiss.

Indeed, he felt reassured, confident that he had learned a solution to his problem. He had to make Holasheeta understand that she must come with him. In order to do that, he would teach her more words of his language, perhaps, or use drawings and sign talk. Then she might see what he wanted her to see and know what he intended to teach her. He must start today.

Rising, he left the cave and knelt beside the fire pit beyond the door hole. The sky was tinged with gray already, and soon the old woman would wake. He would have the blaze crackling when she came out to warm her old bones. He would set stones to heat, put water in her clay basket pot so there would be broth enough for her, as well as for the child.

If she was to survive the long trip to his village, she must be strong and well nourished; he would see to that. The mountains teemed with game, and the canyons held many kinds of small animals as well. He would take home this totem in safety, as well as bringing with him another grandmother who might add her wisdom to that of the tribe.

Having her with him meant that he would not be solely responsible for the child's health, as well. It was an elegant but simple solution, and he knew the Old Spirit Ones had sent him that dream.

When Holasheeta crept out, limping, from the cave, he gestured for her to sit. They had established a certain number of very useful words between them, and he proceeded to explain his plan, as much as those would allow him to do.

She took the gourd from his hand and sipped the broth, when he urged her to. Then, eyes wide, she listened as he explained with words and gestures and drawings in the dust the thing he intended to do.

As if unable to believe what she saw and heard, she drew her own design in the dusty edge of the ashes. A stick figure, bent at the back, crooked of leg. Yes, that must be herself.

A straight figure with two lumps on his back, moving toward a rayed disk that had to be the rising sun, just now peering over the next range. That was himself, surely.

She dotted a long trail of dimples into the ashy surface, curving the trail around the base of the fire pit. Then, at its end, she drew a fair representation of a winter lodge, conical and sturdy. Her people must have built much as his own did.

She drew other shapes—the one with the bundles on his

back, the one with the crooked leg going into the door of the lodge. She looked up into his face, a question in her eyes. He nodded, smiling, and she stared down again at the crude drawings.

She shivered, huddling herself together. He saw tears dropping from her cheek to make more dimples in the trail she had marked into the dust and ash.

When she looked up again, she tried to smile, though it had been so long that her wrinkles seemed about to crack with the effort. She glanced at the edge of the sun, now visible over the adjacent height. "Baby," she said in one of his words that she had learned. "We go."

As she scuttled into the cave to begin putting together the things she must carry on her back as they traveled, Do-na-ti sank onto his haunches. What had he done? She was ancient, crippled, slow in her movements, to the eye, though in actuality faster than one might think.

Would she prove to be so great a burden that he would be forced to leave her to die someplace along the way? The thought made him sad, though he knew that if the child's life, or his own, depended upon that determination, he would make it. Yet he hoped it would not be necessary, for he had a feeling that this woman would be of value to the People.

And what if the Long-Heads should spot them as they moved along? Could she fight beside him? Was she physically able?

He thought of the woman he had come to know. She would fight. He had no doubt of that. Something told him that she had known battle and had killed her own kind. She was not one to shrink from death, either for herself or for others; it was apparent in her stance, the set of her jaw, the chill at the back of her eyes.

It was the child, he understood, who had crept into her heart and opened it, who allowed her to accept the idea of leaving her home. Had she had children, then, back in her distant youth?

There was no way, as yet, to ask her. And if there had been, he wondered if she would have answered his question.

*   *   *

The year was passing, summer moving into its dry time when locusts zinged their raucous songs among the sunflowers and zipped about his trudging feet. His back bent now, under his double burden, almost as sharply as Hola-sheeta's, Do-na-ti found himself glad that she had slowed his pace.

If he had tried to hurry, carrying the heavy child and his pack, he might now be lying beside a mountain track, his bones and the child's picked bare and scrambled together by feeding predators. She had not only slowed but steadied him, keeping him from taking risks that his young heart longed to dare.

After a double handful of suns, he knew that she understood her own limitations and those of the child. She paced them all to their best speed for endurance. They had moved much farther then he had expected or even hoped.

Now they were going north through the wide canyon where he had eluded the Long-Heads on his outward journey. This time he kept close to the line of cliffs, ready to hide them all in one of the crevices or small canyons, if any danger appeared.

The lone bull of the Horned Ones did not surprise him, when it came snorting and stamping out of the brush of the valley and stared at his party with wicked red eyes. He had evidently lost his battle for supremacy and left his herd. Such displaced rogues tended to be angry and dangerous.

Do-na-ti backed into a little runnel and lifted the old woman high enough to climb to a ledge above the reach of the beast. The three of them remained wedged into that crack on the side of the cliff for the rest of that day and most of the night.

When the old bull grunted hoarsely and took himself off at last, abandoning the strange scent that had infuriated him, Do-na-ti breathed a sigh of relief. For a single man, with only an old woman for help, trying to kill one of the huge animals was foolhardy. It was simpler to leap off a cliff or to fondle a rattlesnake, if one wished to die.

This encounter made him even more cautious, which was

a good thing. He kept his spear firmly in hand, his knife ready to be grasped in its loop at his side. He seemed to have eyes that swiveled like those of a frog, so wide-ranging was his watchfulness.

They moved up the line of cliffs toward the break that would allow the old woman to make that climb onto the tongue of prairie beyond. There the village would wait in its fold between the toes of the mountains.

They must go south again, once they were on top of the cliffs, in order to find the summer village. But now it was only a matter of a couple of suns, no more. Soon Do-na-ti would see his wife and his son. The thought made his heart lift, though he did not ease his alertness.

That was why the six Long-Heads, moving casually along the valley, did not catch him unaware. He heard the old woman's hiss as he backed into a narrow canyon running down from the plain above. She would have her own weapon in hand, he knew.

To his surprise, she scrambled up one wall, her feet sure on the rocky incline despite the crooked leg. Compensating for the weight of the child on his back, Do-na-ti ran at the steep incline, and at the top of his surge Holasheeta's hard, wrinkled hands caught his wrist and pulled him up into a crevice that ran to the top, narrowing all the way.

The Long-Heads did not follow their prey into the canyon at once. They were cautious men, even when they obviously outnumbered their quarry. But when they came, Do-na-ti knew that he and the others would be trapped here, within easy spear-cast of the hunters.

Holasheeta seemed unworried. In the dimmer light of the canyon, her old eyes were bright and knowing as she stared into Do-na-ti's face.

"Rocks," she said in his own language. "Throw." She made the gesture of rock throwing, and he realized that she intended to stand off a hand and a finger of enemies by flinging down stones on their heads.

Do-na-ti had only his single chert-pointed spear, although his pouch held a good round of suitable stone and the hammer stone to make more. Holasheeta had her flint-

pointed weapon. Once those were cast, they would be
reduced to rocks alone.

Do-na-ti's mind began working furiously. If the Long-
Heads thought their potential captives were unarmed, they
might be less careful than usual. Pelting them with stones,
injuring all they could manage to hit among them, would
annoy them, make them intent upon capturing those who
dared to resist them. They would want them all alive, in
order to torture them slowly or to take them away into
captivity.

That meant one—or more—might climb the height to
secure their prey. And then . . . Understanding at last,
Do-na-ti laid his spear in the back of the cranny and bent to
pile rocks beside his feet, as Holasheeta was doing.

The motion troubled the infant, and he whimpered softly.
It might be best to set him, too, in the back of the
chimney-like shelter. If a spear was thrown from below, it
would not go into that small space easily, and he would be
safe.

Holasheeta nodded as Do-na-ti made the child secure.
Then together they stacked up a great pile of rocks, which
might well make the Long-Heads uncomfortable—or
worse.

Then there was nothing to do except wait, while the sun
peered down their crevice and moved on toward its goal in
the west.

TWENTY-FOUR

HOLASHEETA RECOGNIZED THE SMELL OF THE LONG-HEADS ALMOST before she knew the shapes of their thin bodies, the warped contours of their skulls. She had breathed that stink before, with the smoke of her burning village and the blood stench of her dying people. Now it brought back everything, and her heart grew strong again, fierce and implacable.

She saw the narrow cut in the cliff wall as soon as she glanced around. Do-na-ti, as was proper, was keeping a watchful eye on the enemy as he backed toward the inadequate shelter of the little canyon. It was up to her to find a way . . . There were too many of the enemies to attack freely, and the child must not be risked.

She spotted the crack, a curve of darkness in the wall of the canyon, and it beckoned to her. She forgot her crippled leg, her exhausted muscles, her abused feet. Taking a long breath, she clambered up, in the way she had when she was a small child, far away in her home village.

To her surprise, she ran up the cliff without mishap. Once in place, she found a projecting knob against which to brace herself; when the young man came up toward her, carrying the child, she was ready.

She had not wrestled with the stones and the wood, the animals and the weather on her mountain ridge for nothing. Her muscles were hard as rawhide, her hands capable of wringing the life even from a rattlesnake. She jerked him onto the footing of rock with little effort.

He turned to look at her, and she tried her best to show him the plan that was forming in her mind. If they kept back the spears, hiding them in the cranny, it would seem they were not armed at all, except perhaps with knives. But the nook where they rested was paved with sharp-edged shards of rock, splintered from the walls of the cleft by weather.

A skillful hand could send such missiles against an enemy, and they would cut, bruise, break bones, or even kill, if they struck the right spot on temple or neck. As she spoke the words she could bring to mind, the boy's eyes lit up with understanding.

He was quick, that one. Perhaps even a suitable guardian-uncle, or whatever he might be, for the small one.

They stacked their rocks and then they rested, and Holasheeta took the opportunity to give the child a bit of dried meat to chew. It might comfort him, in the battle to come. At the least, it would keep him quiet.

One never knew what the Long-Heads would do with a small child. They had brained her own before her eyes—what might they do to this one, even younger and less able to travel on his own?

The streak of sunlight moved at an angle along the canyon, marking its way along the pale golden stone of the wall. Soon they would come, she knew, and she set the child again in his sling of thongs, pushed him into a hole at the back of the cleft.

She told him, "Be still, Nu-ni-he. Be still."

As if he understood, he stared up, his eyes round, his mouth busy with the meat. He made no sound.

But now the Long-Heads were ready to make their foray. Do-na-ti, crouching at the edge of their little patch of stone, whipped one arm. His split of stone spat against the corner around which an exploring head had peered.

That would make them even more careful, Holasheeta thought, as she took up her position and waited, rock in hand, for an opportunity of her own. But it seemed that her throwing skills might not be needed. The young man was a master; she knew that many a rabbit, grouse, or marmot had fallen prey to his deadly aim and wiry muscles.

He caught the next head that passed the opening, with a heavy piece. The man fell backward, though until someone dragged him out of range, his feet thrashed in the patch of dust they could see.

Holasheeta leaned to pat Do-na-ti's shoulder. "Good," she said. "Very good throw. Make them pain, true?"

He nodded, but his gaze was pinned to the mark he had determined to be his target. Any person coming between the cliff and that dark stain was going to be struck, if he was not very quick and agile.

The sun moved so slowly that Holasheeta wondered if it had tangled in a web of the spider-mother and caught fast in the sky. The line of light crept along the floor of the canyon and angled up the wall, moving closer and closer to the place where the two of them crouched.

Once that shaft of yellow light reached them, it might blind Do-na-ti, making it impossible to hit what he saw entering their hiding place. There was no nearby range to the west that might interrupt that steady movement of sunlight. It would come, and when it did, they might be helpless to defend themselves well.

Another head appeared, this one flat against the ground. Do-na-ti kept his gaze on his mark, and Holasheeta half rose and flung her stone, a heavy one with a rounded side. It crunched into something, and there came a yell of pain.

The head, as well as the dark-skinned shoulder that the stone had caught squarely, disappeared around the corner.

The sun was coming. But something told the old woman that their enemies had changed their tactics. No more sound came from beyond the canyon mouth. Were they climbing the cliff in order to get above this spot?

She stared up the narrow cleft and found that at its top a star showed beyond the dark shaft. If she were one of those Long-Heads, young and able to climb almost anything, she would do that. If one was even now climbing the face of the cliff, he might be above, ready to descend upon them, before the sun went down entirely.

She touched Do-na-ti's shoulder. He risked a backward glance, and she pointed upwards. For a moment he froze, his gaze returning to his mark, but his thoughts were evidently examining the thing she had shown to him.

She waited patiently. He was younger, stronger by far, more able than she. It was his decision, and she had only an intuition that the Long-Heads might have taken that way.

At least he turned and gestured for her to keep watch on the opening into the valley. She had proven her skill with rocks. But she was not really fit to grapple with a young warrior, or to meet him with a spear.

Once only, another head appeared, and she sent a rock that clattered off the stone and caused the head to duck into hiding again. Then she heard, even with her failing senses, a scribble of dust and gravel down the shaft.

Do-na-ti turned her by the shoulders and thrust the child into her arms before turning back to meet the invader. She pushed herself against the stone wall, holding the little one tightly against her.

Almost touching her, Do-na-ti stood braced, his rosy-tipped spear shining in the last of the sunlight. The man above could not see below, for his legs and hips all but filled the cleft.

When he was down a fair distance, he dropped, and Do-na-ti met him, spear point first. But he was tough and wily, even with a spear-thrust through his thigh. He grappled with the younger, lighter man, rolling onto the tiny apron of rock.

Holasheeta moved away as far as possible, turning her back so that if a blade found her position it would strike her instead of the child. She could not see what happened there behind her, though she heard grunts, small inhalations of pain, and desperate scrabbling of feet and bodies against stone.

A wet spat, a hot gush of liquid against her bare legs, told her that a death wound had been struck. She turned, ready to defend the child with her last breath.

But Do-na-ti sat on his victim's chest, bleeding from many small wounds and breathing hard. "Dead," he said.

That was a word that both their people had shared, and she was overjoyed to hear it.

He rose unsteadily, and she helped him to lean inside the shaft while she pushed the body off the edge, to thud as if boneless on the rocky floor below. Peering down, she could see only a dim outline, for the sky now was losing all its light, and night had filled the narrow canyon.

Did the remaining Long-Heads wait outside to learn what success their brother had found? If they did, it would be morning before they ventured in, for unless driven by dire need, they did not attack or even move about at night, Holasheeta's people had learned.

Do-na-ti touched her softly. He was a dark shape against the stone as he pointed upward. Did he mean to climb out as the attacker had come, straight up a shaft so narrow that one could not see hand- or footholds?

Yet it made sense. If there had been two, they would have come one after the other, and she and Do-na-ti would now be dead. She tapped him three times on the chest with her free hand.

They would go.

Now her bad leg had stiffened, and her muscles ached with the stress of the past hours. Holasheeta handed the child to Do-na-ti and attempted to hoist herself onto the first toehold she could locate, but the effort was too much, and she fell back again.

She grunted and turned to him. "Go," she whispered. "I stay here."

But he did not begin the climb. Instead, he lifted her bodily up the shaft until her toes found purchase. Once she was in place, she heard him moving, heard the infant whimper, and knew he had realized that he could not climb that skimpy chimney with the child on his back. He must have set him on his shoulders, astride his neck.

Above the base of the cleft, the stone had been ridged by many seasons of rain running down from the grassland above. That offered more holds than Holasheeta had expected. Once she moved again, the stiffness eased and some of her strength returned. She moved up, finally bracing her feet against one side, her back against the other, and working her way toward the top by inching upward.

Bits of rock and grit fell as she went, and she hoped they would not get into the baby's eyes, but there was no way to avoid dislodging loose material as she moved. It seemed to take a lifetime.

At long intervals, she bent her head backward to look up, and a different set of stars shone in the uneven angle of sky that she could see. At last she saw the black edge of the runnel almost within reach.

She whistled softly, the sound hissing down the shaft. She felt a touch on her ankle. Do-na-ti had heard. That was good.

Her energy renewed, Holasheeta shifted her bottom higher while clinging with both hands to slender protrusions. She moved her knees down and found a toehold in the shaft, which now grew too narrow to allow her former method of motion. It was easier, but she was now all but exhausted.

At last she dug her nails into the gritty soil beyond the lip of the shaft and heaved herself upward to lie flat on the ground, her heart pounding in her ears like some ancient drum. Her panting breath was a harsh sound, but she managed to draw her feet up and away, to allow her companion safe passage into the night air.

Spider-woman had drawn her web away down the west, its trapped stars already disappearing below the horizon, as Holasheeta found when she rolled over. A hand touched her.

"Grandmother, are you well?"

Now she understood the words, after sharing this journey with Do-na-ti. She grunted and pushed herself to a sitting position. Even as she did so, she saw movement against the pattern of stars behind the young man.

"Beware!" she shouted, reaching for the spear that still hung from its loop over her shoulder. She raised it just in time to drive it into the chest of a dark body that hurtled down upon her.

She smelled blood, not her own. She longed to go to help

Do-na-ti, but the dead man's weight pinned her to the ground, and now her strength was truly expended. She could not move.

Yet she could see two shapes against the sky, facing a slender form that backed toward her, spear at the ready.

Where is the child? But her voice was gone, along with everything else, and she could only wonder.

TWENTY-FIVE

IT WAS ENOUGH TO HAVE CLIMBED THAT TERRIBLE CLEFT, WITH THE baby sitting astride his neck and the debris from the old woman's passing raining down into his eyes each time he looked upward. Do-na-ti had hoped that once they reached the top there would be a chance to rest, for he was weary beyond belief.

He wondered that Holasheeta had managed to keep moving instead of falling back upon him and crushing them all to the bottom of the shaft. Yet she had, and when he pulled himself free of the constricted space behind him, he could see her dark form lying on the paler grass in the starlight. The sound of her breathing was a rasp on the night air.

Even as he bent his knees to sit, setting the baby well clear of the rough hole in the ground, she shouted. He turned to find two of the Long-Heads upon him, their clubs ready, their eyes glinting in the feeble light as they shifted to take him from two sides. A third seemed intent upon attending to Holasheeta.

Do-na-ti rolled, pushing his pack, which had hung behind him on a thong as he climbed, to hide the child. Freed with one jerk from its drag, he found his feet and held his spear to skewer the first of the men who found the courage to attack him.

There were only two now. He had heard the death gurgle

of the one who'd thought to take Holasheeta, and he found
it in his heart to be glad that he had pushed her up into that
shaft. Old as she might be, she was a bear who still kept her
teeth.

Then he was too busy to think, as first one and then the
other of the pair dashed at him and away, trying to distract
him in order to allow one of them to get beneath his guard.
But he was Do-na-ti. On the day he killed his badger, he had
flung a rattlesnake around the neck of a bear and escaped
from its terrible claws. He had killed a direwolf, as well.

No Long-Heads would find themselves strong and quick
enough to kill or capture him! There were only two, and
they were used to attacking in large groups against much
smaller bands, who were usually taken by surprise.

Do-na-ti was used to moving alone, unassisted except by
the Old Spirit Ones and his own wit and strength. He bared
his teeth as he circled, keeping both of the attackers from
getting behind him.

Puzzled, they kept moving about, and he realized that
they were unknowingly working themselves nearer to the
opening leading down the shaft. It was only a dark blot on
the ground, not unlike a tuft of grass or any other natural
obstruction. These two had not been up here with that one
Do-na-ti had killed earlier, and they might not know exactly
where it lay.

He breathed deeply and moved sideways, at an angle to
the hole, leading his enemies forward as they maneuvered to
approach him. One circled to his left, which was no good,
but the other was going to the right. Do-na-ti inched
backward, sideways, luring the man toward the trap.

The one on the right lunged suddenly. Do-na-ti met his
club with the haft of his spear, knocking him away again and
stepping back still farther.

The other, seeing his chance, sprang forward with a cry of
triumph, which turned into a shriek of terror as his foot
landed on air. He plunged downward, foot first, leaving his
other leg and hip, shoulder and one arm flailing on the
surface, crunched so tightly together that he was helpless.

Now Do-na-ti could attend to a single foe. He grinned,

feeling power run through his body. His weariness had
vanished as if it had never existed. His body thrummed with
energy, his blood singing through his veins and his mind
working with a pure clarity unlike anything he had ever
known.

The single Long-Head backed away now, for fighting
alone against an equal was a thing his people did not
willingly do. But Do-na-ti understood him, thirsted for his
blood, intended to kill him now without hesitation or mercy.

The man lunged suddenly, trying to gain room to run.
Do-na-ti laughed as he plunged the dim sparkle of the spear
point into his throat and saw his eyes widen like dark holes
in his face and go blank. The body sank to its knees and
leaned to one side as Do-na-ti moved the spear haft, laying
his victim on the grass.

He set his foot on the bloody chest and tugged the point
free, letting the body drop back with a thump. He heard a
weak cry and thought of that other enemy, trapped so neatly
in the mouth of the shaft. He was helpless, but he must be
finished.

Do-na-ti turned and looked down into those desperate
eyes. Then he raised his foot and stamped downward again
and again, breaking the man's stressed bones until he could
pound the broken body entirely into the hole.

A thin voice asked, "Dead?"

Holasheeta. In the heat of battle he had forgotten the old
woman and the child. He gathered up the shivering baby,
along with the pack, and went to her. Laying the child
beside her out-flung hand, he tugged free the body that
pinned her and pushed it over the edge of the cliff, which
was some paces distant.

The water gourd gurgled with liquid, and he held it to the
woman's mouth. She took several swallows and said, "I
think . . . we not . . . live," she said in his own language.

He gathered the child into one arm and dribbled water
into his mouth in turn. Gift whimpered, but he did not cry.
His lost mother had taught him well, for if he had wailed as
they moved up the shaft, it would have betrayed their

position and perhaps brought the Long-Heads upon them before they reached the top. Crying babies did not survive in the world of the mountains and the grasslands.

Holasheeta grunted. "We rest now," she said.

Do-na-ti stretched himself on the grass, holding the child in the curve of his arm. He could feel that small heart thudding rapidly, as if Gift had understood the danger that threatened them all. As Do-na-ti's own body began to relax, the child dropped suddenly into sleep.

Good. They all needed that, no matter what might come out of the night to find them helpless. It would be no better to stagger forward through the darkness into some peril they could not foresee.

He woke suddenly. Without moving, he opened his eyes and stared up into the vault of the sky, where brilliant stars laced their patterns between high wisps of cloud.

In the distance, a shrill cry interrupted the whisper of wind over grass. Nearer at hand, chirps and squeaks marked the presence of small creatures stirring in the predawn stillness.

He hurt from neck to knees, his skin scraped and raw from the abrasions gained while climbing the shaft. When he rolled onto his side, his ribs stabbed him, as well, and sitting made his head spin for a moment. The stress of the day and the night had told even upon him, young and tough as he was.

What must those efforts have done to Holasheeta? He would not have been surprised, when he touched her to wake her, if she had been cold and stiff. He had seen mighty exertions kill old people before.

But her sticklike arm was warm with life, and her eyes opened, sparks of light from the stars winking up at him as she roused. At once she pushed herself to sit, then to stand, though her breath was ragged and interrupted by gasps of pain.

"We go?" she asked.

He held out the water gourd, and she drank. He dug into his pouch and found dried strips of meat, and she began to chew, though her teeth were few and she ground the meat mainly between her gums.

The baby woke, as well, taking his share of water and meat and causing no problem as Do-na-ti packed him again into his harness of thongs. Together the three moved toward the east, where the stars were paling with the arrival of dawn.

They came into familiar country after midday, and Do-na-ti knew they were now very near the summer village. As they topped a juniper-studded ridge, he pointed down and to the right. "There are the lodges," he said to the old woman.

She stared intently at the dim huddle of rude shelters that were sufficient for summer living. Clumped in a wide stretch of grass between the two low ridges running down from the heights to the west, the spot was convenient to the river, though not so close as to attract unwanted beasts that came there to drink. It was sheltered from the summer sun by several clumps of pine and juniper, and Do-na-ti felt with pride that his companion was pleased with the sensible arrangement of his people's camp.

They moved down the long slopes, finding the path worn by the feet of hunters and fishers, gatherers of seeds and roots and herbs growing along the water. The soil there was soft to their feet, which had no more moccasins or sandals left to protect them, but by now Holasheeta was near collapse.

He paced himself to her movements, though all the time he longed to race forward to find the birth hut, where E-lo-ni should be recovering from the birth of their son. Still, he held himself in check, helping the old woman to the edge of the village, where his brother Ka-shi came running to meet them.

Close behind came his uncle Ke-len-ne and his sister's son Pe-ti-ne. Ka-shi's shout brought people from the shade of the lodges, the skin-dressing frames, the fringes of brush around the camp.

"Do-na-ti has come!" The words rippled through the

ranks of all the clans of the People until every individual whose tasks had not taken him or her away for the day was gathered about the newcomers.

Ku-lap came out of his own shelter, followed by Fe-ka-na. "You have found the totem for your child?" he asked, but his voice held a strange note.

Do-na-ti gestured for the old people to sit, as Holasheeta had done suddenly, going flat on the ground as her knees gave out. "I have met a stranger totem than any man ever found before," he said. "If you will wait here for me, I will greet my wife and see my son, and then I will tell you the tale."

Fe-ka-na looked up into his eyes, and he could see in her glance that something terrible had happened in his absence. "Come here beside me, son of Ash-pah," she said, and her voice allowed for no objection.

She took his hand between her wrinkled paws and held it as she spoke. "E-lo-ni did not thrive during your absence. The child did not seem easy in her womb, and there were signs that the midwives did not like as she came to term. Her time came while she was gathering plants up the river, and she gave birth there, alone."

Do-na-ti felt his heart thudding heavily in his chest, and a feeling of sickness began to fill his belly. "She lives?" he asked. "Tell me that she lives!"

Fe-ka-na nodded. "She lives, though it was a hard birth. But worse than all, a stranger was there, a man whose wits seemed to have left him. He caught up your son and flung him into the river to drown. We found the infant's body later, after we brought E-lo-ni home."

Do-na-ti leapt to his feet, forgetting how weary he was. "You have kept him here for me to kill," he said, no doubt in his tone. "He will sing like a direwolf before I am done."

"No," the Elder said. "He is dead. E-lo-ni, weak from childbirth and loss of blood, staggering from the sickness that had plagued her through all her time, killed him herself. She bit through his neck and stabbed him to the heart with her flint knife."

Stunned, Do-na-ti sat again. "She lives. The man is dead.

But you have something else to say to me, I think.
Grandmother of the Fox Clan, tell me."

"She sits as one asleep. She lies as one dead. She will not
speak, and her grandmother is hard put to make her eat or
drink. Her spirit has left her, Do-na-ti, and though we have
chanted rituals and dosed her with herbs, it has not
returned."

He turned to look into the eyes of Ku-lap, but the old man
shook his head. "This is women's ritual, Do-na-ti. It is not
in the power of a male to affect your wife or her illness."

Sick with dread, he turned to follow Ku-lap's gesture. "I
will go to her now. She is alone?"

"She is alone. But do not be surprised if she does not
know you. Her own sisters find that she seems not to see
them, when they come with food or other necessities."
Fe-ka-na's eyes were infinitely sad, and Do-na-ti knew that
she would help if she could.

But he must do this, as he had done the search for the
totem, alone. He had played the dog in the Great Hunt.
Surely he had strength and courage enough to face E-lo-ni
and look into her eyes.

And then he remembered the child, whom he had placed
in Holasheeta's lap as soon as she was safely sitting down.
He turned on his heel and went to kneel beside the old
woman. She had understood something of what was said, he
knew, for she nodded gravely and handed the child to him.

"Son," she said. "I know to lose child. Other child might
help to come back from Great Dark."

This was what the Old Spirit Ones had understood, long
before it happened. They had sent to E-lo-ni another child to
take the place of her murdered son.

TWENTY-SIX

E-LO-NI EXISTED IN A FOG. HER SPIRIT SEEMED TO BE SEPARATE from her body, in a chill gray place that held no warmth, no light, no interest in anything except the pain she carried within her. From time to time a voice penetrated the shadows or a face might appear and disappear in a flash of motion, but nothing went deep enough to pull her back from the place where she had gone to hide.

She was dimly aware that regularly an infant was put into her arms to suckle at her breasts, but when that happened, she withdrew even further. Her own child was dead; that was the only fact that stood out in sharp relief against the dreadful gray that her life had become.

She could see the small body of her son in the ripples of the stream, hear the strangled cry that was the only sound he had made in life, once his birth cry was ended. This girl-child was not hers and could never fill that emptiness that lived inside her.

She understood, on some surface level, that one of the Fox Clan women had died in childbirth. It did not trouble her to keep the dead woman's child alive, but its suckling did not engage any part of her that mattered. Most of E-lo-ni remained in a place she had never dreamed existed.

When at last a dearly familiar voice insisted upon an answer from her, she tried to withdraw even more deeply, to shake away the hard hands that caught at her shoulders.

"No, no, no," her spirit protested. "My child is dead. Let me die, too, and rest."

A tiny part of her knew that this was Do-na-ti. He, too, had lost a son. Yet she could not loose herself from the grip of that awful grief. His pain, added to her own, would be too much to bear.

At last the voice quieted and the hands withdrew. Then, as she felt herself slipping into the cold gray semblance of peace that had become her existence, she felt a new presence.

This one was so commanding that there was no ignoring it. A spirit stronger, older, more compelling than any she had known now sat beside her. The words she spoke jerked E-lo-ni cruelly into the present.

The girl opened her eyes to see a withered face, age-tracked yet filled with life and intelligence, very close to her own. Two hands, smaller and yet even harder than those of Do-na-ti, took her by the shoulders and shook her roughly.

"You have lose a son," a cracked voice said in her ear. "Many others lose child, and yet we go not into death because of it. Come back! Listen, for I speak to you truth."

The girl managed to speak, her throat stiff from lack of practice. "You do not understand," she croaked. "You cannot know."

The hands turned her face up, so that her gaze was forced to meet the burning black eyes of this terrible old woman. "I understand all, all, all. My children's skulls the enemy split before my eyes; their brains, their blood I watch run away into soil of my home.

"My man die, too, as I watch, and when I kill and kill until I could not lift the hand, enemies drive me to edge of cliff. I leap from it . . . to death, I think."

The terrible images her words formed in E-lo-ni's mind were like cold water dashed into her face. For the first time in many suns, the girl's mind focused, her attention sharpened, and she really listened as someone spoke to her.

"I not die, because Spirit Ones did not choose that for me. I live and travel until I find place where I be safe. I have live alone for hand after hand of seasons. Only when your man come did I know I was lonely."

The words were oddly pronounced, yet E-lo-ni understood them clearly. They formed a link, stronger than any she had believed possible, between her mind and the world she had tried so hard to leave. Her spirit, so long isolated in the midst of grief, began to emerge from its selfish shell in order to see what sort of woman could bear the grief of which this person spoke.

"Your man find a dream. He find a totem unlike any he ever know. The Spirit Ones know . . . They send totem to comfort your heart. Wake, silly girl; return to life, or waste all you ever do or be."

E-lo-ni shivered from scalp to toes, as if waking from a nightmare. Was she here with a real person, or was this some dream of her own? Yet when she reached to touch that dark face, so near and so strange, she felt warm flesh. This one was real. Her words held the ring of truth.

The young woman swallowed hard, trying to find some word to ask the question that haunted her, drove her so far that she knew her own death had been only days away. "How?" she managed to say. "How did you bear it?"

"All people bear pain. All people lose, all people grieve. Not all people give up." The words were as stern as the voice, but the bitter truth of them struck to E-lo-ni's heart.

She, E-lo-ni, wife of Do-na-ti, killer of the direwolf, who had believed herself to be strong and determined enough to face any danger her world held, had fled before an enemy that offered no actual threat. She had allowed her grief to rule her, though her people prided themselves on being independent and self-controlled.

She bent her head, and for the first time since she was a child, she wept. It seemed that the acid tears washed away a part of the pain—that unbearable part that had poisoned her and sent her to the verge of death or madness. And now she recalled a thing that eased her mind.

"I killed him," she said. "I can taste his blood between my teeth still, and I can feel him twitch as I struck deep into his back with my knife. He died? Tell me that he died." It seemed she might live if she knew that to be true.

"He did," the old woman said. "And now you tell Do-na-ti what he must know. I go. You know him now, I think."

E-lo-ni sat straight on her bed pile, and for the first time she raised her hands to smooth her disordered hair and to braid the tangled locks neatly. She rubbed her face with a bit of leather, trying to remove any dirt that might have accumulated while she was apart from herself.

As she worked, the door hole darkened and his well-loved shape appeared beside her. "E-lo-ni?" There was a world of sorrow in his voice.

"I am again here, Do-na-ti," she said, her voice still uncertain. "I know you now."

"Then listen to me. I have a strange and wonderful tale to tell you. Lean against my shoulder . . . so. Are you comfortable? Now hear the thing that the Old Spirit Ones have contrived."

Safe against his warm shoulder, feeling through her skin the throb of his steady heartbeat, she nodded. She thought she heard another person beside them, breathing, but she was too intent upon his words to pay heed to her own senses.

"I was sent a dream," he began. While she hung upon his words, he told her of the strange outcome of that dream, the wait beneath the ledge. "How long I sat there I do not know, but when I woke it was to the sound of a child whimpering. And when I went forth into the space beneath the cliff I found a small one, tearstained and terrified, waiting for me." His voice changed, becoming deeper and more mature than she had ever heard it.

"We were sent a totem for our son. But our son died, and the *totem* will become our son. Hear me, E-lo-ni. The spirits have replaced the child who was killed, and he will fill your arms and your heart, even as our own baby would have done. Hold out your hands."

Dumbly, not quite understanding, even yet, just what he meant, she did as he asked. And she felt a warm weight against her in the dim light inside the summer lodge. She looked down onto the top of a small dark head.

The child turned his face up to hers. "Mmmaa?" said his small voice. "Mmaa?"

She looked at Do-na-ti.

He sighed deeply and said, "He has said nothing, all the long way home, even to Holasheeta, who saved his life. I think he feels that you are his mother. You *are* his mother, E-lo-ni. The Old Spirit Ones have sent him to you."

She felt the baby nuzzling at her breast, smelling the milk she still produced for the orphaned child of Tu-la-ti. When he began to suckle, a great frozen lump that had filled her belly and her heart for so long seemed to melt away, leaving her weak and disoriented.

Once again she was E-lo-ni of the Terrapin Clan, mistress of herself and no slave to her own pain. "Do-na-ti . . ." The name was warm on her lips, and his presence filled her heart with a living warmth she had thought to be lost forever. "Our son."

She looked down at the curve of cheek and forehead pushed into the curve of her breast. His busy lips seemed to thrill life through her body again and a glimpse of the future into her spirit. Although that other child she had suckled had filled her arms, she had not filled her heart.

This one was different. This was truly her son, older perhaps than the child she had borne, but returned to her in a manner that would, she knew, form tales for grandmothers and chants for the Ritual for generations to come.

Do-na-ti put his arms about them both, holding them close as they formed that bond that is unique to mothers and babies. She understood that he had feared much and now rejoiced that his strange mission had accomplished a magical thing for them both.

When E-lo-ni emerged from the sweat house and waded into the stream to rinse herself clean, she knew that she was not the same woman who had given birth beside this water. She was not the child E-lo-ni or the young wife.

She was a woman who had looked into the Other Place

and returned. There was a deep knowledge inside her
because of that, which she hoped would serve her and her
family well.

Her grandmother waited on the bank with a robe, which
she wrapped about the girl's chilly shoulders. Together they
went toward the lodge that had been raised for her use while
she prepared for the Ritual to welcome this new member
into the tribe.

Do-na-ti had returned to his own Badger Clan lodge, for
until the Ritual was done they would not speak together.
Inside E-lo-ni's small shelter lay a finely worked robe of
deer hide, painted with designs that promised long lives and
good hunting for her and for her new child.

Her grandmother sat beside her as she waited for twilight
to fall and the Ritual to begin. "Did your man tell you of the
fox that guided him through the mountains?" the old woman
asked in her whispery voice.

A strange question. But E-lo-ni nodded. "Yes, he told me
of the fox's dancing paw prints, and of the other prints that
joined his at last. That was a message, I believe, sent to
guide his steps aright."

"A fox has danced along the riverbank," the old woman
murmured. "I saw his track as you went into the water, and
I followed it upstream. Beside the place where we found
you and the man you killed, another set of tracks joined his.
And just a bit farther along I saw prints of very little paws.

"A fox and his family have come to wish you well,
Granddaughter. It is a very good omen."

"So the totem of the totem is the fox? That is fitting. I will
think of that, while they chant the Ritual tonight," E-lo-ni
said. "Thank you, Grandmother, for seeing what I did not
and for telling me the tale. It is a very good omen, indeed."

Night fell, and though the west held a red glare that said
the Burning Mountain was spilling its blood down its sides
and across the plain, it was too far away to offer any threat
to the People. The elders were donning their ritual headgear
and setting in order the drums and the rattle sticks to
accompany the dancing that would follow the Ritual. The

younger people were hoping to find a chance to play or to flirt during the dance afterward.

When the fire was lit in the center of the bare place they had chosen in this summer camp, the People came, each clan moving into its proper place. The Elders sat in the center, their ranks partly filled again by the presence of Ke-len-ne, who now served as an Elder of the Badger Clan.

The rings of waiting people were broken at each level to form a corridor, up which E-lo-ni came, carrying her son. Her grandmother had chosen his tribal name, Su-li-pit, Gift of the Spirit Ones, which tonight would be bestowed upon him.

He was a very good child, and though no infant of the People cried, he did not even fret, as most did. He sat very straight in her arms, his round eyes taking in the fires and the different people they passed as if he understood the importance of this Ritual as well as she.

She walked firmly, not too slowly, to stand before the fire. To her right Ke-len-ne sat, back straight, looking younger than his years; across the flames was the erect form of Ku-lap, and to his right Fe-ka-na bent forward, her old eyes alight with interest.

Ku-lap rose, when she had waited the proper length of time, and cast pollen and pine bark onto the flames, which crackled and spat. The light flared and steadied, and the old man raised his hands and began the chant.

> "There is a new one here,
> a child of our People
> and of the Terrapin Clan.
> He has been sent to us twice,
> once from the belly of his mother
> and once by the hands of his father.
>
> "The totem-quest was long
> and Do-na-ti wondered
> if he would find his child's totem.
> A fox guided him into the mountains,

and he went forward, feeling the presence
of the Old Spirit Ones.

"At last he dreamed,
a ledge, a canyon with a stream
came to his sleeping mind.
When he woke he followed his heart
and found himself there,
looking down
into the place of his vision.

"A totem came to him.
Not a beast, as others have found
but a child, orphaned and alone.
He brought back this totem, this son
to set into the arms of E-lo-ni,
who now stands before the fire.

"Now Su-li-pit,
son of Terrapin and Badger Clans
and of the Old Spirit Ones,
has become one of the People
who live in the plain
at the feet of the mountains."

Ku-lap's old voice wavered to a halt, and he beckoned.
E-lo-ni stepped forward and set the child in the hands of
Fe-ka-na, who examined him closely, nodded, and passed
him on to Ku-lap. When the chief Elder was done, he
handed him to Ke-len-ne, who as paternal uncle was closest
to him and would be his spiritual adviser.

Ke-len-ne marked the round forehead with pollen and red
paint, and E-lo-ni took her son from his hands.

Ordinarily, this would have ended the Ritual, but tonight
there was another to welcome into the tribe. Now Do-na-ti
came from the shadows where he had stood with the Badger
Clan. He touched his hand to his lips in greeting to the
Elders, and then he turned to face the gathered people.

"I have brought to you a woman of strength and knowledge. She saved my son, when he sickened on the trail. She

saved my wife, whose spirit was sick with loss. She is a warrior, a healer, a wise woman, who will be of value to all of the People."

His voice still held that note of maturity that had impressed E-lo-ni earlier, as he led forward the old woman who had returned her to life.

Holasheeta hobbled on her crippled leg, but it was plain that she was strong and still filled with life. She nodded to the Elders, took Do-na-ti's hand, and set it on her own head for a moment. Then she turned to face the circles around the fire.

"I am Holasheeta. If you will it, I will be of your People."

There was no hesitation. Every adult, male and female, thudded heel or staff on the ground in affirmation. Smiling, Do-na-ti led the old woman to stand beside E-lo-ni and the child.

The thing was done. These two, from so far away, brought here so strangely, were now a part of the village as completely as if they had been born to one of the clans.

E-lo-ni felt a new energy rise inside her. She was fast getting well again, and the needs of her son seemed to heal instead of to tire her. She had Do-na-ti beside her, and Holasheeta would not allow her to yield, ever again, to darkness and death.

It was good.

TWENTY-SEVEN

So busy had Do-na-ti been with the demands of becoming a parent that he had set aside, for a while, his determination to hunt and slay the Tusked Ones. Vengeance for the dead must take second place to the needs of the living, and he did not begrudge the delay.

Once his son and his wife and the grandmother he had added to the complement of the village had settled down into the normal routines of late-summer living, however, he turned his thought again to his oath, sworn before the death fires of his mother and his clan's Elder. This was his duty to those who had gone into the Other Place, and he must go forward, as he had promised to do.

E-lo-ni remembered his words, and he knew that she worried when he began preparing himself for this solitary and important hunt. "No single man can hope to kill the Tusked One," she protested, as he set a round of obsidian and a hammer stone in his pouch and checked a new spear haft for flaws.

"You have returned with a son for us. There is no need to go now, so near the time when the village must move to the winter lodges again. Next summer, when Gift is older, will be time enough."

He shook his head, and she dropped her gaze, knowing that if matters were reversed, she would do exactly what he intended to do. "Yet you promised, as the smoke rose from the flesh of your mother. You promised, and I understand your need." Her voice was small, and he heard the pain in it, but he could not back away from this task.

One by one, his kinsmen of his own and E-lo-ni's clans came to speak with him, each giving reasons why he should not go so soon. Ke-len-ne came, of course, and his words were filled with sadness, for no man had ever hunted a mammoth alone and returned to tell of it.

"Nephew, you are valued in our village. You have played the dog in a Great Hunt, and that is no small thing. You have brought Holasheeta to us, and her knowledge of other healing ways has been of great help to the grandmothers. There are still many things left for you to do for your people. Can you not wait to fulfill your promise?" he asked.

Do-na-ti was moved, for already he had ideas for better ways to move the village between seasonal locations, which would expose them to less threat from wandering herds or scavenging predators. He had envisioned a better way to reinforce the winter lodges, so as to withstand the sort of stampede that had killed his mother.

As he thought of such things, he told E-lo-ni, for she would pass them along to the Elders. In that way, he tried to preserve the thoughts that came to him for the use of the tribe, in case he should die on his new journey.

Yet all the while he prepared himself for this all important hunt. He purified himself in the sweat house and plunged into the cold water of the stream every day for two hands of days. He fasted to lighten his spirit; then he ate moose meat to regain his strength.

When he was ready, he prepared to kill a lion on the plain. Its heart, eaten raw over the body of that kill, would lend him the ferocity he would need in his quest.

His weapon was ready, and from the obsidian he could make more points, if he broke the one already in place. As well, the curving shards displaced by his cautious taps would make knives of exquisite sharpness, with which he could slice meat from his prey or mark his symbol onto his kills.

E-lo-ni had made him a new robe from the underside of

a pelt from a Horned One. It was tough, warm, and its thickness would shed water, if the weather turned wet earlier than usual. She had made moccasins with four layers of soles, so that he would not wear through them as he had those he wore for his totem trek.

Now he was ready, first to kill his lion, and then to hunt a Tusked One to send into the Other Place as a gift for all his kindred who now were there. When he left the lodge of the Terrapin Clan, E-lo-ni did not follow him. He knew that her pain was great, and his own matched it, for it was unlikely that he would live to enter her door again.

His son had crowed as he held him high and touched that small cheek to his own. The feel of the plump, warm body between his hands went with him as he moved out onto the grassland, knowing that the lions would be hunting among the herds of saiga antelope and moose that grazed there after the rains of the past week.

When night fell, he curled into his new robe beneath an outcrop of rock, feeling the earth under his body quiver with the restless sleep of the Burning Mountain. He was used to that, and it lulled him to sleep.

The next morning he watched flights of birds crossing the sky. After a time he saw a distant circle of vultures wheeling ahead and to the east. There were very many, which told him that some predator had made a kill large enough to feed multitudes of the scavenger birds.

He marked the direction, using the mountain peak far to his left to keep his bearings, and headed toward the area about which the creatures circled. He ran, his pouch bouncing at his side, his spear secure in its loop.

Before midday he came over a ridge and looked down into a long, flat stretch between two low ridges. At its bottom he could just pick out a featureless lump toward which an occasional vulture dipped a wing before going in to land.

The herd would not be there, of course. It would have run downwind after the kill. For all of today the wind had come out of the northwest, off the mountain range that was now beyond sight, over the horizon. He must head east and south to cut the trail. The lions should be pacing the herd, picking off stragglers or younglings or old animals.

Again he ran, his deep lungs never straining or panting, his wiry legs devouring distance without tiring. His purification, followed by his diet of heavy meat, had given him stamina and energy enough for more difficult things than this.

He ran until he could see a distant straggle of grazing shapes, long-nosed and prong-horned. Saiga antelope, without a doubt, just as he had thought. Now it was time to go warily, for a lion relished a man as much as it did any other meat, and Do-na-ti had no intention of falling prey to one of the hungry cats.

He slowed to a walk, bending so as to remain below the level of the scrubby growth that studded the plain. That was very little slower than his former pace, for his people had perfected the technique of running stooped. At last he was near enough to see tawny shapes, almost the color of the late summer grasses, as they moved, checking their potential prey.

There were four—three lionesses and a lion. Two of the lionesses were young, smaller than the third, and they remained behind the older one. The male waited in the shadow of a thicket of scrub, while his pride stalked a slow-moving mother with a half-grown fawn at her heels.

The lion's attention was focused on the hunt, and Do-na-ti knew that, coming from downwind, he might slip up on the giant cat and kill him before he could resist.

Or I might die. The unbidden thought was something to push away instantly, as he crept in a wide arc on the downwind side of the animal's resting place.

He felt quite cool and steady, and hardly a blade of grass crinkled audibly as he crept toward the great shape of the resting lion. He could hear the sounds of the antelope grazing, the thuds as the hooves of playing youngsters romped over the ground, the shrill chirp of a nearby bird. Dust sifted into his nostrils, tanged with the acrid scent of the soil and a sharp odor of cat urine.

Wriggling as quietly as a snake through the sun-dried grass, over the new growth pushing up after the recent rain, Do-na-ti approached the big cat. Now he could smell his dusty coat, his strong male scent, and he could see the sun rippling through the thin branches of the bush in stripes across his tawny fur.

There came a snort from the grazing antelope; hooves pounded as the intended prey dashed frantically to avoid the lionesses. Do-na-ti heard everything, noted the moment when the desperate animal found itself surrounded by all three of the female cats, but did not glance aside from his quarry. He noted the antelope's anguished bleat as one of the hunters took it by the throat.

All the while, the lion's gaze was fixed upon the kill, and Do-na-ti came very near. Now, in order to use his spear, he must stand, and that would be the supreme test of his skill and nerve. And if the lion heard him . . . He breathed deeply and silently, filling his lungs with air, his heart with boldness.

He rose straight up from the ground, setting his feet, bracing his stance, raising the spear so that its rosy point glowed in the sunlight. Before he could cast, the lion turned his massive head and looked the young man straight in the eyes.

That long breath went out of Do-na-ti in a gust of shock. For an instant, it seemed that he looked out through the eyes of the lion, seeing this skinny brown figure, without claws or fangs, that held a ridiculous stick over its head.

A lazy curiosity washed through him . . . and suddenly he was back behind his own eyes, looking still into those of the giant cat. That golden gaze seemed to penetrate him to the bones, seeing all that he was, all that he had done, all that he might still do, if he lived.

The lion's whiskers twitched, and his tongue curled as he yawned widely, showing terrible white fangs inside a mouth that was like a cavern.

Do-na-ti found himself, without willing it, speaking softly to the beast. "You are . . . I see it now. You are of the Old Spirit Ones. Perhaps you are one of them, resting inside this animal body for a time to watch the hunt on the plain. I see your strength, Old One. I see your wisdom.

"You are not for me to kill, just in order to eat your heart. That is not a thing that a man should need. To steal courage from a lion is an unbecoming thing, the act of a child.

"An adult of the People should possess the strength and the courage to do anything he finds needful, no matter how dangerous or difficult it might be." Do-na-ti heaved a sigh and stepped backward slowly.

"Go in peace, Great One. I will trouble you no more. You have taught me the thing I needed to know, and now I shall go on my own hunt, knowing that it is my sole responsibility. I should no more concern you in my affairs than I do the other hunters among my clan and village."

The golden eyes narrowed, and the lion closed them in a long wink. He did not offer to rise or to attack. It seemed that he found this man-thing too unimportant to pose any threat. He looked for a moment longer, but at last he turned his head to watch his mates' progress with the antelope.

Do-na-ti sank into the grass and backed away among the scrubby growth behind him. Even as he hid, the lion rose with majestic indifference and moved toward the meat that his pride had killed for him.

Do-na-ti took the opportunity to turn and run at top speed back toward the ridge from which he had spotted the herd and the lions. Even as he fled, he knew that he was not afraid. Awed, yes. Astonished at the thing he had been taught by the lion and the Old Spirit Ones, but not frightened. He would not be frightened, he thought, when he took his spear and went against whatever of the Tusked Ones he found when he went on his hunt for vengeance, even if he found his death in that attempt.

But before he made his way toward the deeply worn trail used by the migrating tuskers, he must go back to his village and tell his people of the thing he had learned. They had believed for many lives of their kind that it was a strong and virtuous matter to devour the courage of the lion.

Now they must be warned. The Old Spirit Ones found no

virtue in such things. Instead, they had sent a warning of their own, through Do-na-ti, son of Ash-pah, that this was no longer something to be attempted by those who lived on the plain at the foot of the mountains.

TWENTY-EIGHT

DO-NA-TI SAW THE HUDDLE OF SUMMER LODGES RISE ABOVE THE grassland with a strange feeling in his heart. He had not truly thought to come here again, if he lived, until the next summer came.

His people would be astonished at his return. It was probable they might resist the idea that the hunt for courage was no longer acceptable to the Spirit Ones. Yet he had been given that vision through the eyes of the lion.

He knew within his heart that this was the message he must bear to his kind. This was a duty he must perform, no matter how he longed to go about fulfilling his oath.

It was, as usual, Ka-shi who saw him first. The boy was on his way homeward, carrying three grouse and a rabbit that dangled limply from his hand by its long ears. His sharp eyes recognized Do-na-ti at once, and he came pelting toward him, his game dropped to be retrieved later.

"Brother! You have come again! Have you slain the tusker so soon?" He panted as he drew near.

"I have come with word for the Elders, but I have not yet taken the trail after the great ones. Go, Ka-shi, and tell Ku-lap to gather the others before his lodge. I will bring your meat, for I am weary and do not wish to run with you."

He watched the boy dash away, the rear of his skimpy loincloth fluttering in the wind of his passing. Do-na-ti smiled. He hoped that this brother would live, as his older

185

brothers had not, to become a man, for Ka-shi showed
promise of becoming one who could help the People.

By the time he had gathered up the dropped grouse and
the rabbit and made his way to the first lodge at the edge of
the village, Ku-lap was coming from his own shelter to meet
him. It saddened Do-na-ti to see how feeble the old man was
becoming.

"Ho, Do-na-ti! The boy tells me that you have word for
the People. Come with me and tell us what you have found."
The old man turned and moved with some difficulty toward
his sitting pad before his lodge, and Do-na-ti followed him
without speaking.

Since looking into the eyes of the lion, he had felt an
inner urge toward silence and deep thought. It seemed that
he had been given more than a single piece of information,
but a part of it had not yet become clear to his mind. Until
that happened, he would speak as little as possible, for he
felt that words might muddy the clarity of the idea that was
being born.

He nodded to his Badger Clan kin as he moved through
the camp. He smiled when E-lo-ni came near, saw that he
was in the grip of some vision, and dropped back to walk
beside him, not touching even his hand. His wife knew
when to deny her own wishes, and she understood, it
seemed, things that he could not yet put into coherent
words.

Followed by most of those who remained in the village at
this time of day, he moved to the space before Ku-lap's
lodge and sank onto his haunches beside the Elder. Fe-ka-na
hurried from her own place, and Ke-len-ne came into view
from the direction of the stream. A hail from Ku-lap hurried
his steps as he saw that a meeting of some importance must
be taking place, and soon he dropped into his own spot
among the Elders.

There was no need for Ritual. All knew Do-na-ti. All
understood that he had been singularly chosen by the Old
Spirit Ones, receiving visions unlike any others among their
tribal members. They simply waited for him to speak,

knowing that he would not have returned so soon if he had not brought information that was important to his village.

He looked about, smiled at E-lo-ni again, at Holasheeta, who held his son, and at each of the Elders. When he spoke, his voice was husky, and he had to clear his throat.

"I have come with a strange matter that overturns the beliefs we have had since the time of the most ancient of grandmothers." He coughed, and Holasheeta passed him a gourd of water.

"I looked into the eyes of the great lion. I stood over him, spear in hand, and I might have slain him, though it is likely that I would have died in the doing. He looked at me, gazing deeply into my heart, and for a moment I was inside him. I saw through his eyes, and I felt with his spirit.

"The Old Spirit Ones spoke inside, and this is what they said:

"'It is not the work of a man to steal courage from a beast. If a man has no courage, that will not provide it. A dangerous act is only worthy if done through the strength and courage of the one who performs it.

"'All beasts are of the spirits, and all have value. Only when a person must eat or provide clothing or shelter for himself and his people is the slaying of an animal an act of virtue. And when that is done, the People must give thanks to that animal for its gift of life to your kind.'"

To his surprise, Do-na-ti could not recognize his own voice as he spoke, for it boomed out, deeper and more authoritative than ever before in his life. The feel of it in his throat was strange and alien, and he felt that the voice of that lion-spirit had spoken through his mouth to the ears of his people. Its echoes seemed to travel away and echo back from the nearby mountains.

For a long moment there was silence, and he could see a stunned look in the eyes of the Elders. Not even the smallest child whimpered or gurgled, and only the sound of the wind, rising as the sun began to set, interrupted the stillness.

A distant hail broke the spell at last, as a group of boys returned from checking their snares. Ku-lap drew a long breath and shook his grizzled head. Ke-len-ne looked at his nephew as if seeing him for the first time. Fe-ka-na wheezed and leaned forward to take Do-na-ti's hand between hers.

"You have brought a true word, Do-na-ti. I felt it in my heart, in my belly. The voice of the Old Spirit Ones came from your mouth, and we all now understand what we must do. Go and fulfill your need and your promise. Then come back to us in the winter village, if you succeed and live."

Do-na-ti rose and stood over E-lo-ni, who looked up at him, her eyes warm. She did not raise her hand to his but touched her fingertips to her lips in greeting and farewell.

He looked down at Holasheeta, who nodded, her expression closed and secretive. She knew, that one; more of the spirits than most. Living alone on her high ridge for so many seasons had attuned her inner being with those of the Old Ones, he suspected. Now she foresaw something that she would not reveal by look or by word.

He did not want to know. Whatever the outcome of his quest, he must go. So thinking, he turned and left the village in the twilight, moving toward the edges of the mountains that formed dark, jagged shapes against the rose and gold of the evening sky.

He did not look back but moved into the growing darkness, without thought of any night-borne danger. His life, he felt, was not in his own hands but in those of spirits beyond his comprehension. He would follow as he was led, and he could only hope that he might live to return to his family.

He moved up the edge of the plain, keeping to the foothills so as to see far across the lower country. At this season, the heights were growing colder, driving those animals that grazed or hunted there into warmer places, and already he could see the tracks of moose and small deer on the game trails leading down to the streams he crossed.

The peaks above the foothills were powdered with white, and the higher ones, the great gray upthrusts of stone, were deep in snow. That meant that the Tusked Ones would be turning their trunks toward the south, moving along their ancient trails toward chosen spots where they would winter.

He had picked his time well for locating a herd and confronting one of its members, if he could find one alone or injured. Yet his former burning need for its blood had cooled since he met that lion on the plain.

He had caught a glimpse of what it might mean to be a beast, compelled by needs and purposes that no man could understand. Anything that might frighten the lion would be so terrible that it might well paralyze a man beyond the possibility of intelligent reaction.

What had frightened those tuskers, on the night they stampeded? He wondered if they had been blinded by their panic, as he had sometimes been in his childhood, before he learned control.

He was finding in his spirit a sort of pity for the great beasts, lumbered with bodies that were impossible to hide, burdened with mysterious fears beyond his power to guess. Dimly, he groped toward a thing that no one of his kind had ever thought before.

How did it feel to be an animal? What did the beasts think, and how did they react to this grim world they shared with so many other species? The questions ran around in his head like squirrels.

On the day when he saw a distant blur of motion out on the plain, he knew that a time was coming when he must comprehend fully what he needed to do. He could no longer go ahead blindly, as he had seen boys and very young men do all his life. The vision he had been given forbade that, now.

When he came face-to-face with the Tusked One he must slay, it would be with full recognition that this was a creature whose blood ran red, like his own. It would be in the understanding that death came to all; the respect and gratitude he might offer his victim might ease his own death, when that time came.

He sat cross-legged in the shadow of a juniper, watching the distant herd plodding, head to tail, along the trail that generations of their kind had worn into the grass and soil of the plain. Tomorrow he would follow them and wait for one to injure itself and fall behind the rest of the herd.

At dawn he was on his way, moving down through the foothills toward the spot he had set into his memory. By the time he arrived, the line of tusked marchers would have moved a long way down their trail, he knew, but that was a good thing.

They must not know that he tracked them. Usually they ignored man as being too small for their notice, but at times one of the big bulls would raise his trunk, trumpet a terrible challenge, and trample a hunter into the grass until he was only a smear of red on the grass.

No, he would travel behind the group; it was one of fewer and fewer left, he realized, thinking back. Even in his short life, the Great Ones had dwindled until mere handfuls walked the ways that had been worn by huge groups in the past, according to the oldest of tales among the People.

He would wait for some straggler, some lame youngster or slow-moving old cow or bull that might fall behind. No man could hope to slay a healthy adult, but it might be possible to kill a disabled tusker and live to tell of it . . . he hoped, though there was no tale of such a happening among the stories of his clan.

When he came to the deeply worn rut in the tan-green grasses, the big piles of dung and the tracks told him that the last of the herd had passed less than a day before. Even though it was growing late, he ran after the herd, guided by their trail, knowing that no predator would approach their route until the rank smell of them had dissipated.

That would protect him as he traveled behind them, he was fairly certain, although nothing in his world was ever without peril. He did not run along the track itself, for plowing into one of those huge piles of droppings was nothing he relished; instead, he dropped to one side and ran southward over the prickly growths and the clean grass.

He felt that he might have closed his eyes and still kept to the trail. The rank scent that repelled lions and direwolves was strong enough to guide him, even if he only followed the promptings of his nose. Indeed, he closed his eyes for moments at a time, resting as he ran, yet keeping his other senses alert for any danger.

Night found him far out on the plain, where the track ran beside a deep ravine that carried spring snow melt running down from the mountains. When he curled into his robe, huddled beneath a bush, he slept deeply, without fear of death that might creep through the night.

If it came, it came. If not, tomorrow he would resume pursuit of his great prey and the fulfillment of his promise to Ash-pah and Tu-ri-nit.

TWENTY-NINE

THE BIG BULL REELED A BIT AS HE WALKED AT THE HEAD OF THE HERD. His cows, his calves and yearlings, and the grown young males that would soon dispute his leadership marched steadily in his tracks, but he was becoming slower with every day of the migration.

He did not think, and yet some instinct told him that he would not make this journey again. The pain in his joints with each step, as his great weight descended upon his knees, had become more and more troublesome as the year progressed.

Now he began to limp, long before a good place to stop and browse came into view. He must locate a spot where the herd could find small trees and bushes the tops of which they could devour.

The light moved westward, and shadows crept across the swells of grass and bushes. He must stop now, for he was staggering. He raised his trunk and trumpeted, but instead of sounding a challenge, his call was more a signal of distress. One of the cows pushed her way up beside him and laid her trunk over his back, but her closeness gave him no comfort.

The herd spread out among the scanty growth in that resting place, leaving him to close his eyes and sway restlessly from foot to foot, his trunk swinging rhythmically. If he could only regain his strength . . . Yet he understood

*in some dim way that this would not happen. He was old,
and he was tired.*

*The young bulls had sensed the change in him, he knew.
The strongest of them would challenge his leader tonight,
while he was weary and in distress. A huge sigh rumbled
through his chest, and he curled his trunk around a sapling
and pulled it absently from the ground, stuffing the dusty
leaves into his mouth.*

*Food no longer strengthened him. He had no mind for the
scent of a cow in heat. No, he was old. He was finished,
although some deep instinct refused to give up without a
struggle.*

*When the young bull came sidling toward him, trunk high
in a shrill challenge, tusks ready for battle, the old one
backed off a bit and shook his head, trying to regain
something of the old spark that had sustained him for so
long. However, the youngster didn't wait. Instead he
charged, raking a tusk along the side of the older animal
and using his weight to push him off-balance.*

*But those tree-like legs had withstood terrible trials,
holding that bulk steady in the teeth of storms and earth
tremors, battles and stampedes. The old bull did not waver
but lowered his head and jabbed a tusk into the leg of his
opponent.*

*Even the scent of his challenger's blood did not warm his
own blood to its old heat or give his muscles the vigor they
once had. Yet he did not retreat. He would die as he had
lived, battling for survival.*

*The two backed and rushed together, heads down, tusks
ready. The old bull gave all he had, but the younger backed
him relentlessly toward the edge of the ravine alongside
their old trail.*

*He stumbled up the lip of the worn track, over the grass,
and felt his hind pads scrabbling on the rotten lava rock
forming the sides of the canyon. The ground was quivering
beneath him, but he was used to that.*

*The earth shook frequently, and its increasing tremors
had not disturbed him. Yet even the soil itself seemed in*

league with his enemy, for as he braced to hold against the
weight of the younger male, the ground gave a heave.

The edge of the cliff fell away into the depths below, and
his great feet found no purchase as he followed it. His huge
body bounded off out-thrust ledges and buttresses as he fell,
and when he crashed into the rocky soil at last, a section of
the cliff came down on top of most of his great body.

It was the end. With the fatalism of all animals, he
accepted that, though his crushed bones and torn flesh were
a torment.

If he had been injured up there with the herd, perhaps the
older cows would have helped him to leave the rest, coming
up beside him to brace his feeble steps to some quiet spot
where he might die in peace. Down here, out of sight, he
would be forgotten at once; that was a thing he knew
without knowing it and accepted without question. It was
the way of the world.

Yet as the night crept past, he groaned faintly, his breath
coming painfully. His trunk was free, and he managed to
touch it to a bit of his shoulder and back, but the rest of him
was buried in broken rock. He did not even try to heave
himself free . . . It was time for him, oldest of his herd, to
die.

As morning lighted the sky above the rift to purple, rose,
and gold, the ants found him. That was another agony, to be
expected and ignored. He closed his eyes, curled his trunk,
and waited to be released from his pain.

Do-na-ti followed the herd for two days. At night,
protected by their rank scent, he slept in safety, but on the
third evening he realized that something was changing. The
herd stopped earlier than usual, and he could see from the
top of a lava ridge that the lead bull was confronting a
smaller one.

He had seen such battles before, from a much greater
distance. Although the large herds that the greatest of
grandfathers had known had dwindled to only a few, from
time to time his people came upon the scene of such a battle

for leadership, sometimes while it went on, sometimes afterward.

One of the beasts must lose, and the loser might well be crippled enough to allow a single hunter to kill him. Do-na-ti watched for a moment, while the shadows crawled across the ridges of lava and the grasslands between. If he came closer, he might know better how to deal with that survivor, if it were possible to approach him at all.

He crept over to the edge of the ravine and looked down. At this point it was very deep, but the walls were etched and creased by weather. He could climb down and run along the winding bottom until he was near the herd's position. Then he might be able to see what was best to do.

It was not an easy descent, for the rock was brittle and tended to break free from the cliff. He had to test every toehold before trusting his weight to it. Even as he went down, the ground tremor began again . . . a slow shaking, tumbling small stones onto his head and raining grit and pebbles down his back.

He dropped the last couple of man-heights, landing on all fours amid rough-edged splits and chunks. Nothing was broken; bruises and scrapes were a part of life that none of his kind particularly noticed, so he rose at once and ran along the dry channel.

Above him the cliffs shook still, and he had to dodge occasional falling stones and even entire sections of wall that came down with a crash and filled the ravine with dust. He ducked and twisted, moving forward toward the herd.

He could not see, of course, from the depths of the canyon, so at last he found a place where he could climb the wall on the other side from the trail. From there he could observe without going too near the perilous battle that must be taking place.

It was no easier than the climb downward had been, principally because of the continued tremors; he reached the top at last and gazed across the dark chasm. He was still some distance from the bulk of the herd, and he ran along the edge until he could see the triumphant bull standing, trunk raised to trumpet, above the paler stretch of stone where the cliff had fallen away from the land above.

He could see no huge shadow that might be the old bull. Feeling suddenly light-headed with discovery, Do-na-ti realized what must have happened: as the cliff dropped into the ravine, the older animal must have fallen with it. Surely he would be too badly injured by the fall to pose too great a danger to a lone hunter.

He found a tree tall enough for climbing and went up into its prickly top, where he sat on a slanting branch, wrapped both arms about the trunk, and dropped off to sleep. Tomorrow he must be rested, ready to put forth the most terrible effort of his life.

If he lived, it would be a thing for making tales to instruct many generations to come.

He heard, when he woke from time to time, the uneasy movements of the herd. Scrunching sounds told him when they ripped the tops from trees or jerked bushes up from their roots. Occasional gusty sighs or trumpetline snorts marked the position of the great beasts.

He slept again, knowing that they would move away before dawn, following the strange instinct that moved them across the plains. Then he would go down again to see what waited for him at the bottom of the canyon.

He woke before daylight, when dawn made black and gray images of rocks and trees and a black streak of the ravine. There were no shadowy shapes across the chasm, no sounds of chomping and crushing. The tuskers were gone, and as soon as full light came he would know if his quest might succeed.

As he climbed down his tree, a great tremor shook the land, and he fell the rest of the way, landing in a prickly bush with a thump and a gasp of pain. Thorns studded the side and hip where he landed, and he pulled them out of his flesh as he waited for the sun.

He would not lose enough blood to weaken him, though he knew he must poultice the wounds or risk having them go rotten and begin to stink. Many deaths among his people were caused by untended wounds, and the grandmothers had found plants whose leaves and roots helped to heal such injuries.

Do-na-ti knew that he must go home again quickly, once he dealt with what lay below, or he might die out here alone, without anyone to sing the Ritual. But first he must do the thing his oath demanded.

When the light penetrated to the depths of the chasm, he lay on his belly and stared down at the tumble of broken stone that slanted down from the other side. Tops of bushes and trees stuck out at strange angles, and soil still trickled down from time to time, when the land trembled. He could see, at the edge of the rubble, something dusty that moved.

It was the old bull, he was sure. He checked his spear, making certain that the heavier point, like those used by the ancient grandfathers against the ancestors of this kind, was securely fastened, the bindings tight and well secured. He fastened his pouch to fresh thongs, pitched his bundled robe down into the ravine, and began climbing down.

He clung fast as a lizard when the land quaked, and it did not succeed in shaking him off. When he reached the bottom of the cleft, he laid his pouch beside his bundle and turned to move toward the trapped animal.

As he drew near, he saw one great sad eye regarding him patiently, without fear or surprise. The head and one shoulder of the tusker were free of the tumbled rocks, but the rest of his great body was covered with layers too thick for even an entire clan or village to move. That was a pity, for the huge carcass would have fed many of the People for a very long time.

The creature uncurled his trunk and extended the tip questioningly toward this intruder into his death. Again Do-na-ti had a flash of insight into the animal's spirit, as he had felt when he faced the lion.

This Great Tusked One was dying a most agonizing death, but he did not struggle against his fate. Time would end his misery . . . or Do-na-ti would.

Suddenly excited, Do-na-ti looked into that long, tragic face and saw there the same knowledge of death that he had seen people show, when their time had come. There was no

fear, no resistance. This one would not object if Do-na-ti,
son of Ash-pah, small and weak as he was, should end his
suffering.

The young man felt strange. He had thought he would
feel triumph at avenging his dead mother, his dead Elder,
upon the body of one of those who had killed them. Instead
he was filled with sadness.

A breeze wandered down the ravine, bringing the scents
of bruised greenery, broken rock, and suddenly bared earth
to his nostrils. Life was sweet, running hot in his veins,
throbbing in his heart. He felt sudden pity for this great
animal, who had led his kind for so very long, that must
come to his end at the hands of one so unworthy.

But the beast groaned deeply as the great weight of the
cliff side pressed into his trapped flesh, and the eye blinked
shut, opened, shut again. Blood trickled from the corner of
a drooping lip.

It was time. Instead of taking vengeance, he would give
a merciful death to this suffering beast. Perhaps that was the
thing the Spirit Ones had intended from the first, when he
made that rash promise over the bodies of his dead.

He raised his spear, heavier now with its larger point, and
looked for a place where a thrust might be instantly fatal.
But the body he could see was so thick that he could never
hope to penetrate to the heart that still beat inside that living
mountain.

The hide was too tough to cut to the jugular vein. Only
that great sad eye offered any hope of killing this giant of his
kind.

Do-na-ti stepped forward to brace himself for the thrust.
The dusty trunk snaked out and touched his knee, gently,
almost caressingly. It moved to finger his hair, touch an ear,
drop to his shoulder. Then it curled back into the huge face.

"Go forth, Great One, to the Other Place," Do-na-ti
murmured, putting every bit of strength into his back and
arm as he pushed the spear tip into the eye; he leaned into
his thrust as the point dug through into the creature's brain.

The bull gave a huge, shuddering sigh, and the trunk
dropped, limp, onto the rocky soil.

The pile of rubble over the body quivered, seeming to sink as the life left the creature. Blood bubbled up around Do-na-ti's hand and arm, which were almost flush with the eye socket. When he tried to retrieve his weapon, one tug told him that he would never draw it out of the lifeless hulk.

The spear and the beast would remain together, here at the bottom of the ravine, and the falling rock would cover them. Perhaps, one day, the earth would crack again, and some hunter of a future generation would find the beautiful spear point among the massive bones. It might be that another would use it, in time to come, as he sought other game to feed his clan.

THIRTY

STINKING OF BLOOD, ALREADY WEARY WITH THE EFFORT OF KILLING the tusker, Do-na-ti sank onto his haunches, breathing hard. He must replace his spear. It was not sensible to travel the plain or the mountains without such a weapon, and that was the first thing he had to accomplish, even before obtaining a part of the tusker to place in his pouch.

When he had regained his breath, he rose and searched the slant of rubble for a sapling of suitable size. Green wood did not make a good spear haft, but it would be better than nothing. Soon he found a slender trunk, which he cut off with his flint knife. He notched the butt end and sliced the other away cleanly.

He sat on a stone and scraped the rod free of bark, smoothing it so that it ran easily along his palm. Then he took from his pouch a round of obsidian and his hammer stone. Setting the oblong carefully upon a handy rock, he struck its edge with the hammer stone, and a neat arc of dark glassy stuff chipped free.

He set that aside, for he would need to cut some part from the carcass to carry home; the blade-sharp glass formed a very effective knife. He struck again, turned the piece, and kept chipping away slivers, shaping the point with great care, making it smaller than the one now entombed in the flesh of the tusker.

He would no longer hunt the Great Ones for revenge, so

he had no need for that heavy spear point. He would need a spear capable of killing a predator or small game, on his way to the village, and the smaller fluted ones worked best for that.

It took most of the morning to chip out his point. By the time he had bound it into the new haft, vultures were circling high above the crack in the land, sensing the presence of enough meat to feed them all and more. But as long as Do-na-ti worked there, moving about, they kept their distance, and he was left in peace.

Using several of the slivers he had freed from the round of obsidian, he began slicing the tough hide of the beast, baring the visible shoulder. The meat would be tough and stringy, but he could chew the juices from it as he traveled. That would mean that he could go quickly toward the healers, instead of taking the time to hunt.

Already his puncture wounds were festering, and when he had freed the meat he could carry, and chipped away the tip of one of the tusks with a pair of stones, he knew he must clean the wounds if he was to make the journey back to E-lo-ni and his son.

The shadow of the western cliff covered him from the pitiless sun now, and he arranged his burdens carefully, ready to carry forward. Then he found the smallest, thinnest of the glass blades and sat to dig out the dirty and swelling flesh from his injuries.

Without hesitation, he sliced cleanly around one of the deepest punctures, cutting out a neat cone of disturbed flesh. Blood spurted, and he let it flow for some time to clean the cut, before packing it with a roll of limp but fragrant leaves from his pouch. One by one he tended the rest, slicing lengthways along the cuts and digging out the other thorn holes.

His blood mingled with that of the tusker as he worked, and the dust at his feet became red and sticky mud. It was somehow fitting, he thought. In death, the animal became his blood brother, as in life it had taught him the kinship of their spirits. When Do-na-ti came at last to the Other Place, he might find that beast browsing there, waiting to reclaim this strange friendship.

When he was done, all his many wounds and abrasions tended as best he could without extra water and with his limited supply of medicinal leaves, he rose. He must move, for if these stiffened before he began his journey, they would make the thing almost impossible.

It was hard to carry the meat, even wrapped in his robe, but he trudged down the canyon, hoping to find a lower place where he might climb out easily. Behind him he left drops of blood, but they were relatively few and would not drain him of strength.

The sun went down, and he found a niche in the wall of the canyon and barricaded himself with loose stones. The smell of the meat and of his own blood would attract any predator that might be prowling along the ravine.

With solid rock at his back and his new spear to defend the frail barricade, he should be able to survive the night. Tomorrow, whatever came, he would climb out and spend the next night in a tree.

But the wall of the canyon became steadily lower as he moved along its twisting length, and he came at last to a runnel from the plain above that afforded an easy climb to the surface again. It was late afternoon, but he oriented himself by the smoke rising from the Burning Mountain to the west.

Yes. If he went east and south again, he would find the winter village, where his people should now be settling in for the cold season. The jagged peak that broke the skyline to his right would help him to keep to his route, and the occasional clumps of trees that studded the plain would give him a safe place to sleep when the sun went down entirely.

Do-na-ti felt strangely light, not quite weak but not entirely strong and fit. He took to the first good-sized tree he found, and though it was fairly low, it took him above the reach of a bear's claws or a direwolf's leap. He tied the meat to the scaly trunk above him and again wrapped himself about the bole to sleep.

In the night he heard growls and snarls beneath his perch.

Wolves? Perhaps, or a wolverine. The tree shook from time to time as whatever it was tried to climb to this tempting prey, but Do-na-ti didn't really worry. More and more, he believed that the Old Spirit Ones were guiding him and taking care that the worst did not quite happen along the way.

He woke stiff and dizzy, barely able to unbend his legs from their cramped position around the tree trunk. He retrieved his bundle with difficulty and dropped to the ground, unable to manage the branches between.

Now he did feel weak, but he chewed the meat of the tusker, finding strength in the stringy stuff, and it allowed him to begin walking straight toward his goal.

The People shared an inner compass that guided them over the long swells, the deep grasses, the thickets and rivers and canyons of their world. Now that he was going home, he did it with the sureness of a swan flying south for the winter or a swallow going north with the spring.

He did not need to think, for his heart told him how to set his feet and where to aim for on the horizon.

Now Do-na-ti knew, in his occasional fits of awareness, that he must not stop again. He would not be able to start when morning came. He must go until he died or came home again, and his legs worked automatically as his spirit drifted away into some time and place of its own choosing.

His brother Ka-shi, running his newly set traps for the first time that season, was, of course, the one to find him. Ka-shi, the sharp-eyed, Ka-shi the ever-curious, appeared before him like a ghost or a dream.

"Do-na-ti!" The voice was Ka-shi's. Do-na-ti's spirit swept like a vulture overhead before deciding to descend again into his body.

He found to his surprise that his eyes were closed. Now he pried them open, the lids feeling gummy and difficult, and stared into his brother's face.

Instead of flashing his usual grin of joy, Ka-shi looked very serious. That alone brought his brother back to full awareness.

"I . . . have slain . . . the Great Tusked One. But

it . . . was not . . . for vengeance. Take me . . . to E-lo-ni . . . my brother." Then Do-na-ti felt the darkness closing in from all sides, and he seemed to fall asleep standing up.

He was warm, and his belly felt full. Feeling with both hands, Do-na-ti found that he lay on a soft fur instead of the worn and gritty robe. Quiet sounds came to his ears, and he listened for a while before venturing to open his eyes.

A gurgle—that was Gift, he was certain. A laugh. E-lo-ni, to be certain.

A voice that belonged to Holasheeta, her words strangely accented, said, "He will wake, now. We give him meat, for the broth he drink in sleep will not be enough."

Do-na-ti opened his eyes and looked up into the face of his wife. "Pouch," he said. He took a long breath. "I have brought . . ." He pushed himself up to sit, knowing that he was well, if somewhat weak. It had been weariness that had made him sleep for so long.

"I have brought a part of the tusk of the Great One I slew. There is no more bitterness in my heart, E-lo-ni. I lost my mother to the tuskers, and it poisoned my spirit, as losing our first son poisoned yours."

He paused to think carefully about his next words. "Holasheeta and Gift removed the poison from your heart, leaving you healed. The lion and the Great Tusked One have healed me of the poison that sickened me, as well."

She smiled, but she said nothing. Instead she handed him their son, who crowed joyfully at seeing his father again and wrapped his arms about Do-na-ti's neck.

Holasheeta patted his shoulder wordlessly, and he knew that she, too, was glad to see the black spot in his heart pale and heal.

"I will tell you, tomorrow, of my dream," the old woman told him.

Even as he rose to go and visit the Elders, he wondered what she might mean. He sat in the circle of wise ones and told his tale, hearing their murmurs of wonder, and still he thought of the ancient woman's words.

What would she tell him that he had not learned on his terrible journeys, from his great and perilous enemies and the beasts that had taught him pity and gratitude?

He had thought that nothing could surprise him now, after the spirits had led him so far. He found that he had been wrong.

THIRTY-ONE

HOLASHEETA HAD BOTH HOPED FOR AND DREADED THIS TIME. SHE had watched Do-na-ti leave the village with something of the same feeling of loss she had known when her children were slain. It seemed unlikely, at best, that he would survive to return to his people, and the thought saddened her.

Now that he had returned, changed and matured by his confrontation with the injured Great One, she knew that she must find the words to tell him of the thing she had learned in a dream of her own. It was not easy, speaking in this language that was so like her own in some ways and so different in others.

When Do-na-ti and E-lo-ni sat with her on the sheltered side of the lodge, looking across the frost-killed grasses toward the mountains that rose to the south, she drew a long breath before beginning. Then she said, "I am like child of the mountain, for I live there long, alone, with no other companion.

"I talk to rocks, and at times I think they speak back to me. I listen to the bird, to the animal that cry below my ridge. My heart become hard, like stone, from living so long alone. I think I turn to stone, in time, and sit there forever.

"When you come with the little one, something break apart inside me. I *feel,* though for long I push away the feeling, for it is too hard to bear. But then I know—the Spirit Ones have send you to me.

206

"There is work for the woman who sit on the height and mutter curse against Long-Heads. I see that curse is no good, no use to me or to any. I see that my work must be for you and the child."

She paused and wiped her face with her robe, for the effort of putting such thoughts into words was very great. "I think what work may be, but I do not find. But after you go to hunt the Great One, I dream. That dream show me great and terrible thing that is one you must know." She looked deeply into Do-na-ti's eyes, straining to make him understand how important this thing was that had been revealed to her.

"Do-na-ti, you dream, too. You see what others do not. You feel and understand new things, like lion and Great One in mind and heart. The Spirit Ones have use for you, but you must understand more. There is another journey for you, another task before you rest for winter."

"No!" That was E-lo-ni, who put her arm over her husband's shoulder and held him tightly as if to prevent his leaving her again. "He has been hurt and weary. He should rest for the winter before he follows any other dream!"

Holasheeta shook her head. "This is a thing that cannot wait." Now words flowed more easily, as if the Spirit Ones helped her choose the proper ones. "It happens soon, soon, with barely time to get there. You must go at once, very fast. Take with you a companion . . . and your son."

Again she leaned forward to hold the young man's eyes with her own. "Go toward the Burning Mountain, Do-na-ti, son of Ash-pah. Go toward the Burning Mountain and see the thing that will happen there."

A great burden seemed to shift from the old woman's weary heart. She smiled, feeling herself lightened of the burden of her life. With the last of her strength, she reached a hand to touch the baby, who sat beside her on her cloak, and stroked his soft cheek.

Then her hand fell, limp and useless, beside her, and she knew that her work was done. She would soon join her children and her man and her kin in the Other Place. When

her eyes dimmed, there was no fear inside her, only
boundless joy.

Do-na-ti had felt a strange curiosity along with a stranger
hesitation as he went to hear Holasheeta's words. He was
battered, stiff and sore from his falls and his efforts in the
past hands of days. He felt that this was going to be another
demand upon his exhausted body and his overfilled spirit,
and he was not wrong.

As the old woman spoke, her words clearer and less
broken than usual, he felt a terrible sense of desolation. He
was at home with his family and his kindred. Why should
he, of all the People, be chosen to do such tremendous and
unheard-of tasks?

He had opened his mouth to protest, as E-lo-ni had done,
when Holasheeta smiled and her eyes seemed to dim. She
reached and touched his son, and then she was dead, a
crumple of robes and withered flesh and bone, left like a
scavenger's meal beside the lodge.

He bent over her, lifted her light weight, and took her to
her bed pile inside the lodge. Outside Gift began to
whimper, as if understanding that this one of the lodge posts
holding up his world was gone forever.

Do-na-ti felt like whimpering, too, for he had grown fond
of Holasheeta, grim and wary as she had seemed. It was
almost like losing his mother again, but this time it was
without bitterness.

She had faced him as she died, and he had seen joy in her
eyes. She had seen the Other Place, he knew, and he
rejoiced for her. She would find again those lost ones of
whom she had spoken to him on their long trek together.

The grandmother came to stand beside him. "She brought
us good things," the old one said. "And she saved my
grandson. She will go to the Ritual dressed in the best that
we can find for her, for she became one of the People before
she died."

Do-na-ti was content. Once the Ritual was done, the body
burned to ash and scattered on the wind, he would obey her
last wish and go again from his tribe and his family. He

must, as badly as he hated to make the attempt, visit the Burning Mountain and find what the dream concerned. What secret waited there?

Despite himself, despite his fatigue and his grief, Do-na-ti found himself wondering about the journey as he went out to inform the Elders that this new member of the tribe was gone from them so soon. He thought of taking his son again into the open country and exposing him to its dangers. It was a perilous thing to do, and yet he must—that had been the word sent to him on Holasheeta's dying breath.

He would take E-lo-ni also, and together they would make the long trek over the chilly distance to find what waited for them beside the Burning Mountain where the Ancient Ones rolled and tumbled beneath the earth.

THIRTY-TWO

=============
=====

Aᴌᴛʜᴏᴜɢʜ ᴡɪɴᴛᴇʀ ᴡᴀѕ ᴛᴏʏɪɴɢ ᴡɪᴛʜ ᴛʜᴇ ᴘʟᴀɪɴ ѕᴏ ꜰᴀʀ, ᴡɪᴛʜᴏᴜᴛ
any blizzard to make travel too hard for a family, the peaks
toward which Do-na-ti set out were already deep in snow.
Once he topped the ridges, he could see jagged teeth of
white beyond the flare of the Burning Mountain.

E-lo-ni had been doubtful of taking her son on such a
risky mission. Yet she had not argued when Do-na-ti told
her what they must do. She had seen Holasheeta die with the
command upon her lips, and she knew, as he did, that they
must obey.

The wind sliced through even the heavy bison hide of
their winter robes, and Do-na-ti carried Gift on his back,
beneath the cover of the robe, to keep the child from
freezing. The only good thing about the weather was the fact
that it sent predators and other animals to cover.

A storm would come soon on the heels of the blast,
Do-na-ti knew, but once they drew near the Burning
Mountain the ground would warm beneath their feet. They
would survive, he understood, if they could reach that area
soon.

It was not very far from the winter village to the mountain
Do-na-ti sought. Two days saw his family drawing near, as
the ground shook beneath their feet. Though the grassland
still stretched away, broken by occasional ridges, toward the

foot of the smoking giant, already the soil was warm enough to feel through thick winter moccasins.

Another day's travel would take them too near the mountain for safety. Do-na-ti began to wonder what he should do—he could not risk their lives on the whim of an old woman, no matter if the spirits had sent her dream. But he plodded onward, E-lo-ni beside him, his son tucked snugly against his back.

Then the ground began to shake harder, so hard that it threw him to his knees. He felt E-lo-ni clinging to his shoulder as they knelt on the ash-covered grass, staring at the thing that began to burst upward between their position and the mountain toward which they traveled.

The earth seemed intent upon flinging them off into the murky sky. He put one arm over his wife and tucked Gift, retrieved from the sling on his back, under his other arm. Together they lay flat, riding the bucking ground as it heaved beneath them.

A sound, too huge, too sharp, too booming to hear properly, exploded into the afternoon. Do-na-ti raised his head and uncovered his eyes, peering into the chaos before him. A plume was shooting into the sky, like smoke, but much whiter. As it rose, it opened out to form a wide cloud on the air, and as it plumed it turned pale gray.

Now the ground shook even more strongly. A rain of ash and heavier debris began to pelt down upon the small family so near that new opening into the underworld, where surely the Ancient Ones must have flung a spear to pierce the rock and burst into the free air above.

Do-na-ti felt that he was seeing the thing the spirits had promised him, but he had no understanding of what it might mean. What he did know was that he must retreat with his family to the shelter of the ridge to the south, for if larger rocks began raining from the sky, they would surely be crushed.

He nudged E-lo-ni, for even a shout could not have been heard above the bone-shaking rumble of the earth. They rose together, holding the larger robe over their heads to

shelter them all from the deadly hail of stuff that the plume
was dropping upon their heads.

Gift was crying now, his training lost amid such noise and
confusion. Do-na-ti could feel the round body heaving
against his chest as he ran beside E-lo-ni toward the ridge,
which was their only chance of survival. Tears dampened
his chest and trickled along his neck as the child wept.

It seemed that herds of Tusked Ones must be stampeding
at their heels, bellowing and tearing up the ground, so great
was the tumult. Ahead a crack opened in the ground before
the fleeing feet of Do-na-ti's family.

He knew that to pause was to die, and he caught E-lo-ni
against him and leapt with all his might. They landed with
a thump. Without pausing, he urged them onward, for now
the rocky ridge was near, although when he peered through
the thick air, it, too, seemed to be dancing before his eyes.

As they came to the first slopes, loose rocks and patches
of shale broke or rolled beneath their steps, but Do-na-ti
kept his balance somehow, half-clinging to E-lo-ni and
half-supporting her. Now the ridge itself was cracking, parts
of the lava cap breaking free to tumble toward them.

But Do-na-ti felt a sudden surge of strength. He had made
great journeys, guided by the Old Spirit Ones. This journey
had been ordered by their messenger. They would keep his
family safe, and with that for comfort he moved forward
more steadily, ignoring the terror of the bellowing monster
behind him.

They came to the spine, now broken and perilous, and
moved over the ridge into the deep canyon beyond. A
segment had fallen across the narrow cleft, roofing it over
for quite a long distance. There, if anywhere, Do-na-ti's
family should be sheltered from the rain of cinders and ash
that now was becoming more and more dangerous.

They rested there for a long time, holding to one another
to keep from being thrown flat. It was hard to breathe, for
the air was filled with steam and smoke and ash. Do-na-ti
knew they must move again soon, for if so much stuff
continued to fall, it would fill the area around the hole into
the underworld and even this canyon where they hid.

When he and E-lo-ni could move again, they fastened Gift to his back and raised the robe again. When they moved out of their shelter, the level of the canyon floor had risen to the height of their knees. It would have very been easy to fall asleep and wake again to find themselves buried alive beneath that stony roof. Do-na-ti shuddered, thinking how nearly he had decided to ride out the catastrophe in that place.

Beyond the canyon, they climbed breathlessly, clinging to each other and to weathered lava rock that threatened to come loose and tumble them back into the canyon. To stop was to die, and neither of them hesitated, flinging themselves recklessly down gullies and across opening gaps in the stone.

When they had run as far as they could possibly go, Do-na-ti realized that they were again in the flat grassland, which undulated far less disturbingly than the land closer to the steaming and smoking mound that now could be seen rising above the broken ridge.

Even as Do-na-ti looked out from beneath his robe, it was growing higher and higher, though the debris seemed to be falling nearer to its foot. Only an occasional bit fell this far away, but that dark cone, steaming and fuming, pushed upward and upward beyond the broken ridges, as if to reach the sky itself.

Panting and gasping, for the breath of the new mountain filled the air with hot gases, Do-na-ti stared at the thing the spirits had brought him here to see. He could not speak to E-lo-ni, for still the voices from the earth howled and growled and rumbled, but he thought of that long-ago day when he had wondered if his son might have a mountain for a brother.

That son had not lived, but the spirits had sent this one; Holasheeta had said the child must come on this dangerous journey. Totem-Gift was present as his mighty brother came into the world with more lament than any mortal woman had ever uttered. That tall cone would remain to carry on their kinship, even when Gift himself went to ash.

Then perhaps they would join in the Other Place, spirit to spirit, mountain to man, while the kindred who had gone before marveled. Do-na-ti sighed. There was no time to dream now. He must get his family clear of this place, away from the falling ash and the swirling gases.

He turned to look into E-lo-ni's eyes, but they were fixed with terrible comprehension upon the plume of steam and smoke and the rising black cone that had been born so near to them. She rose at once when Do-na-ti touched her, taking the child this time upon her own back.

The wind had not paused, although now, as it swept past the new mountain, it became warm instead of icy. With it pushing at their backs, they went away across the grassland. They reached the first of the forested hills long after darkness had fallen; yet they were guided by the intermittent light from the belched fires of the Burning Mountain beyond the cone.

There the wind was neither warm nor cold, and the ash was left behind, for the moment. They had to sleep, Do-na-ti knew, and this was the best place they could find. No animal of any size would be left within range of the explosion, he knew, for all would flee from such noise and bombardment. They would be safe here.

They did not think of making fire. Exhausted, now that the need to run was past, they fell into a heap, all three rolled into Do-na-ti's heavy robe, and slept at once. Even the occasional heavier explosions did not do more than half-rouse him.

When Do-na-ti opened his eyes, there was no dawn. The sky was dark still, but it was with smoke and ash, he knew, for beyond the pall to the east he could see a clear edge of gray-blue. Day was there. It was only beneath the cloud caused by his son's brother-mountain that night still held sway.

He stood, having laid the robe over his wife and son, and wrapped himself in his hide cloak. They were now high enough to see that entire cone, from whose ever-widening base a line of scarlet crept out into the ruined land. It, too, bled burning blood, Do-na-ti thought, as he saw the trickle become a stream and the stream a torrent that moved more and more swiftly toward the ridge that had sheltered them.

The top of the cone was sharp and black against the red-lit cloud. Do-na-ti's son's brother would make a handsome mountain, worthy of the child.

Now E-lo-ni rose to stand beside Do-na-ti, holding Gift up to see. The small one pounded a fat fist against his father's shoulder. "Ahhh!" he yelled, more loudly than Do-na-ti had ever heard him speak. "Pretty!"

Do-na-ti looked down at his wife, and she lost the grim expression she had worn. "Is this the thing the spirits brought us here to see?" she asked, and now he could hear her, for they were far enough from the noise for a shout to carry.

"Yes," he cried. "We have seen a mountain born, and it is, I think, the brother and totem of our son. It is a thing that no one, not even the most ancient of grandfathers, has ever seen before, and we will make a chant of it for the Ritual, if we live to return to the village."

The child laughed aloud and clapped his hands, watching the red tide flow around the foot of the distant mountain. His eyes were bright, and his face was flushed with pleasure.

Do-na-ti took him from his mother and set him again into his sling. Then Do-na-ti caught up his spear and gestured toward the east and north. "We will go home, now," he said.

They walked for some time, and he knew that E-lo-ni, too, paused from time to time to gaze back at the awesome thing that rose, still growing taller, on the edge of the sky. Beyond it, the Burning Mountain dribbled its own burning stuff down its side, and the lurid light made Do-na-ti feel half-afraid.

"What have we learned here?" he asked his wife.

She shook her head, frowning, trying to think what great and important thing they might bring back from this experience.

It was no use, Do-na-ti realized at last. Some lessons taught by the spirits were obvious, like those he had read in the eyes of the lion and the tusker. Others, like this one, might take a long lifetime to understand, and even then, he thought, he might never learn all the things it might teach him.

He sighed and trudged forward, his wife close by his side, his son warm on his back, and the mountain that was the new totem of his clan and his kind growing ever taller behind him.

AUTHOR'S NOTE

O<small>F THOSE WE NOW CALL</small> C<small>LOVIS AND</small> F<small>OLSOM HUNTERS, NO TRACE</small> remains except the beautifully worked spear points that give them their names. Only postholes in the plain, discolored by the presence of wood where there should only be soil or rock, tell us that they sometimes built earthen lodges supported by posts set into the ground.

It is impossible to work backward from existing American Indian cultures to what might have been so long ago. Cultures evolve relentlessly, and on this continent most of the native cultures were remorselessly exterminated by the invading whites. The re-creations that are now happening in different tribes are probably only pale shadows of what actually existed for the ancestors of those now surviving.

Although no possible hint remains of the social/ familial/religious structures or beliefs of those who lived on this continent from nine to six thousand years before our present millennium began, there are patterns of behavior that the novelist can use as guidelines for their lives and habits. The American Indians, shortly after Columbus but before the arrival of settlers from Europe, were observed by early missionaries and explorers, both Spanish and French, who described them with much accuracy.

Other primitive societies have been discovered in remote parts of the world and described knowledgeably in relatively recent years. All of these observations can provide valid patterns of primitive behavior.

For my own village of the People, I have used elements from many sources. The clan is the family, basically, although young men who marry go into the clans of their wives, and their children are considered to be totally members of that other group. Siblings include those born to siblings within the clan structure, so what we might call cousins are called brothers or sisters.

Ritual is something seemingly built into the human psyche, and chants and dances go back as far as any record of mankind exists. Therefore, my People use both in their important rituals, and the chants deal with things they see and know, as well as those they intuit from observation of nature and from dreams.

Primitive societies are metaphysical to a degree almost unknown in our present Western culture. Therefore visions and dreams are taken most seriously and often are used to guide the individual, his or her family, or even the entire village in crucial or perilous circumstances. In particular, listening to the wind, the earth, the rain, and the growing things is important to primitive people.

Farmers who tune their senses to such matters, as I myself did in my youth, can foretell with some accuracy upcoming changes in weather, if nothing else, by making such observations. For those without any other source of weather information, living in country prone to tornados, blizzards, and occasional floods, this is a vital skill, to be nourished and treasured. But such intuitive connections may well have provided other insights into the world of nature that are now lost to our civilized society.

The world in which the People live is one only dimly reflected in the modern geography of northeastern New Mexico. The weather was milder then, wetter, and there were more trees and deeper grass. The last generation of volcanoes to rise there was in the process of forming, and the one that Do-na-ti saw being born might well have been Capulin Mountain, east of Raton, New Mexico, or one of its near neighbors.

The method of that birth is accurate, as far as I can make it. I used as a model Paricutin, in Mexico, which rose in the space of a few weeks, and the birth of which was recorded on film. As well, geologists have pretty well worked out the mechanics of such upwellings from the magma beneath the earth's crust.

During the time of which I write, many animals ranged the plains, most of them of tremendous size, compared with today's fauna. Ground sloths twenty feet in length shared the land with the last remnants of the woolly mammoths, giant bison, short-faced bears with very long legs that were highly adapted for speed, grizzly bears, direwolves, and arctic foxes.

There was also a variety of lion (*Panthera leo atrox*), far larger than any modern species. Badgers were there, also much larger than their counterparts of today, along with saiga antelope, moose, horses, and wolverines.

At some time during the early era when hunters went after such tremendous and dangerous animals, there must have occurred some revelation that told the human predators the value of their prey and its kinship to themselves. Every later mythos among American Indians stresses that link between beast and mankind and the duty of the hunter to give thanks to his kill for giving up its life for his benefit. I have used such a revelation, within the context of the culture I have invented.

The bones left from such hunts have been found, sometimes with those beautiful spear points still in place. It is such discoveries that proved to us that the early people on the plains lived and hunted before the last of the mammoths succumbed. Indeed, the harsh hunting methods they used may have contributed to that extinction, for their method of driving entire herds of bison or tuskers into deep canyons surely was devastating to the creatures.

The lands I describe, as Do-na-ti travels about on his missions, are shaped after those in existence now, with as much geologic backtracking as I can manage. In the history of the earth, ten thousand years is a very short time indeed, and while I may not have given accurate descriptions of the places he visits for the time when he was there, I feel that nobody alive can say with complete certainty that this or that particular bit is completely wrong. At least, not from firsthand knowledge.

As always with re-creations of prehistory, this is fantasy. There is simply no hard evidence upon which to attempt to write history of such a remote time on this continent, particularly as it deals with humanity and its behavior.

People tend to be unalterably human in their needs, feelings, and actions. It is my purpose to show human beings not too unlike ourselves, with at least as efficient brains, dealing with the conditions among which they must survive.

They were tough, intelligent, persistent, and inventive. No other kind could have survived. The human brain has changed little if at all in such a short span of time, and my people are in some ways more fit and quick-witted than we are now.

Whatever their other attributes, however, they have human problems and failings and depressions and triumphs. We probably don't change that much, no matter what length of time passes.